I0572818

UNBREAKABLE

THE WAR ENDED—HIS STORY DIDN'T

The Remarkable True Story of a Holocaust Survivor's Six-Year Journey from Nazi Labor Camps to Buchenwald

EDMUND A. KRUSZYNSKI

PRAISE FOR *UNBREAKABLE*

UNBREAKABLE is based on the true story of Rafal Kantor, a Holocaust survivor with deep roots in the Cincinnati community. Rafal's journey illuminates the lived experiences of those who endured one of humanity's greatest moral failures and found the courage to speak.

Told with compassion, and unflinching honesty, *Unbreakable* underscores the critical importance of preserving local survivor stories. Through Rafal's voice, readers bear witness to the horrors of the Holocaust and are called to confront the enduring consequences of hatred and indifference. Rafal's harrowing account stands as both a warning and a powerful reminder of why personal stories are essential in the fight against forgetting.

At the Nancy & David Wolf Holocaust & Humanity Center, we are committed to inspiring upstanders—individuals who use their character strengths to make a positive difference in the world. *Unbreakable* embodies that mission. It is a deeply moving and urgently relevant reminder that the choices we make today will shape the future we all share.

Jackie Congedo
Chief Executive Officer
The Nancy & David Wolf
Holocaust & Humanity Center

Unbreakable is both devastating and uplifting—a powerful reminder of one man's courage, endurance, and the will to live when everything was taken from him. As the granddaughter of Holocaust survivors, Rafal Kantor's story will stay with me forever, and reminds me why these stories should never be forgotten.

Melissa Hunter
Author of *All She Lost*

Unbreakable shows how faith—in God, in others, or in the will to endure—can guide us through life's darkest chapters.

Daniel Epstein
Author of *Portraits in Faith*

Rafal Kantor's story reminds us why it is so important to teach every generation to be Upstanders—because even in the darkest times, one voice can make a difference.

Joyce Kamen
Author of *Upstander Stories*

In memory of RAFAL KANTOR and his family.

Wife
LIDKA KANTOR

Parents
TOVYA AND CHAVA KANTOR

Brother
SHLOMO KANTOR

Sister
RIVKA KANTOR

May they all rest in peace and be eternally remembered.

Table of Contents

PREFACE

IN FEBRUARY 2023, I received an unexpected phone call from the Nancy & David Wolf Holocaust and Humanity Center in Cincinnati. They informed me that Ron Kantor, son of a local Holocaust survivor, was interested in writing a book about his father's experiences and wondered if I would meet him to discuss the project.

Just a few months earlier, I had published *The Medic's Wife*. For three years, I had immersed myself in the life of my own father, an American combat medic, retracing his harrowing journey across France and into Hitler's Germany. I walked alongside him through the D-Day landings, the Battle of the Bulge, and the profound moments of saving—and losing—human lives. Despite his experience as a battle-hardened soldier, the horrors he witnessed at Buchenwald concentration camp haunted him for the rest of his life.

Writing about my father's WWII experiences had been both rewarding and emotionally draining. I told myself I needed a break. But something compelled me to take the meeting—and I'm so grateful I did.

I met Ron at a cafe in Cincinnati. As we sipped our coffee, he shared his father Rafal's harrowing story and asked if I'd be willing to read his dad's written testimony. I agreed out of courtesy—but once I began reading Rafal (Raf, Ray) Kantor's Holocaust account, something unexpected happened.

As I dug into his words, I uncovered a chilling connection to my own father. On April 17, 1945, Rafal lay barely alive in the hospital barracks at Buchenwald—the very same day my father, Staff Sergeant Edmund Kruszynski, a U.S. Army combat medic, entered the camp and bore witness to its horrors.

Nearly eight decades later, Ron and I sat together, unaware that our fathers' paths had once crossed in one of history's darkest places. That realization sparked a two-year collaboration to bring Rafal's journey to life. We both agreed it was bashert—meant to be. Writing Rafal's story has been one of the greatest honors of my life.

UNBREAKABLE is based on the true story of Rafal Kantor, a Polish Jew from Czestochowa, Poland. This novel chronicles his extraordinary six-year journey of survival—from the Nazi invasion through the Czestochowa ghettos, forced labor camps, and ultimately the Buchenwald concentration camp.

The story is drawn from Rafal's own written account (1979), hours of videotaped testimony (1996), and various newspaper articles. To enrich his personal story and provide a broader view of this tragic chapter in history, I also integrated insights from other survivors—particularly through the important work of The World Society of Czestochowa Jews and Their Descendants (TWSCJ), which has preserved many eyewitness accounts from that community.

To bring Rafal's experiences to life for readers, I've taken some creative license while staying faithful to the historical record and true to Rafal's voice. This includes expanding descriptions of pivotal events, adding dialogue, and reconstructing characters and interactions where details were omitted in his original testimony.

The story is told in first-person narration to preserve the intimate, deeply personal feeling that Rafal himself is sharing his story directly with you.

It has been an incredible privilege to help tell his story. I hope you find *UNBREAKABLE* as meaningful to read as it was fulfilling to write.

PROLOGUE

Selection

Czestochowa, Poland — Septermber 1942

"MOVE THE LINE FASTER," Degenhardt barked. The SS soldiers responded with rifle butts and clubs, smashing legs and shoulders without hesitation. He stood there, fat and smug, flicking his crop and screeching "left" or "right" without hesitation. When it came to children—even babies—his voice only grew more gleeful. That sound—that smug look—would haunt my nightmares forever.

At last, we made it to the front of the line. Degenhardt stood all powerful, and he jabbed both Tatte's and Shlomo's right shoulders. "Right!" he proclaimed, one after the other. Now it was Mama's turn.

Mama turned toward me, her eyes pleading, and gestured toward Rivka. I circled my arms around my sister's waist, then Mama turned around to meet her fate. I could barely breathe as that beast stared at my beautiful mother longer than most—licking his lips like she was edible.

PART I

INVASION

CHAPTER 1

Last Day of School

Czestochowa, Poland — June 1939

THE SUN SPILLED GOLDEN LIGHT over the narrow streets of Czestochowa's Jewish quarter, bouncing off the Warta River like scattered diamonds. It was the kind of light that made you forget the dark threats rising in the east. School was out for summer, and freedom buzzed like a melody waiting to be sung.

Ishak, Shlomo, and I walked home together, our voices cutting through the warm air.

"Junior class president and vice president!" Ishak grinned, puffing out his chest. "We'll run the whole school next year. Mark my words!"

I laughed and shook my head. "We make a great team. You've got the brains, and I'm the schmoozer."

Ishak Goldberg was my best friend—and the smartest kid in school. With his beak-like nose and ever-slipping glasses, he always looked like he was solving the world's next big problem. Before speaking, he'd lift one finger like he was about to share a life-changing secret.

This time, he pointed at me. "Rafal, everyone listens when you talk. Speeches, plays—and don't even get me started on your singing. If I had your voice, I'd own this town."

Shlomo, my younger brother by a year, piped up from behind. "Yeah, and you love it when the girls swoon over your singing." Before I could turn around, he locked me in a reverse bear hug.

It was hard to stay mad at Shlomo. He was always in a good mood and funny as heck. His skin was a shade darker than mine, and his unruly black curls always looked like he'd just rolled out of bed. He had the same Kantor family chin dimple I did—the same one Rivka had, too. A mark that bound us unmistakably as siblings.

We didn't have much, but in that moment, it felt like the world was ours.

Ishak's eyes turned dreamy. "I'm going to be editor of the school paper and star of the debate team—challenging every quota and rule that holds Jews back."

I cleared my throat, suddenly shy. "I was thinking I might take singing lessons this summer. You know, to get better. Maybe one day… I don't know."

Shlomo slung his arm around Ishak's neck and pulled him close. "Hey Ishak, do you think Rafal will give us his autograph when he's famous?"

"Mock me all you like. When I'm famous, you can carry my bags." I punched Shlomo in the arm and nodded at Ishak. "Eat our dust, little brother!" We bolted ahead, laughing, with Shlomo close behind.

As we neared our synagogue on Nadrezeczna Street, we heard children playing in the open lot beside it. The building stood like a beacon of love and faith, its upper floors looking out over the Warta. Tatte had been bar mitzvahed there—so had I, and more recently, Shlomo. The path home from the synagogue was so familiar I could walk it blindfolded.

Out of the corner of my eye, I spotted Rivka—a streak of electricity hurtling toward us. At nine, my little sister was a force of nature. Her raven-black braids bounced wildly as she ran, her brown eyes sparkling with mischief. She skidded to a stop and slipped her small hand into mine.

"Rafal! Did you miss me?"

"Of course," I said, grinning as Shlomo jogged up and took her other hand. Together, we swung her into the air. She shrieked with delight, her feet kicking skyward.

"Raf was just telling us he wants to be a famous singer!" Shlomo teased.

"Wowee, Rafal!" she beamed, spinning in circles, her braids whipping around her face. "I'll be a famous dancer!"

"Oh, brother," Shlomo groaned. Ishak snorted so hard he had to pinch his nose.

Rivka blinked at us, confused. "What's so funny?"

I took a slow breath. For Jewish boys like us, opportunities—whether securing a role in a national music production or getting a university education—were often a wish and a prayer. For Jewish girls? The odds were even worse.

"Nothing," I said, forcing a smile for her sake. "Becoming a famous singer is just a silly dream."

"You should pray to the Holy Madonna! She makes dreams come true, you know." Rivka crossed her arms like she knew something I didn't.

My mouth dropped open. "The Black Madonna? At the Jasna Góra Monastery? Rivka, you know we're Jewish, right?"

"So?" she shot back, squaring her shoulders. "Miracles are for everyone. My friend Beatrice says the Madonna makes Czestochowa the most special place in all of Poland."

Shlomo snickered, but Rivka stood firm. I ruffled her hair, letting her talk.

As we walked the rest of the way home, the streets smelled of fresh-baked challah, and mothers leaned out of doorways calling their children in for an early supper. It was the only world I'd ever known. Familiar. Solid. Unbreakable.

But just beneath the surface, like a splinter I couldn't reach, whispers of war troubled me. I looked down at Rivka, her small hand swinging in mine as she skipped beside me. Her spirit was so bright. I vowed then and there I would do anything to keep it that way.

CHAPTER 2

The Black Madonna

Czestochowa, Poland — August 1939

RIVKA TUGGED AT MY SLEEVE for the hundredth time, her brown eyes pleading. "You promised we'd see the Holy Madonna before summer ended!"

I sighed, glancing out the window. Neighbors had been stopping by nonstop all morning, sharing news about a non-aggression pact between Germany and Russia. The entire city was standing on a precipice, waiting for the world to tip over. People were nervous—we were nervous. Jews like us had every reason to be, as the papers wrote about Hitler's intense hatred for all Jews.

Rivka remained blissfully unaware of the world outside our Jewish quarter, sheltered from the things I experienced whenever I left our neighborhood—the mean stares, the whispers, the taunting by the Christians—or gentiles, as Mama and Tatte called them. Whatever they were called didn't matter to me. There were far more of them than of us. And that gave them all the power.

I put my sister off for weeks, but school would begin soon, and I couldn't bear to disappoint her. "Ok, you win. Let's go now!"

Rivka's face lit up like a Sabbath candle. She darted around the house, grabbing her black and white saddle shoes and black patent purse.

As we walked through the wide boulevards of the non-Jewish area, I suddenly remembered that every August, Catholic pilgrims made their way to the monastery to pray for miracles. It was bound to be crowded, but Rivka was bursting with excitement, and it was too late to turn around now. During the entire walk, she talked about all the amazing things the Holy Madonna would grant her: a pony, a chocolate cake, and a new wool coat among them.

By the time we reached the monastery, the grounds were already thick with people, dressed in their finest clothes, clutching rosaries, and murmuring prayers. With our plain clothes and black hair, it was obvious that Rivka and I didn't belong here. But she didn't notice. She fixed her eyes on the enormous spires of Jasna Góra, awe shimmering in her gaze.

We slipped into the back of a long line that led into the chapel. She bounced on her toes, rubbing her hands together, while I stood stiff as a board, hoping to remain inconspicuous.

I told myself to remain calm. We'd get a glimpse of the Madonna, Rivka would ask for her miracles, and then we'd leave. But the two ruddy-faced teenage boys ahead of us kept turning around, their eyes flicking back and forth between me and Rivka. I tried to ignore them, yet Rivka tugged on my sleeve, wide-eyed with curiosity. "Rafal, can I ask them something?" Before I could stop her, she stepped forward. "What miracles are you going to ask for?"

The older boy loomed over my diminutive sister. "We're going to pray that all the Jews leave Poland and never come back!" He brayed like a donkey, and his father howled with him. The mother lowered her head but didn't utter a word against their hatred and prejudice.

Rivka froze, her smile vanishing. Heat climbed up my neck and into my face. As if that weren't bad enough, others weighed in.

"Go home," someone hissed from a few paces behind us.

"You don't belong here," another voice grumbled.

"Stinking Jews! As if the Madonna would bless them!" The whispers became a torrent of vitriol and hostility, all directed toward us.

Rivka's hand slid into mine. She didn't understand the venom behind those words, but I did. I'd heard them before, felt their sting. I bent down and whispered, "Rivka, we need to go. Now."

"But we haven't seen her yet," she protested.

I squeezed her hand as I pulled her away. "We can pray to the Madonna when we get home." The mutters and stares chased us until we left the monastery grounds.

Rivka was unusually quiet beside me, and the walk home felt twice as long as the walk there. When we entered our apartment, she ran straight into Mama's arms. "They were so mean to us! Why do people hate us?" A flood of tears uncorked and streaked down her cheeks.

My mother's face fell, and she shot me a look that implied I should've known better. I tried to explain, but all she did was shake her head.

Mama was the glue that held our family together. She didn't dress like the more traditional Jewish women, and her lighter skin and high cheekbones made her appear almost regal. My wavy, thick hair came from her, though she always kept hers pinned back in a neat chignon. She rocked Rivka gently, whispering soothing words.

Later that evening, my father came into my room and sat on the edge of my bed. In the next bed over, Shlomo let out an exaggerated snore—too deliberate to be real. Usually, he was the one on the receiving end of these talks, so I knew he wouldn't miss the rare chance to witness the roles reversed.

"Why, Tatte?" I asked before he could say anything. My voice cracked with frustration. "Why do they hate us? We believe in the same God, who teaches us to treat others with compassion and understanding."

Tatte rolled up his sleeves and perched his reading glasses on his head. He wore modern clothes, never the black garb of the more pious Jews, and unlike them, he was clean-shaven. He was not yet 40, but gray peppered his dark hair.

"I wish I had a simple answer for you, Raf. Hatred is a poison that seeps into people's hearts. People often use religion as an excuse for bad behavior, but it's not about faith. It's about fear, and fear breeds hatred."

"But we keep to ourselves!" I pressed. "What possible reason do they have to fear or hate us?"

His eyes filled with deep sorrow. "Because we're different, the way we look, the way we hold onto our traditions. And sometimes, people can't accept different. But that doesn't mean we should stop being who we are. We must hold on to our faith, our family, and our values, no matter what the world throws at us."

I shook my head. "I just don't understand why they can't see that we're all the same underneath, no matter the faith we practice or the color of our skin."

"Not everyone sees it that way. It's a hard truth, Raf, but one we must accept."

I hung my head in shame. "I was supposed to protect Rivka. I completely failed."

Tatte sighed. "Your heart was in the right place, but we must all be extra vigilant in these turbulent times." He patted my shoulder and left me with my horrible guilt. Even Shlomo, ever the joker, knew enough to stay quiet.

Sleep never came that night. I lay there, tossing and turning, replaying those hateful comments and nasty looks over and over. Each time, I imagined that I'd reacted differently. I didn't run. I didn't freeze. I fought back—shouting, striking, refusing to let them demean us.

But that wasn't what happened.

Next time, would I have the courage to stand my ground or push back? Or would I let their hatred bury me and my siblings in shame?

CHAPTER 3

War

Czestochowa, Poland — September 1939

WHEN I ROSE, the sky was a predawn gray. I rubbed the sleep from my eyes and padded into the kitchen. The smell of tea usually perfumed the air where Tatte sat at the breakfast table. I prized this time before the rest of our family awakened, when Tatte shared news about his shop, and I'd talk about school. Today, though, the tea wasn't brewing, and the table was empty.

Occasionally, Tatte liked to walk before breakfast to clear his head while our corner of Czestochowa still slumbered. But when I opened the front door to check, I spotted him among a group of neighbors gathering on the sidewalk. Normally, these Jewish men would exchange a few quick words before heading off to their jobs, not cluster in a conspicuous group.

With their troubled expressions, I knew something terrible must have happened. As I approached them, I heard the words Hitler, Danzig, and an ultimatum. They were so absorbed in discussing the news, they didn't even notice my presence when I slipped among them.

Our building was a narrow, four-story tenement, one of many in the cramped, bustling Jewish quarter. Weather and use had worn the walls, and the stairwells always smelled faintly of yeast and kerosene. Laundry lines stretched from building to building, crisscrossing in a connective web. Typically, children played in the court-yards, and peddlers called out their wares, their voices rising with the morning sun. But today, unease thickened the air, silencing the usual street murmur.

Tatte's voice rose above the rest. "If Poland gives up Danzig, we have a chance to remain neutral. If we resist, they will invade us, just as they invaded Austria and Czechoslovakia.

I could barely breathe. Give up Danzig? That was unthinkable.

"Moscicki has already refused," said Mr. Abramowicz, our nearest neighbor. "Whether or not we give up Danzig, I guarantee Hitler will get his hooks in us."

"We have allies," an older man I didn't recognize countered. "France and England have pledged to stop Hitler in his tracks."

There was a pregnant pause. If Britain and France didn't help Austria and Czechoslovakia, they would never come to Poland's aid. Even I knew that.

Tatte sighed heavily. "We can hope, but we must also prepare for the worst."

I had heard the rumors—everyone had. Our Jewish news-paper featured a grainy photo of Nazi soldiers doing their "Heil Hitler" salute in startling symmetry.

A younger man spoke up, stress turning his nasal voice shrill. "Danzig is a free city, protected by the League of Nations. It's the pride of the Baltic. Surely, even Hitler wouldn't mess with that!"

"Nothing will stop Hitler's quest for world domination and drive to stamp out all the Jews," Mr. Abramowicz countered sol-emnly. "My family is leaving tonight. I urge you all to do the same."

There was a moment of silence as the truth washed over the gathering. A loud debate ensued, and I became lost in my churning thoughts. *Was Mr. Abramowicz right?* I couldn't imagine leaving Czestochowa, the only home I had ever known.

Tatte's voice broke through. "Whether we remain or flee, we all need to be extremely careful. We can't afford to draw attention to ourselves, else we put targets on our backs. Remember, we are a minority in this country, and many people hold prejudices against us."

With my head full to bursting with the terrible news, I retreated into the safety of our kitchen. Collapsing onto my seat, I ran my hands against the knots in the pine table and stared at the striped dish towel covering the loaf of bread in the center. I couldn't bear the thought of eating after learning that Hitler had turned his sights on Poland.

Mama walked in and began preparing for what she assumed would be a day like any other. How I wished that were true.

$$\triangledown \quad \triangledown \quad \triangledown$$

I WATCHED MY FATHER PACE back and forth across our apartment, too restless for the small space to contain. Mama sat at the kitchen table, reading aloud to Rivka, her voice steady despite the unease in the air.

"Raf, help Shlomo and Rivka pack two days' worth of clothing," Tatte ordered. "Your mother and I will gather food and supplies. We must be ready to leave at a moment's notice."

Nodding, I rushed to help my siblings. Shlomo needed reminding to pack socks and underwear, but otherwise, he was quick. Rivka, as expected, was more difficult.

"I can't go anywhere without Leo." She clutched her stuffed lion and stomped her foot.

"I know you love Leo, but he's too big to pack. Besides, he'll be more comfortable staying here, keeping watch over your room."

She pouted, hugging the lion closer. "Maybe… but I'm packing my hair ribbons and my favorite book."

"Deal!" I folded two dresses and a cardigan while she added her underthings. We told her we might go on a trip if Tatte found someone to mind his shop. Thankfully, she accepted the story. After settling Rivka, I went to pack my bag.

Peering out my bedroom window, I saw the streets below already crowded with people—some fleeing, others talking in groups, their unease unmistakable. When I returned to the kitchen, Shlomo was at the table, wolfing down a slice of bread while Rivka helped Mama chop vegetables.

"Where's Tatte?" I asked.

Mama chopped with extra vigor. "He went out for supplies."

I grabbed a glass of milk from the icebox and slid into my usual seat. "Do you think we're safe here? Ishak told me his family is staying in a shelter tonight. Many families are already fleeing."

Mama brushed back her brown wavy hair, revealing her high cheekbones and regal dark brown eyes. At that moment, I thought she was the most beautiful and strongest woman in all of Czestochowa.

"Your father and I discussed it. Leaving now would attract too much attention. We believe we are safer at home." She smiled, but it didn't reach her eyes.

"Mama, how can you be so calm?" Shlomo blurted.

She placed a hand over his. "I draw strength from our faith. We must prepare, yes, but worrying will not add a single second to our lives. God will provide what we need."

Rivka squeezed Mama's waist. "I'll pray for the Holy Madonna to save us! She grants miracles, you know."

The three of us exchanged grimaces at the reminder of the ill-fated trip. "Yes, little sister, you've mentioned that *only* once or twice before," Shlomo teased in an obvious effort to break the tension. Before he could crack another joke, there was a sharp knock on the door.

Mama nodded at me, but before I could move, our neighbor Mrs. Rosenberg let herself in, wringing her hands and blinking rapidly. "The Germans have breached our border! They'll be marching down our streets tomorrow!"

Mama pushed Rivka toward Shlomo and me. "Boys, take your sister to her room."

"I want to stay! I can be brave," Rivka protested, gripping my hand.

"You're the bravest person I know. But Leo might be frightened," I told her.

Rivka wiped her eyes with her sleeve and nodded.

After settling Rivka with Shlomo, I slipped back into the kitchen. With Mrs. Rosenberg gone, I was ready to ask about Tatte when he walked in and hung up his hat. Though his shoulders slumped, relief flooded me.

Mama poured him a glass of water, which he drained before speaking. "The Steinbergs invited us to their cousin's farm outside the city. I turned them down."

"Why?" I was stunned. "Wouldn't that be safer?"

"There are no guarantees anywhere. We stay where we have beds, food, and shelter for as long as possible. And I must protect my store."

Mama rested a hand on his shoulder. "Agnes Rosenberg said families are staying in our supply cellar tonight. I think hiding together is wise."

Tatte wiped sweat from his brow. "For tonight, at least."

After our rushed midday meal, we grabbed blankets and headed down to the cellar. It was a small, musty, underground crawl space with a dirt floor used to store coal, potatoes, and some larger items. Even though it was cleared out, the space could barely fit the Rosenbergs and their grown son Max, plus the Steinbergs with their two young girls. Adding the five of us would make it cramped. At least it seemed like a good hiding place, being in the back of our building, underneath a stairwell, and covered by floorboards.

"I don't want to go down there," Rivka whispered, her eyes pooling with unshed tears.

I knelt beside her, pasting on a smile as Tatte lifted the floorboards. "Think of it like camping. We'll tell stories and sing songs, and the night will pass before you know it. Soon we'll be able to return to our apartment, and everything will be back to normal." My brave sister nodded, pulled her shoulders back, and slipped her hand in mine. I prayed silently that I would be worthy of her trust.

The others squeezed together as we descended the rickety stairs. Tatte brought a large candle to use as a nightlight in the otherwise dark, dank space. We could barely move a muscle, we were packed in so tightly but I did my best to keep everyone's spirits up by leading them in songs we knew from synagogue, though I sang quietly and some only hummed or moved their lips. The girls beamed when Shlomo spun a tale about a brave princess who saved the last unicorn. But as the night stretched on, the distant rumble grew closer. We all knew it wasn't thunder, and the mood turned somber.

"Tatte?" I leaned over Rivka and cupped his ear so no one else could hear. "Do you think they'll bomb Czestochowa?"

Tatte sighed. "Try to sleep, or at least close your eyes. We all need our energy for what's coming. What that will be, only God knows for certain."

CHAPTER 4

The Occupation

Czestochowa, Poland — September 1939

CONSULTING THE TIMEPIECE he kept in his shirt pocket, Tatte alerted us that the new day had arrived. It remained so dark in our enclosed space, we wouldn't have known otherwise.

"It seems quiet," Mama murmured, but no one moved.

"I'll check," I volunteered. Careful not to step on anybody, I made my way to the stairs, removed the planks, and popped my head out like a turtle. Seeing and hearing no one, I tiptoed over to the nearest window and peered out.

"All clear!" I called out. "No Germans in sight!"

One by one, people emerged, drowsy, wrinkled, but smiling.

A few hours later, we learned the Germans had bombed the nearest airfields and military installations, and then seemed to vanish. Maybe they'd moved on, chasing after the "mighty" Polish army they had referenced in their newspapers and which no one from Poland had ever seen.

Later that morning, I was lying in bed, unable to shake off the anxiety when Ishak appeared and poked my shoulder. "You can't mope all day. Let's go exploring."

I lifted my head. "Explore? Are you sure? I mean, what if…"

"Come on, Raf. The Germans aren't here, and besides, don't

you want to see what happened? I, for one, am tired of listening to rumors."

Curiosity won out over my lingering fatigue. "Fine. But we shouldn't venture far."

"Deal," Ishak said with a grin.

The rest of my family was resting, and I didn't have the heart to wake them before we left. The sun peeked through the gaps in the clouds, warming our faces as we started our journey. While we walked, our conversation shifted between normal things like school, girls, and the absurdity of the German threat.

"It's crazy how quiet it is out here," I said, as we crossed the street onto Aleje, the major boulevard. Usually, carts, pedestrians, and the occasional horse-drawn carriage packed this street. Today, there was nothing—just the long stretch of road and the occasional bucket being dumped out of a window.

"Yeah," Ishak agreed, kicking a small rock as we plodded. "Where is everyone?"

"Probably hiding. Or trying to get out of the city." I paused, thinking of the panicked families we'd heard about, stuck on the roads, trying to escape. Fearing we had made the wrong choice made me uneasy, but Ishak seemed unfazed.

When we reached a bridge over the Warta River, my mouth dropped open at the sight before us. At each end of the bridge, German soldiers stood behind anti-aircraft guns, the black swastikas stark against their light green sleeves. I remained frozen, as did Ishak. The soldiers didn't seem to notice us at first.

"We should head back. Now," I whispered to Ishak. But he ignored me and walked toward them, his head held high like he hadn't a care in the world.

"Come on, they don't bite," he called back to me, wiggling his eyebrows. I swallowed the lump in my throat, every instinct alerting me that this was a colossally bad idea.

One soldier finally noticed us. He didn't appear much older than my twenty-year-old cousin, David. "Hallo, Jungen! Was macht ihr hier?" (*What are you doing here?*)

Luckily, Ishak understood German, though he didn't speak it fluently. He waved back and answered, "We are just... exploring."

The soldier chuckled and nudged one of his older comrades, who scrutinized us with a bemused expression. "Go home, boys," he ordered in thickly accented Polish. "It's not safe to be out. You see these guns? We use them to shoot down planes." He pointed up to the sky, to emphasize his point.

I nodded, swallowing hard. "Planes? Not people?"

He nodded. "Go home or we might change our minds," he snickered and elbowed his friend.

Ishak remained undeterred. "You shoot down Polish planes?" He kept his tone light, but I could hear the tension underneath. Morris, a guy we knew who graduated two years ago, had joined the Polish air force.

The older soldier shrugged. "I'm not sure there are any left to shoot down. Go on home, boys. You're trying our patience."

I tugged on Ishak's sleeve. "Enough questions. Let's go." Luckily, he didn't fight me.

We trudged back in silence, the streets still empty. I kept replaying the image of those soldiers standing so casually at the bridge, enormous guns pointed at the sky. I wondered what might have happened to Morris and the other members of the Polish Air Force. I sure hoped they were okay.

"That was... strange," Ishak confessed when we were back in our neighborhood. "They didn't seem like monsters. If those were

Nazis, they were a lot more polite than I imagined. I mean, they could have blasted us if they wanted to."

"We're fortunate they didn't. We should lie low, not pretend they're our friends." My voice came out harshly. I was angry at Ishak for suggesting we treat this like a game. But I was madder at myself for lacking the courage to refuse him. The Nazis might have turned their guns on us if they had realized we were Jews.

When we entered our apartment, my parents demanded we both sit down. My eyes darted to Ishak, communicating without words. *Don't you dare tell them where we went.*

"How could you go outside? You needlessly endangered your lives!" Mama yelled, her face flushed with anger. "I thought you both had more sense than that!"

Tatte banged his fist on the table, a vein in his forehead throbbing. "It's a tinderbox out there. The calm before the storm. You didn't just endanger your lives, you endangered your families, too. If you're captured or shot, how long before they come for us?"

"I'm really sorry," I croaked, biting my lip until it bled. If they knew that we'd flirted with the enemy, I feared that Tatte might have died on the spot.

"I'm sorry, too," Ishak said, contrite. "I should go home."

After Ishak left, I escaped to my room, grateful that my parents didn't press me further lest I crack. Shlomo was on his bed, scribbling in his journal. "You're in hot water," he smirked. "What's up with you? I'm supposed to be the troublemaker in this family."

I collapsed onto my bed, turned to the wall, and shut my eyes—a clear signal I didn't want to talk. When I finally got up, the afternoon sun had already climbed high, and my family stood huddled by the living room window. I joined them and froze. Czestochowa had transformed. Just hours earlier, the streets lay quiet. Now, they bristled with German soldiers.

They rolled in with incredible precision. In contrast to the pitiful Polish Army, the Germans were fully mechanized with tanks, trucks, and weapons that looked like they hailed from the future. After an hour or two, Mama, Tatte, and Rivka tired of watching, but Shlomo and I remained glued to the window, absorbed by the endless parade of soldiers marching in lockstep. Czestochowa and all of Poland were theirs for the taking.

Then came the declaration, blasted through a bullhorn on repeat. "Poland is no more. You are now citizens of Germany."

We were stunned into silence, unable to process what that would mean for us or our neighbors. Could the entire country suffer, no matter whether people were Jewish or not? Only time would tell. The parade continued for twenty-four straight hours—the endless sounds of engines rumbling, boots striking pavement, and horses clopping making the whole apartment shake. The German army seemed immense enough to swallow the entire world.

"They aren't stopping," Mama said, her eyes bloodshot.

"They appear to be passing through," Tatte added. "But we must remain vigilant."

"There's an early curfew tonight," Mama said during our light afternoon meal of bread and yesterday's stew. She had been too distraught to cook, and I could barely taste a thing anyway. "I think we should spend another night in the cellar."

We all agreed, nervous that the relative calm couldn't last. Back to the underground crawl space we went, packed like sardines with our same neighbors. This time, fear and sweat permeated the enclosed space, and there was no singing, stories, or talking at all. My thoughts wavered between hope and dread. Would the Allies come to our rescue? Would anyone?

The damp air of the cellar felt heavier that night. We sat huddled together, the flickering candle casting silhouettes against the cold stone walls. Sleep came in restless fits, but when Tatte announced the dawn of a new day, a collective sigh of relief rippled through the group. The night had passed without incident.

Mama and Rivka were the first to venture back upstairs, eager to clean up and use the bathroom. Others followed suit, slipping in and out, reclaiming their meager belongings, moving between the fragile safety of the cellar and our homes above.

I was back in my room and had just pulled my shirt over my head when a deafening explosion hurled me backward. The force slammed me against my bed, knocking the air from my lungs. Glass shattered, and my arms took the brunt of the jagged projectiles as I protected my head.

"Raf!" Shlomo skidded out of the bathroom, his face pale with terror. "They're coming!"

From the kitchen, Tatte's urgent voice cut through the chaos. "Get to the cellar!"

Gunfire crackled outside like a violent thunderstorm and shouting erupted in the streets, peppered by harsh commands in German. My pulse beat in my ears as we sprinted into the hallway, away from the pounding of jackboots. We had just cleared the entryway when the front door exploded behind us, splintering under the force of rifle butts and kicks.

"Raus! Raus! Kommt heraus!" (*Out! Out! Come out!*) The harsh voices sliced through the air like a knife, assaulting our ears.

We ran toward our basement hideout. I lunged forward, my hands fumbling to yank the loose floorboards aside.

An accented Polish voice bellowed behind us, "Out! All males surrender with your hands up, or we will shoot everyone in this building!"

I dared a glance over my shoulder. There were no German soldiers in sight, but the pounding of boots was drawing nearer.

That moment of hesitation nearly cost us, but with frantic urgen-cy, the four of us slipped inside, dragging the boards back into place just as the soldiers stormed the hall.

My feet struck the cellar floor, and I crouched like a cat, silent and tense, praying we remained unseen. It was supposed to be pitch black in the cellar, but in our haste, we must have not fully sealed the floorboards covering the steps. The tiniest sliver of light beamed through a minuscule crack above us.

I scanned the cramped space, doing my best to count body shapes in the dark. Like before, we were the last to arrive. Tatte crouched at the base of the rickety steps, and Mr. Rosenberg whispered in his ear. I saw Tatte's shoulders sag.

Something was wrong.

Shlomo nudged me and leaned in close. "Mrs. Rosenberg isn't here."

The rumble of explosions shook the ground beneath us. I caught my mother's eyes. She clutched Rivka protectively. Terror gripped us as we sat in silence, praying to avoid discovery.

We heard a door being bashed in overhead. "Out! Out!" a thick German voice commanded.

Someone shrieked, "No! No!" just before gunshots rang out. The young Steinberg girls whimpered, and I feared my heart would escape my chest.

Mr. Rosenberg lunged toward Tatte, trying to rush upstairs, but Tatte used his body to block him. They tussled, and Tatte managed to restrain him. When he whispered, "We must protect the children," Mr. Rosenberg's body flagged.

We all flinched when another detonation rattled the building. This one was closer, jarring the dust from the beams above. Shlomo cursed, burying his face in my side.

Then we heard it—a new sound, one that sent a tremor down

my spine. The heavy thud of boots stomping on the floor above us. We all froze, barely breathing.

Suddenly, the cellar became shrouded in darkness. The soles of German jackboots stood right over our heads.

"Raus! Raus! Surrender now or we will shoot everyone!" the Germans bellowed. Little did they know we were hyperventilating just beneath them.

I closed my eyes to calm my body down. *Would they capture the men and let the women and children go? Or would they kill all Jews on sight?*

A soldier banged the butt of his rifle on the floorboard just above us, making sawdust and dirt rain on our heads. Rivka jumped and mother covered her mouth, stifling any potential shrieks or cries. The silence between heartbeats was unbearable, and I could smell that at least one person had lost control of their bodily functions.

The soldier moved on, and tears pricked my eyes. "All clear," a German voice boomed and miraculously, our tormenters marched away from our building,

Still, no one dared move, all of us shell-shocked by the violence that had occurred right over our heads and how close we had come to being discovered.

Finally, with the immediate danger past, Tatte spoke. "The men can't stay. The Nazis are relentless. They may not find us today, but when they do, they'll drag us out and make examples of all of us. We must protect the women and children." After haggling, crying, and exchanging of ideas, the men agreed to surrender.

"Tatte, no… please don't go…" Rivka grabbed his arm, tears coursing down her cheeks.

Father knelt in front of her, taking her hands. His voice was soft but firm. "Rivka, listen to me. You must be brave and take care of Mama. Can you do that for me?"

Rivka nodded and said, "I can be brave, Tatte."

Tatte kissed her on the forehead and stood.

One by one, the fathers rose, exchanging quiet words with their families. As I saw Mr. Steinberg embrace his wife and children, I remembered Mrs. Rosenberg's absence and prayed for her survival. Tatte took a deep breath, then told me and Shlomo to follow him.

I turned to Mama, hugging her.

"Take care of each other," she whispered.

I nodded, too choked up to speak.

Tatte took the lead, pushing open the trapdoor. Daylight poured in. I took one last glimpse of my mother and sister. Would we see each other again? I willed myself to believe it. If I didn't, I wouldn't have found the courage to move forward.

"Wave your handkerchiefs high above your heads," Tatte instructed as we shuffled past the foyer of our apartment building. After we complied, Tatte squared his shoulders and pushed open the front door. "Follow me."

The world outside was a nightmare come to life. Black columns of smoke twisted into the sky, making it hard to breathe. The air was thick with the anguished cries of those caught in the streets. Bodies lay scattered along the road—some deathly still, others being dragged away. I struggled to take in the devastation's scale.

Tatte raised his white hanky high. "Come," he murmured, and we followed his lead. Shlomo and I mirrored him, holding our own scraps of cloth in the air—fragile shields against an unstoppable force.

At the center of the mayhem stood the Gestapo, secret police of the Nazi Party, responsible for persecuting all political opponents, ideological dissenters, and, above all, Jews. They were nightmarish conductors in steel helmets, green-gray uniforms, and black jackboots. Their faces were cold and expressionless as they moved through the chaos, barking commands at frantic soldiers tasked with rounding up Polish men. Batons hung at Gestapo's sides, ready for swift punishment, and they used them without hesitation, striking anyone who didn't move fast enough. The street had become a blood-soaked battlefield.

We were just ordinary people, caught in a horror beyond our comprehension. Had we known what awaited us—that Hitler had commanded his forces to "kill without pity or mercy all men, women, and children of Polish descent"—we would have fled like so many of our neighbors did. But our bags remained packed, still sitting in the corner of our apartment. And here we were— trapped like flies in a spider's web.

A group of soldiers surrounded us, the barrels of their rifles raised and aimed at our heads. Tatte stepped forward, placing himself in front of Shlomo and me. His voice was steady, though his German was halting.

"Don't shoot. We are surrendering." Still clutching the white handkerchief, Tatte held his hands high above his head.

"Zu spät," their leader sneered. (*Too late.*)

With a flick of his hand, soldiers rushed in and yanked us into a line. I stumbled as one of them gripped my collar and shoved me next to Shlomo. Were they going to shoot us right here in front of our building?

Their leader barked another command. My eyes drifted and then froze.

Mrs. Rosenberg.

She was on her knees, just beyond a row of soldiers. Her floral dress hung in tatters, her hair tangled wildly, and blood streaked down her face. A soldier towered over her, yelling something I couldn't hear over the din.

Mr. Rosenberg spotted her, too. His strangled cry tore through the air as he lunged forward, but two men held him back. The Gestapo officer didn't blink as he delivered the order.

A Nazi soldier raised his pistol to Mrs. Rosenberg's head. The gunshot was deafening.

Mrs. Rosenberg crumpled to the ground.

A silent scream lodged in my throat. The world blurred—the soldiers, the shouting, the acrid smell of smoke, the crushing weight of Shlomo's grip on my wrist.

My eyes refocused as the Gestapo leader turned to face us, his cold eyes sweeping over our group. Behind him, the soldiers kept their rifles pressed against our backs, their fingers resting on the triggers.

"Resistance is futile!" the Gestapo officer shouted, white foam flying from his mouth. "The penalty for resisting is death!"

CHAPTER 5

Bloody Monday

Czestochowa, Poland — September 1939

THE GESTAPO HADN'T FINISHED with us. One by one, they slammed the butts of their rifles into the backs of our knees. I cringed at the sound of Tatte's groan before collapsing beside him, pain shooting through my legs.

I pressed my hands into the dirt, trying to steady myself, as their brutal, methodical weapons search began. They knew we had nothing, yet they struck us anyway. When Mr. Rosenberg cried out, a soldier slapped him hard across the head, sending him sprawling to the ground.

Our captors ordered us back on our feet and made us march in line. To speed our pace, the Gestapo unleashed police dogs on us. One sank its teeth into my calf. I tried to kick it away, but it kept snapping at me.

The dogs were finally called off. Tatte hobbled forward, his pants torn, blood dripping from his leg. I grabbed his arm, steadying him as they force-marched us down Warszawska Street toward Plac Daszynskiego.

The city square, once filled with market stalls and cheerful conversation, had become a war zone. Trenches crisscrossed the area, with machine guns mounted on piles of dirt. German soldiers stood at every corner, aiming their rifles at the city's remaining population. Lifeless bodies lay scattered everywhere, discarded like garbage.

I tripped over the corpse of a young girl, about Rivka's age, a bullet hole clean through her forehead. It was the first time I ever saw a dead child. I had read about the horrors of the Great War, but nothing had prepared me for this. This was pure savagery. Shlomo clutched my sleeve. He was heaving, his eyes wide with terror.

"Raf," he gurgled and wiped his mouth with his hand. "What will they do to us?"

"I don't know," I whispered, feeling a strange numbness wash over me. "Let's focus on staying alive."

They marched us into the old Catholic church. Once a place of peace and beauty—with its tall steeple and candlelit services—it had now become a prison. Inside, people packed the space wall to wall. The air was suffocating, a mixture of blood, sweat, and human waste.

A man beside us, broad-shouldered with straw-colored hair, whispered to Shlomo. "They just shot ten people in cold blood. They begged for mercy but…" His words cut off, strangled by the horrible memory.

Soft murmurs, quiet prayers, and stifled sobs filled the church. Jews and Gentiles huddled together, equal in our suffering. Non-Jewish boys had taunted us for years and beat Shlomo more than once for daring to fight back. Now, all those divisions seemed meaningless. We were all prisoners of the Nazi invaders. I was surprised because I had always believed that Hitler held a special hatred for the Jews.

As the hours dragged on, my thoughts flickered to Mama and Rivka, hoping and praying they remained unharmed. Tatte hadn't spoken since the dog attack, and I feared his spirit had broken. I squeezed his hand, relieved when he squeezed back.

"Think they'll blow up the church?" Shlomo whispered.

"I hope not." I blinked hard. "If ever there was a time to pray, this is it."

Morning arrived with a brilliant wash of filtered light through the stained-glass windows. German soldiers entered with buckets of water, and for a brief, foolish moment, hope surged through the crowd. But it was a trick—they flung the water into the air, soaking us but offering none to drink. Shlomo muttered a curse under his breath, his face tightening with anger. I grabbed his arm and shook my head, warning him to stay silent.

"Sixteen and up—step forward!" a German voice ordered.

I tightened my grip on Shlomo's hand. "Let's go."

"But I'm not sixteen," he protested, his eyes wide.

"I know. Just stand tall and act confident." I squared my shoulders, trying to project a bravery I didn't feel. Tatte nodded, and I gave him a quick kiss on the cheek before pulling Shlomo with me, blending in with the other boys.

Miraculously, the Germans waved us off, releasing us into the streets. We didn't waste a second. We sprinted home, the wind biting at our faces, the gruesome carnage behind us driving us forward. When we burst through the door of our apartment, Mama and Rivka screamed and pulled us into a fierce hug.

"Where's Tatte?" Mama asked. "He's not with you?"

"They only released teenage boys," Shlomo explained. "But I'm sure they'll release the men next."

The night passed in tense silence, our nerves stretched thin. Mama kept patting our heads, forcing food into our hands, though none of us had much appetite.

At 11 a.m. the next day, Tatte wandered through the door. His face was pale and drawn, pants ripped and stained with blood. Mama sobbed with relief, holding his face in her hands. "How? How did you get out?"

Tatte sank into a chair, his voice hoarse. "The Nazis told us we could leave—as if it had all been some kind of sordid test."

Being together again felt like a miracle. I thought I could sleep for days. But Rivka kept slipping into our room, checking to make sure we were still there. After the third time, I tucked her into my bed and lay on the floor beside her.

Our relief was short-lived. By midday, whispers of the death toll spread like wildfire.

"Four hundred lives lost in a single day," Tatte told us. "Half of them Jews."

The Germans claimed it was retaliation for an attack, but we know the truth—there was no resistance. They killed and tortured for sport, to ensure obedience.

We fell into a heavy silence. Then Tatte led us in the Shema, our voices soft but resolute. We offered prayers not only for ourselves but also for the dead—especially for Mrs. Rosenberg, whose life was taken so callously.

"Shema Yisrael, Adonai Eloheinu, Adonai Echad..." (*Hear, O Israel, the Lord is our God, the Lord is One...*)

September 4, 1939, would forever be known in Czestochowa as Bloody Monday.

CHAPTER 6

Ishak's Apartment

Czestochowa, Poland — September 1939

A FEW DAYS LATER, the tension in the streets eased. Despite the relative calm, a growing worry had taken root in me. I hadn't seen or heard from Ishak since Bloody Monday. Knowing him the way I did, he should have been the first to check on me and my family. But there had been no word or sign of him.

I spotted Tatte patching our front door and noticed how his hair had gotten grayer in the past few days. I cleared my throat to get his attention. "Can we go check on Ishak's building? Just to see…" I couldn't finish the sentence.

He studied me for a moment, the lines on his face deepening. "All right, but stay close to my side. No wandering off." Shlomo overheard our conversation and insisted on coming. The three of us set out together.

The streets were eerily quiet, the scars of Bloody Monday etched everywhere—in shattered windows, bullet holes, blackened doorways, and crumbling facades. Every step felt like walking through a graveyard, the silence screaming louder than any sound.

When we arrived at Ishak's apartment complex, the building stood unscathed. It seemed like an oasis of calm amid the destruction and desolation we'd passed to get there. For a few heartbeats, I dared to believe everything would be fine.

The hallway was as I remembered it—the same green carpeting stretched beneath our feet and the familiar murals of flowers and trees adorned the walls. But I could tell something was wrong. Normally, the sound of pans clattering and voices mingling in lively conversations would reach the entryway. But it was silent as a tomb. Ishak's immediate family lived on the third floor, and as much as I wanted to rush up there, I dreaded it, too. Since his entire extended family lived in the building, all of whom we knew, we agreed to check every apartment for survivors.

We approached the first apartment. The door was ajar with splintered wood around the frame. The ransackers had overturned the furniture, emptied the cabinets, and scattered belongings across the floor.

"Is anyone here?" Tatte called out.

There was no answer.

We moved to the next apartment where the same scene awaited us. Each apartment on the first floor was empty, the contents in disarray. The second floor was a mirror of the first.

Shlomo glanced at me, his eyes wide with worry. I was so unsettled, I turned away.

As we climbed up to the third floor, my pulse quickened with every creak of the old wooden steps. Reaching the floor, I raced down the hallway to Ishak's door. The door was shut, a hopeful sign, but it hung loosely on its hinges, barely attached. I rapped my knuckles against the frame, the sound echoing in my ears.

Nothing.

Tatte laid a hand on my shoulder as he and Shlomo joined me. We stood there for a moment, straining for signs of life. I was ready to burst in when I heard a muffled sound from somewhere down the hall.

"Did you hear that?" Shlomo said, his voice softer than I'd

ever heard it before. The sound came again, and he pointed down the hallway. "There."

Thank God.

We stepped toward the open door, my heart pounding like a snare drum. Inside, we spotted Mr. Avrum Goldberg, Ishak's uncle, slumped in the corner of his living room, head in his hands. Avrum had always been a large man with broad shoulders and a square jaw, known for his booming voice. Now he was shrunken, practically unrecognizable, crushed beneath the weight of unspeakable sorrow.

"Tatte…" I whispered, my voice cracking. His hand on my shoulder steadied me, though I could feel them trembling.

"Avrum?" Tatte said gently. "It's Tovya Kantor with my sons."

Mr. Goldberg lifted his head and blinked. "Come in," he rasped.

Tatte crouched down beside him, his tone soft but urgent. "What happened?"

Avrum swallowed hard, his voice like broken glass. "They made us bury them… my family, my brother's family… all gone."

He gestured toward the corner, where his son Saul sat on the floor, rocking back and forth. His presence startled me, as I hadn't realized he was there. Saul had always been the picture of strength, tall and athletic, with dark curls and a mischievous grin. But now, his eyes were vacant, and his once-muscular frame seemed to have withered. I was bursting with questions, but Tatte shook his head. "Give him time."

Avrum stared at the floor. "We hid in the attics… we didn't want to give ourselves up. We just wanted to stay together. But the babies cried, and the Nazis found us. They accused us of resisting."

Resisting? They were families just like ours, not fighters. Desperate people, hiding like we did, praying they wouldn't be discovered. I didn't want to hear the rest, but I couldn't move. I could barely breathe.

"They dragged us down one by one—grandparents, men, women, children. In the courtyard behind the building, they lined us up against the fence, out of sight. Then came the words: we were a threat to the Reich," Avrum continued, his voice choking up. "I tried to tell them... we weren't... we had no weapons. But they wouldn't listen. Soldiers pulled Saul and me aside and forced us to watch."

Shlomo clutched my arm and dared to ask the question that I could not. "Ishak, too?"

Avrum's eyes squeezed shut. "Just before they lined us up," he choked, "Ishak made a run for it." His chest rose sharply, his breath catching in his throat. "They shot him in the back," his words coming out strangled. "But he wasn't dead. The soldier stood over him, and... and..."

From the corner of the room came a guttural, broken sound.

"STOP!" Saul screamed.

He was curled on the floor, arms locked around his knees, rocking like a wounded child. His voice cracked open with raw pain. "Don't say it, Papa. Please—don't make us see it again." His eyes were wild with grief, his face twisted with a kind of terror that came from remembering too much. "I was there," he gasped. "I saw it. I still see it. Every minute I see it. That's enough, Papa. That's enough!"

The room fell into a stunned silence. Even the air seemed to pause, thick with sorrow that clung to the walls like smoke.

I stumbled back, my knees giving out as I leaned against the doorframe. My brave, foolhardy, brilliant best friend. Gone. We'd shared everything—our dreams, our secrets, our disappointments, our joys. He was the brother of my heart. And now he was dead.

CHAPTER 7

Nazi Rule

Czestochowa, Poland — September 1939

THE NAZIS WASTED NO TIME setting up their puppet government, headed by H. Belke, a Volksdeutsch, a Pole who'd betrayed us to serve the enemy. I saw him once in the square, swaggering in his crisp new uniform, ruling over his own people like he was a god. With him came the laws, each more brutal than the last. The Nazis aimed to crush us completely—mind, body, and spirit—with special vitriol against the Jewish population, as we had feared all along.

Our rights vanished like smoke. They shot Jews on the spot, with no explanation or warning. Germans bearing the Nazi swastika on their armbands burst into our homes and helped themselves to our food, furniture, and treasured possessions without repercussions or mercy.

"I don't understand," Shlomo complained one evening as we sat huddled around the table, discussing the terrifying situation. "Why are they singling out the Jews? I thought the Nazis wanted to wipe out all the Poles."

Tatte leaned back in his chair, his hand running over his chin. By now, his hair had turned completely gray, and deep worry lines had carved themselves into his face. "Throughout history, Jews have always been a convenient scapegoat." He rolled his wedding ring around his knuckle and stared at the floor. "And sadly, that may never change."

That night, Rivka slept in our parents' room, while Shlomo and I moved our beds together. We lay close enough to hold hands in the dark. Neither of us uttered a word. Eventually, sleep took us, though it wasn't the peaceful kind.

More laws followed. First, they froze all Jewish bank accounts, allowing each family to withdraw only one hundred zlotys—barely enough for a loaf of bread. A week later, they demanded every piece of jewelry and heirloom we possessed. In the center of the square—where guns still loomed and batons slashed the air like threats—we handed over rings that had belonged to our grandparents, and pewter kiddush cups engraved and passed down through generations. We watched helplessly as the treasures of our family history piled into a growing heap behind our merciless captors. My hands clenched at my sides, the humiliation burning through me, making me want to scream or lash out. "They're only things," Tatte said gently, trying to calm me, but I saw Mama blinking back tears.

Every day brought a new restriction against the Jews. The schools closed their doors to us. The local Jewish newspaper stopped publishing. Then came the ban on radios, to keep us isolated from the outside world and dependent on Nazi propaganda. Police dragged people hiding valuables to the station. Entire families disappeared in the dead of night, never to return.

The looting came next. I'll never forget the sound—mobs filling our streets, shouting racial slurs against us. Polish Gentiles we once called customers of Tatte's store became looters, smashing windows and kicking down doors. They worked alongside the Nazis, hauling out whatever they could carry. Some didn't even wait for permission—they just helped themselves.

I stood on the sidewalk in stunned silence, watching them tear apart the storefronts we had walked by our entire lives. They carried away crates and furniture, their arms full of items they hadn't bought or paid for. Criminals, pure and simple, yet emboldened by the Nazis.

Tatte's business had been distributing colonial goods like coffee, tea, and cocoa across Czestochowa. Customers from all walks of life shopped at his store, both Jewish and non-Jewish alike. He dreamed that one day Shlomo or I might take an interest in the business and carry it on. But now, that dream lay in ruins.

I'll never forget the afternoon we returned to his shop. Shelves lay overturned, crates of coffee and tea torn open, the contents stolen or strewn across the floor. The smell of cocoa lingered in the air, a scent I'd previously associated with celebrations. My temper simmered until we made it back to the apartment. Once inside, it boiled over.

"They *knew* us! How could they?" I was poised to grab a cast iron pan and seek retribution, but Tatte shook his head and ordered, "Sit! All of you."

He cleared his throat and looked at each of us in turn. "Whether they were jealous of what we had or destroyed the store just for the thrill of it—it doesn't matter. Never forget who the real enemy is." Tatte pointed out the window at the soldiers patrolling the street. "The Nazis are behind all of it. They're orchestrating the chaos."

▽ ▽ ▽

IN THOSE EARLY DAYS, the Gestapo stalked the streets like wolves. It wasn't long before their eyes fixed on any Jew they could snatch and force into their perverse version of "work." But it wasn't work at all, just a brutal display meant to crush our spirits. They delighted in targeting Hasidic Jews, as the skullcaps, prayer shawls, and traditional attire made them easily identifiable. Attackers tore the devout from their homes and ripped off their beards—their sources of pride. The cries of those men echoed in my head, haunting me endlessly.

I'll never forget the Rosh Hashanah of 1939. One of the two High Holy Days, it marked the Jewish New Year and the beginning of the period of atonement. Traditionally, we celebrated with apples dipped in honey and daylong services in the local synagogue. But that year, we could only pray at home, and apples and honey were scarce, as stores sold only the dregs to "Jewish scum."

The holiday fell in late September, and at midday, we gathered for prayers led by Tatte. Suddenly, we heard heavy jackboots in the hall, followed by the clang of a rifle. Moments later, a Nazi soldier burst into our apartment and leveled his bayonet at our heads.

"Out! Now!" he demanded, his harsh, clipped voice making us flinch. When my whole family rose, he pointed the rifle at me. "Nein. Just him."

He ushered me, along with others from the building, down the stairs and into the street. The moment I stepped outside, I saw a long line of men guarded by more soldiers. They drove us forward, marching and prodding us through the streets like we were criminals.

Gentiles lined the footpaths, jeering, spitting, and throwing rotten vegetables at us.

"Filthy Jews!" one man shouted, his words cutting like glass.

"This is what you deserve!" a woman yelled, hurling a rotting apple that splattered against a helpless man's shoulder.

My cheeks burned—not just from humiliation, but from anger that fellow citizens from Czestochowa reveled in our suffering. It seemed like they were competing to show the Nazis who hated us the most. But then my thoughts traveled to the horrible treatment we had received at the Jasna Góra Monastery. This hatred wasn't new. The only difference was that the Nazis gave them permission to unleash it.

The Gestapo waited for us in a fenced-in churchyard, where cinder blocks and lumber lay scattered from construction work the invasion had halted. Soldiers strolled down the line, yelling things like "War criminals!" and "Parasites! Your end is near!" One officer cracked his wooden billy club against a man's back, sending him sprawling.

At gunpoint, they dragged me to a pile of cinder blocks. "Pick them up!" Each cement block was cold and heavy, and before I found my balance, the Nazi yelled, "Run, you useless piece of filth!"

His club struck my back to urge me forward, and my arms quivered under the strain of the heavy load. I struggled to run to the other side of the churchyard, where another soldier waited to greet me. "Drop it!" he ordered.

I obeyed, relieved to be free of the weight. "Now pick it up again and run back to the other side!" he snarled.

After hours of this torment, back and forth, an older man near me collapsed, unable to take another step. He fell face-first into the mud, blood trickling from his mouth where he'd bitten his lip in his struggle to keep going.

"Get up!" an officer bellowed, bringing his club down again and again on the fallen man's back. I gritted my teeth as I watched. What kind of monster would enjoy this?

I whispered a silent question to God as I toiled. *Why do you let them do this to us?* But the heavens remained silent.

Just when I was about to collapse myself, the guards ordered us to disperse. I staggered out of the churchyard like I was drunk, my body aching and muscles screaming with each step. Somehow, I found the strength to help the poor old man the guards had beaten. He clung to my arm, too weak to make it alone. As I limped home, a dark premonition filled my thoughts. A creeping certainty that this day was only the beginning of my suffering.

CHAPTER 8

Illegal Trading

Czestochowa, Poland — Fall 1939

LIKE SO MANY OTHER JEWISH FAMILIES, we pledged to persevere despite the hardships and continued restrictions. We learned to endure random torture, sporadic looting, and food shortages. Every day, we gave thanks to the almighty God that our family unit was still together and our home was intact.

Following the looting of Tatte's storefront, he wisely broke his stock into smaller stashes and stored them in secret hiding places. If the Nazis came through for inspection, they'd seize whatever they found. By scattering the products, he hoped that even if they uncovered some, the rest might stay safe. We did what we had to, trading with Poles who still had the means to buy and who pledged not to betray us. It was risky, but it was our only means of survival.

One fall day, Tatte sold a small package of cocoa to a friend. It was just a tiny parcel, about the size of a tea bag. I was in the courtyard with Shlomo, tossing a ball back and forth, when we heard the commotion.

"Stop!" a Polish police officer's gruff voice echoed through the street. As we arrived on the scene, the officer—an immense man with a neck like a bull—yanked the parcel from the hands of

Tatte's friend. I watched the man crumble as the officer interrogated him. Then he pointed his finger at our apartment.

"Shlomo, we've got to warn Tatte!" We bolted up the back staircase and burst through our apartment door.

"Tatte!" I huffed. "There's going to be trouble!" Before I could explain, there was a violent pounding on our front door.

"Open up! Now!" The officer kicked the door for emphasis.

Mama went pale but remained calm. "Tovya," she whispered, "answer the door before he breaks it down."

Tatte drew a deep breath and opened the door. The officer bullied his way into our apartment and pushed Tatte against the wall. His eyes swept across the room like a predator out for blood.

"Where is it?" he yelled, spittle flying from his foul mouth. Rivka clung to Mama. Shlomo and I ducked into the living room, praying he'd overlook us, as neither of us were as calm as our parents.

Tatte lifted his hands in a placating gesture. "It was just a gift, the last of the supply from the business I once owned."

The Polish officer sneered and yanked open drawers and cabinets and tossed aside the paltry items he found. Every time one of Mama's dishes cracked against the floor, I cringed.

Tatte strode to a cabinet, pulled out a small bag of cocoa, and handed it to the policeman. "I was saving this tiny bit for a special family occasion. I swear to you, this is all that's left."

The officer grabbed the bag and shook it to feel the weight. Sweat dripped down my back.

The officer's tone was unforgiving. "There are dire consequences for illegal trade. Authorities can arrest the head of the household, and the family will lose everything." Tatte nodded, standing his ground.

"Yes. We understand."

The officer's eyes flicked to Mama, and then to us. For a second, his expression shifted, his anger melting into something more like pity.

"You're lucky today," he raised the bag of cocoa in the air. "I'll accept this as payment for your indiscretion. But if I see you again, I won't be so accommodating."

The policeman gave us one last stare, then spun on his heel and left. Tatte shut the door behind him and exhaled mightily. "That was too close," Mama whispered, and began sweeping up broken plates.

Tatte stepped toward the kitchen cabinets, his expression hard as stone. "We all need to be more careful," his voice carrying the weight of what happened. "We can't even lend a grain of sugar to a neighbor."

"Could they really take you away from us, Tatte?" Rivka asked, her eyes wide. Tatte patted her on the head, softening his stance.

"Supporting the family is my burden to bear, and I promise you, I will be cautious. Try not to worry, okay?"

From that day on, every knock at the door, every stranger's voice on the street, sent a chill through us. But we needed to eat, and the threat of discovery loomed over us daily. It wasn't just about the cocoa, tea, or coffee. It was about keeping our family whole in a world that was falling apart, piece by bloody piece.

CHAPTER 9

Judenrat

Czestochowa, Poland — Fall 1939

THE STREETS WE ONCE KNEW now felt foreign—every corner patrolled by soldiers bearing the Nazi swastika, their suffocating presence poisoning the air we breathed. Hope for our freedom was fading into a dream, and I wondered if we could possibly survive. The takeover had been swift, crushing us like fingers smothering a candle.

Autumn was dying, and the winter ahead promised to be more dreadful than any in my known memory. Food was already slipping out of reach, and while the Gentile Poles suffered, too, we Jews had it worse.

Toward the end of Sukkot, I heard whispers about the formation of a new group called the Judenrat or Jewish Council. The Gestapo summoned Mr. Leon Kopinski, a man known for his dedication to the Jewish community, and ordered him to lead this council. Kopinski agreed and had the unenviable task of persuading other Jews to join him. The Gestapo tasked the Judenrat with administering all facets of Jewish life, with the Gestapo's demands looming over them like the Sword of Damocles.

That evening, as we huddled in the kitchen, Tatte muttered under his breath. "That traitorous swine!"

"Kopinski had no choice," Mama reasoned, stirring watery potato soup over the stove.

Tatte's voice sounded rough and irate. "No choice? I would die before becoming the Nazis' puppet and doing their dirty work!" He banged his fist on the table, his frustration palpable.

Mama leveled him with her sternest stare. "Fellow Jews will at least try to protect us. Better Kopinski than the Gestapo, don't you think?"

Tatte didn't answer. He stared into the candle flames, as if they held the answer to all that plagued us. After a long silence, he muttered, "The Judenrat will be our overlords. You'll see."

There was no calming Tatte when he was in such an argumentative mood, and we all saw how much the Nazi presence had aged him. In the quiet that followed, I weighed both of their positions. I agreed with Tatte that the Nazis would use the Judenrat to squeeze us dry, to carry out their warped orders. But I agreed with Mama, too, that the Judenrat would do their best to protect us.

Luckily, Rivka was reading in her room and Shlomo was scribbling in his journal, sparing them from Tatte's wrath. But I wasn't so lucky, and as much as Mama tried to defuse the tension, her eyes reflected the worry she tried to hide.

One of the Judenrat's first orders was that all Jews needed to wear an armband when in public, a white band with a blue Star of David stamped on it. The first day I wore it, the thin cloth felt unbearably heavy, not because of its physical heft, but because it targeted us.

"Rafal, do you have your armband?" Mama called from the other room as I prepared to leave. It was my turn to stand in line at the butcher's.

I ran my fingers along its rough edges. "Yes, Mama."

"Because, if they catch you without it…"

"I know, Mama. Trust me."

The punishments were brutal enough to remind us daily that this wretched armband wasn't a choice. So, I took a deep breath and walked outside. As I left the Jewish quarter and entered the main part of town, icy stares and taunts clung to me with every step. Strangers passing by didn't bother me much. But the ones who knew me—customers from Tatte's store—those were the stares that cut the deepest.

Some muttered curses, and some even spat in my direction. I had to endure that and worse when the butcher made me stand in line until all Gentile customers had been served. At the end of that mentally and physically exhausting day, the only meat left was tough and gristly—barely fit for a dog.

One night, after enforcement of the armband decree, the smell of smoke seeped into our apartment. When I flew to the window, I could spy roaring flames rising near the Warta River.

"Tatte," I called out. "They're burning down our synagogue!"

Tatte dashed to my side and let out a bone-deep wail. "No! Not our beautiful synagogue!" He slammed his fist on the lamp table next to the window, splintering the wood.

I understood his distress—the loss of our hand-inscribed torah, with its embroidered velvet covering, was unfathomable. Whenever Rabbi Roth lifted the torah out of its sanctuary, hushed awe would flow through the congregants. Then there was the display case filled with a collection of kiddish cups crafted from glass, pewter, and porcelain. I had stared at that case so many times, wondering whose hands had created such beauty.

"Grab your coat!" Tatte barked, throwing on his. But when we were two blocks away, a small band of Wehrmacht soldiers prevented us from getting any closer. My father broke down and cried as soldiers fingered their guns.

"There's nothing we can do," I said as I dragged him back home. The fire was already an inferno, our treasures and memories reduced to acrid smoke.

CHAPTER 10

Forced Labor Decree

Czestochowa, Poland — March–July 1940

FOOD AVAILABILITY HAD GONE FROM SCARCE to only available through the black market. I was sure the Nazis stole all the food for themselves and their army, while the rest of us stood in line at the Judenrat office for free soup. It was a full-day affair, as the line stretched as far as the eye could see, with people from Czestochowa and refugees from Lodz, Krakow, and other nearby Polish cities. New faces, withered and haunted, told us that as bad as we had it, they had endured worse.

The Judenrat was trying—they set up ration cards, a health board, and even pulled together a small police force for our protection. They did what they could, providing one free bowl of soup per day for each person. But that paltry ration was not enough to sate anyone's hunger, least of all the bottomless appetite of teenaged boys like me and Shlomo.

That night, Shlomo turned to me as we tried to fall asleep in the cold room we shared. We no longer had any money for heat. "Raf, do you think this will ever end?"

I took three deep breaths before answering. "The Judenrat's doing everything they can for us and for so many others. But I don't think the Germans will stop until we all disappear."

"Why don't they just shoot all the Jews? Boom! Done." Shlomo snapped his fingers.

I laughed so I wouldn't cry. "I suspect they don't want to waste any precious bullets on us." Shlomo cracked up, a sign that we were both losing it.

Tatte must have heard us as he entered our room. "I couldn't sleep myself. I'm glad you're both able to find humor in this wretched situation. Just promise me you won't share your grim jokes with your sister or mother."

We nodded, and Tatte leaned against our tall dresser with a sigh. "I take back every awful thing I said about the Judenrat. Kopinski and the others, they're working tirelessly to sustain us. Unfortunately, the Nazis take more than they provide."

$$\triangledown \quad \triangledown \quad \triangledown$$

WHENEVER I THOUGHT our lives couldn't get any worse, our tormentors were determined to prove me wrong. By May 1940, the streets felt like traps, ready to snap shut on any unsuspecting Jewish man. The Nazis could seize any of us without warning and haul us off to a forced labor site, much like my cement-block-carrying "adventure," as I called it for sanity's sake. Our oppressors didn't care who they took—we all looked the same to them. At least, they hadn't stooped to using women and children. Yet.

Over time, the labor demands grew, and some jobs were legitimate. The Nazis required Jewish men for individual tasks and hard labor. Jews were skilled, and best of all, free labor.

To cope with the incessant demands, the Judenrat organized Jewish laborers into pools to meet these demands more systematically. The hope was by assigning men with the proper skills to meet each task, it might prevent the Nazis from yanking random Jewish men off the streets.

This led to a decree that every Jewish male over fifteen had to register for forced labor. As Tatte, Shlomo, and I made our way to the registration building, I could feel the noose tightening around my neck. Still, we were more fortunate than most.

Some of my high school friends had landed administrative jobs with the Judenrat, and they got me work as an office clerk. The role was tedious and monotonous, and the pay was a ration of bread and soup, but it kept me off the lists for distant hard labor sites.

Shlomo was lucky, too, finding work at the nearby railway. Unlike the brutal Nazi SS, the supervisors were Gentile Poles, which offered a small degree of protection. For now, we allowed ourselves to breathe. Our jobs provided just enough cover from the relentless harassment on the streets and let us sleep at home most nights.

Tatte, meanwhile, had secured a "Wichtiger Jude" (Important Jew) card, which granted him a reprieve from forced labor. To get it, he had to bribe an official, risking everything to pull it off. Bribery was dangerous, but Tatte's card saved him from the random labor calls that tore men away from their families without warning, and from which their return was never guaranteed.

IN JULY 1940, I TURNED SEVENTEEN. I didn't expect any type of celebration, but Mama had enough ingredients to bake a single sufganiot, an oven-baked jelly donut, to commemorate the occasion. My family sat around our scratched but sturdy kitchen table, and after singing to me, Mama cut the sufganiot into five pieces so each of us would enjoy a little taste of sweetness. I'm not embarrassed to admit that all of us licked our fingers until the last traces of jelly were gone.

I'll never forget that birthday. Despite all the hardships, we were together and remained in our own home. Shlomo raised an imaginary glass of wine and made a toast: "May we outlast our Nazi overlords and remain together as a family."

"From your mouth to God's ears," Mama proclaimed.

PART II

ENTRAPMENT

CHAPTER 11

Hell Revisited

Lublin, Poland — August–October 1940

IN AUGUST 1940, THE JUDENRAT issued a call for labor. "Only three months," they promised. "You'll return after that." But most people believed this would be dangerous work, and those who volunteered might never return. Thankfully, Shlomo and I had "good" jobs and believed we were exempt from this work detail. Tatte, with his important status and middle age, wasn't worried about being chosen.

One afternoon, I stood in the street and watched a line form outside the Judenrat. They were all young men—some only a few years older than me—many with their hands buried deep in their pockets and shoulders hunched against the weight of uncertainty. Each carried a small sack of personal belongings and a blanket, lending weight to the growing belief that they would be gone for a long time. I stood, transfixed, as guards loaded them onto open-air trucks and drove them out of the city.

The entire operation made me uneasy, and I shared my concerns with Tatte at home later that night. "They'll be back in three months," he insisted, his voice barely audible above the loud sound of boots marching in unison past our apartment block. "The Judenrat would never lie about that."

I didn't think the Judenrat would lie. But I wouldn't put it past the Nazis to lie to the Judenrat. "I guess we'll see soon enough."

I didn't want to be right, but weeks passed, then months. It was as if they had dropped off the face of the Earth. Nazi propaganda didn't breathe a word about them, and no one from the Judenrat could shed any light. The rumor mill went into overdrive. The disappearance of those poor men proved the Judenrat, despite their honorable intentions, was just as powerless and uninformed as we were.

"I'm scared," Shlomo murmured one night in our bedroom.

"Me, too," I whispered back. "It won't be long before they come for the rest of us."

In October 1940, the authorities issued a new forced labor decree that spread terror throughout the Jewish community. The Germans were back to hauling men straight from the streets, and every time we left for our jobs, Shlomo and I hugged Mama, Tatte, and Rivka like we might never see them again.

A few days after the decree, I was finishing my work at the Judenrat administrative building when German soldiers stormed in, shouting at us to follow them. It was happening—all that we had dreaded. Outside, we found the street filled with young men. I scanned the crowd, hoping that Shlomo wasn't caught in this net.

When I saw him, I cried out and ran to his side, "What happened? I thought you were safe."

"I thought you were, too! Shlomo fired back. The soldiers trapped us when we were coming home from the railroad."

We heard someone calling our names, "Hey, there's Cousin Ephraim!" Shlomo said, pointing.

Cousin Ephraim was two years my senior, and much to my regret, I hadn't connected with him in months. He clutched a bundle of clothes, his face bleak, but his eyes lit up when we greeted him. The three of us stayed close during our march to the Czestochowa train depot. I was relieved Tatte wasn't among this group, but I could hear him telling me to watch out for Shlomo and Ephraim, no matter what.

At the railway station, they directed us toward a grassy lot that abutted the cattle cars they would use to transport us. Night had fallen, and with it, the temperatures. It was cold enough that frost crunched under our shoes as the guards lined us up in front of the cattle cars. With their doors pried open, the cars looked like monstrous, gaping mouths ready to swallow us whole.

Huddling together for warmth, I caught a movement in the nearby parking lot and nudged Shlomo and Ephraim. Shlomo's eyes were keener than mine. "They're civilians, exchanging packages with the guards," he said. "Money? Cigarettes? What do you think?"

I laid a finger against my lips, a sign to keep our voices down. But to our great surprise, a supervisor called out our names, and a package flew toward us. Unfortunately, as Shlomo reached out to grab it, a guard intercepted.

"What do we have here?" he mused, rifling through the contents. "Don't mind if I help myself." He shoved an apple in his mouth and pulled a wool blanket over his shoulder. After taking what he wanted, he tossed the rest of the package to us.

We set the box on the ground and took stock of its contents. Thankfully, there were extra blankets, clean clothes—and to our astonishment—a full Sabbath meal. It came complete with a small chicken and the traditional braided challah, covered in Mama's handmade striped linen cloth. Our parents must have moved mountains to get this package to us.

"They'll go hungry for this," Shlomo remarked, his expression a mixture of gratitude and sorrow.

I sighed. "I know, but they would want us to enjoy it." I broke off a piece of challah for each of us. The taste was bittersweet, a reminder of the family we were leaving behind.

Eventually, the soldiers shoved us into the boxcars, prodding our backsides with their bayonets, loading our car so full of bodies that I feared we might suffocate. All around us were sobs and whispered prayers. So tangible was the angst, I could taste it.

The boxcar jolted forward, and with the package wedged between my feet, I clung to Shlomo and Ephraim as the train rolled eastward. I tried to rest, but the stench of sweaty bodies and the fear of losing our sustenance kept me wide awake.

It was a relief when morning sunlight filtered through the boxcar's tiny openings. Some people had taken care of their bodily needs where they stood, though most agreed it was better to press closer together and designate a corner for refuse. But despite our best intentions, there was nowhere for it to go, so it sloshed under our feet and made several men throw up.

All any of us could do was to pray for this nightmare to end, for someone to open the doors and let us out so we could breathe. But no one came. We were trapped in this moving hell, questioning whether it would become our tomb.

CHAPTER 12

Separated

Lublin, Poland — August–October 1940

I HADN'T TASTED A DROP OF WATER in two days. My lips were cracked and bleeding, every breath burned like dry gravel. But when the boxcar doors finally burst open, a rush of fresh air surged in, and I drank it down like a man saved from drowning.

For a fleeting moment, it felt like salvation.

Then I saw them.

German SS—dozens, maybe hundreds—advancing in a sea of black uniforms, red-and-white swastika armbands blazing, Death's Head patches grinning from their collars. They moved like predators. And we—trapped, weak, blinking in the light—were the prey.

The Ukrainian SS were with them, their cruelty already a dark legend whispered among the prisoners. They eyed us with twisted glee, as if we were vermin needing extermination.

With the butts of their rifles, they beat us out of the boxcars, cursing, spitting. The guards forced men to leap from the train, falling eight feet to the ground below, legs buckling, arms flailing.

There was no mercy. Only orders—and pain.

I pressed myself against the back wall of the car, hoping to avoid their blows, but the madness inside the boxcar was inescapable. Men shoved past me, desperate to escape. I didn't think—I shoved through the chaos, ducking rifle strikes, and before I knew it, I was airborne.

Bodies were piling up on the ground, men struggling to stand, many knocked down as more of us fell from the train. When I hit the ground, I felt nothing, not the pain of the landing, not the weight of the men who crashed on top of me. Adrenaline took over, fueled by my survival instinct.

I rolled away from the mass of bodies, trying to stand, but each time I rose to my feet, someone else knocked me back down. Finally, I found an opening and scrambled through, stepping on arms, legs, any body part that got in my way.

Then the SS unleashed their police dogs, and my body convulsed with terror as memories of the horrors of Bloody Monday flooded back. I spotted a gap between the boxcars and bolted straight toward the waiting SS, who were forming us into columns.

I was free of the chaos, miraculously still clutching the care package, but where were Shlomo and Ephraim? I couldn't see them anywhere, not even where the SS were manhandling lagging Jews into lines. It was my responsibility to keep us together, and I had already failed.

"Raus!" A rifle butt slammed into my ribs, knocking the air from my lungs. I stumbled forward, my legs forced to obey, but my thoughts remained on Shlomo and Ephraim. *Where are you? Did you escape this madness?*

SS soldiers forced us to run in formation. All I could do was keep my head down and focus on staying upright as they drove us through the streets of Lublin. Dust rose thick from the dirt road, burning my eyes and turning my parched throat raw. Behind us, dogs barked and snapped at the heels of the slowest men. I kept up my pace, desperate to stay clear of their slavering jaws.

After what felt like an eternity, we arrived at the camp, a

former Polish army base now surrounded by barbed wire. Another group of fresh SS soldiers stood at the gate, waiting for us with guns primed should any of us cause trouble. Guards shoved me into a barracks with nine other prisoners. I was so overwhelmed, distressed, and exhausted, I found an open bunk and passed out.

It was before dusk when I woke, cradling the package in my arms like a security blanket. My back and legs throbbed in pain, and my throat was parched like the Sahara. I limped outside, desperate for water, and that's when I thought I saw a mirage—Shlomo and Ephraim, standing by a well. *Is that really them?*

When they rushed toward me, I knew they were real, and I would have wept for joy if I had an ounce of hydration in my system. For the first time in what seemed like forever, I felt a glimmer of hope. We hugged, and after drinking our fill, cleaned each other's wounds.

"I'm so sorry I left you guys behind in the boxcar," I croaked, unable to look them in the eyes.

Shlomo snorted. "You didn't leave us. You shouted, 'Go!' and plowed through the guards. Ephraim and I followed in your path."

I blinked, trying to remember the scene, but it was all a blur. I didn't know if he was telling the truth, but it didn't matter. What mattered was that we were together.

That night, after we shared the Sabbath meal with our bunkmates, we rolled our spare clothes into makeshift pillows and tucked the remaining food safely inside. I turned to face the wall, still emotional and not wanting Shlomo to see my tears. But then his arm wrapped around me, pulling me close—he knew exactly what I needed.

CHAPTER 13

Train Depot

Hrubieszow, Poland — October 1940

THE FOLLOWING MORNING, I discovered my right eye had swollen shut, the sting of infection lingering from yesterday's dust-covered march. Shlomo, ever the joker, grinned at me. "You look like you lost a few rounds with a heavyweight fighter!" His words brought a weak smile to my lips, but the infection throbbed with every movement. I rinsed it with water from the well, but it still stung.

After we choked down a slice of stale bread and sipped the bitter swill they called coffee, the SS barked at us to line up. "We will hang anyone who tries to escape—along with two others we choose at random. Disobedience means death." Death wasn't far off anymore—it hovered around us, and we all stood on edge, waiting for the unthinkable.

Remarkably, over the next few days, the beatings lessened, and the taunts became more subdued. The SS added an extra bowl of soup to our noontime meal, a blessing since we had polished off the food from our parents. By the time they shoved us back into the boxcars, I allowed myself to believe that perhaps they didn't want to kill us after all.

My tentative optimism was reinforced at our next stop, a town called Hrubieszow. When we arrived at dusk, the guards didn't rush us off the train. The doors opened, and I breathed a tremendous sigh of relief that there were no new tormentors to harass us. We filed off in an orderly fashion, inhaling the fresh air.

Then I spotted the volunteers—local Jews whose faces radiated warmth, making me feel human again. They hugged us, kissing both our cheeks like an auntie, and I couldn't help but blush.

"You're safe for now," one of them whispered as she embraced me. She held me longer than I expected, and her voice cracked as she whispered, "You look just like my son."

I hugged her again, as I didn't know what to say. Nearby, I saw Shlomo grin as a man handed him a roll. He held it up like it was the most valuable treasure in the world, which, in a way, it was. The volunteers brought not just sustenance but luxuries such as cakes, sliced meat, and wonders of wonders, wine. I couldn't fathom how they managed it.

"Here, eat this." A young man pressed a roll in my hands, his eyes radiating kindness. "There's more if you need it."

"Thank you, but are you sure you can spare this? I know how hard life has been for everyone since the Nazis invaded Poland." I pushed the bread back to him.

"Jews must take care of each other. I know you'd do the same if our positions were reversed." He passed it back and placed his other hand over it. "Take the food. It brings me great joy to offer it."

German and Ukrainian SS stood on the sidelines, their cold eyes watching but not interfering. We were allowed to revel in community with our Jewish brothers and sisters, a genuine gift I fully cherished.

One volunteer, an older man with a long white beard, stood up and addressed us. "Your ultimate destination is Wereszyn, a village close to the Soviet controlled territory. Your task will be to build roads. Stay strong, my brothers. You'll need every ounce of strength for what's in store." Despite his solemn words, we were grateful to know where we were heading. Knowledge gave us power and increased our chances of survival.

"Stay strong," I murmured, savoring a bite of the roll. We stayed with the volunteers for several hours, sharing stories, prayers, and quiet conversations. When it was time to leave, tears flowed freely as they had all become dear friends. The townspeople hugged us goodbye, wished us luck, and pressed more food into our hands, which we accepted with gratitude.

Labor trucks arrived, and the guards ordered us onto them. As we rolled out of the Hrubieszow station, the faces of those generous and thoughtful volunteers stayed with me. Our Jewish brethren had given us something more powerful than food or blankets. Their kindness, their warmth, created a light so bright that no amount of darkness could extinguish it.

Shlomo poked me in the side and kept his voice low. "I'll never forget them as long as I live."

I tapped my heart. "Neither will I."

CHAPTER 14

Labor Camp

Wereszyn, Poland — October 1940

IN THE MIDDLE OF THE NIGHT, we stumbled half-asleep onto different trucks to continue the journey. When the trucks finally ground to a halt and the guards ordered us to march, we jolted awake. A full moon lit our path, keeping us from tripping over rocks—or our own feet. I don't know how far we walked, only that by the time we reached the village of Wereszyn, dawn had not yet broken. We were running on fumes—Shlomo, Ephraim, and I all dragging our feet under the same invisible weight.

The guards shepherded us into barns, and the hay served as our beds. At least we had a roof over our heads, though the scent of animals permeated the enclosures. Water came from a well, but there were no latrines, just the open fields. There was no fighting our circumstances, and the hay, though itchy, was soft and comfortable.

The sun rose, bringing with it a new group of Ukrainian SS guards. "Up! Out!" they barked. My back ached as I stood, and I heard moans all around me. They directed us to a central square where an enormous kettle of soup cooked over an open fire. As the cook stirred, soup spilled out, covering the ground with mold and wriggling maggots.

Shlomo stared at the maggots, his mouth twisting in disgust.

"I'm not touching that."

Ephraim blanched. "Me neither." I nodded in agreement, too sickened to speak.

Back in the barn, we huddled together and pooled the money we'd brought with us. "We've got enough to last us two, maybe three weeks if we're careful," Ephraim reasoned as he flipped through the crumpled bills.

Shlomo cracked open the door and peered outside. "The coast is clear. Maybe we can barter with the locals. Someone might trade food."

As the oldest, Ephraim volunteered to be the first to try his luck. He took a handful of bills and slipped out of the barn. The hours dragged until he returned, a grin on his face and precious food in his hands.

"Bread, cheese, even a few potatoes!" he announced. It felt like a feast, enough to soothe our grumbling bellies. As long as the money lasted, we would avoid eating that awful slop they called soup.

The next day, they marched us back to the same square, to the same blackened kettle. This time it held grain coffee. I winced but drank it down, forcing myself to swallow the sludgy bitterness. Ephraim handed me a slice of black bread, mercifully free of weevils, and we ate in silence.

The village of Wereszyn was small but colorful. As we passed by a church, its onion domes gleaming in the gray morning light, I almost forgot we were there to work. That was, until we reached the equipment depot, and they thrust shovels and wheelbarrows into our hands. We were building roads—roads for *their* army to travel.

My body screamed at me as I lifted the heavy wheelbarrow. Filled with dirt, it weighed as much as a horse. But I had no choice and inched forward, my legs wobbling beneath me. The supervisor, a Ukrainian SS soldier with a sneer etched onto his craggy face, took delight in tormenting me.

"Too slow, you weakling!" he yelled, swinging his baton at my legs. The sting of the blow sent me stumbling, and the wheelbarrow tipped, spilling its load. I bent to refill it, but airborne dust burned my eyes, mixing with the tears I fought to hold back. My infection wasn't entirely gone, and this was the worst thing for it.

Ephraim caught my attention from across the worksite, giving me a nod of solidarity. Shlomo was a few yards away, making ridiculous faces to lighten my mood. Honestly, I didn't know how I could have managed without them both.

"When we get home," Shlomo muttered during one of our breaks, "remind me never to complain about chores again!" We managed a weak chuckle, though neither of us believed we'd ever see Mama, Tatte, or Rivka again.

▽ ▽ ▽

THE KINDHEARTED JEWS from Hrubieszow were right—we could never have imagined the oppression, indignity, and abuse we would face at the Wereszyn camp. The guards delighted in beating us as we worked, robbing us of our strength. Illness and fatigue assaulted us, and now we had an insidious new enemy—lice.

These minuscule invaders peppered my scalp and private areas with tiny landmines. I could feel them marching through the seams of my clothing, their horrible legs sending a relentless tickling sensation across my skin, especially on my scalp. The itching was maddening, and the unsanitary conditions in camp made it impossible to get rid of them.

"There's got to be something. We can't keep living like this," Ephraim complained as he scratched his underarms.

Shlomo tried to keep our spirits up by offering ridiculous suggestions. "We could strip naked and run over our clothes with the wheelbarrows. Or we could beat the lice to death with bricks." He motioned for us to come nearer.

"I have one more idea. A two-for-one deal!" We huddled close, intrigued despite our lack of confidence in his suggestions.

Shlomo turned his head from side to side, making sure the coast was clear. Satisfied, he crowed, "We should shave our heads and stuff the hair inside the guards' pillows!" The three of us laughed and wished we had the guts to try it. Nothing would have made us happier than to know that our guards suffered as much as we did.

CHAPTER 15

Foraging

Ukraine-Poland border — November 1940

WE MADE A FEW MORE RUNS for food, and our money was quickly running out. The labor demands didn't let up, and the meager rations were woefully insufficient. Desperation began to set in, as we knew finding nourishing food was a matter of life or death. Shlomo, Ephraim, and I decided our only option was to appeal to local farmers for help. We hoped that some might have enough compassion to risk feeding us without demanding payment in return.

"I'll go first," I volunteered, sounding braver than I felt.

Ephraim had handled most of the food purchases to this point, and he counseled me to wait for the right moment. It came on a miserable, gray afternoon, with visibility obscured by sleet. I hoped the guards would be too busy keeping themselves warm and dry to notice my absence. "Cover for me," I told Shlomo and Ephraim before breaking away from the work detail and dashing into the forest. An hour later, I spied a farm on the edge of the village.

The house was a simple, weathered cottage with a thatched roof and faded wooden shutters. Chickens pecked at the dirt, clucking softly as they roamed the yard, but I couldn't see any people. I knocked on the door, my stomach doing somersaults. When the farmer's wife opened the door, I pulled off my hat, placing it against my chest.

"Please," I begged. "They're starving us. Anything you can spare would be a blessing."

To my amazement—and immense relief—she let me inside. She called for her husband to come in from the backyard, and together they offered me more food than I'd seen since before the Nazi invasion. Bread, yams, cheese—simple fare, but fresh and nourishing. I ate as quickly as my body would allow. When they pressed a parcel of food into my hands for Shlomo and Ephraim, I thanked them again and again, overwhelmed by their kindness.

My brother and cousin rejoiced over the bounty. They agreed that since I had built a connection with the farmers, I should be the one to return. I snuck away several more times, and each time, the family welcomed me and shared what they had.

But one day, when the wife opened the door, something had changed. Her eyes flitted nervously across the yard, scanning the shadows. Without a word, she grabbed my arm and pulled me inside, closing the door quickly behind us. Her hands trembled as she bolted the lock, then quietly called for her husband to come into the kitchen.

I should have left, but ravenous hunger overpowered my better judgment. As I devoured the food they offered, my ears pricked at the sudden mention of a single word—"Gestapo." The wife gestured toward me, then pointed to the back door, where children stood watching from behind the screen. I froze. I had never noticed them before—never stopped to consider who else might be in the house. In that moment, the full weight of my selfishness hit me. By continuing to accept their kindness, I was endangering them all. I swallowed the last bite, a surge of unease creeping over me, and stood.

"Is the Gestapo coming for me?"

"No, you are safe for now," the father said. "But the Gestapo are making surprise visits to search for Jews, and our neighbors would sell us out for a few coins. My wife and I feel you shouldn't come back here again. It's too risky for all of us." His shoulders slumped, and his gaze turned downward.

I knew I could never forgive myself if harm came to this family because of me. I pushed back from the table and started for the door, but the wife stepped into my path. Wordlessly, she handed me my half-filled glass of milk. Her hands trembled, but she stood still, waiting as I drank every last drop. I wiped my lips and set the glass gently on the table.

"Thank you," I said in her language, my voice low, steady, and aching with sincerity.

Then, without warning, she pulled me into a fierce embrace. When she finally let go, she cupped my face in both hands, her eyes shining. She kissed my cheek—softly, deliberately—the way a mother might when sending her child into a world she can't protect him from.

"Go," she whispered, her voice thick. "Go, and live."

The farmer motioned for me to leave by the back door. I knew this would be my last visit. Taking a breath, I removed my worn hat. Inside the front hem, I had tucked the last of our paper money—just a few notes.

"Please," I said, holding it out, "take this—for everything you've done for me, my brother, and my cousin. I can't ever repay you, but it's all I have."

He looked down at the money, his face a blend of weariness and compassion. His rough, calloused fingers brushed mine as he gently pushed my hand away.

"No," he said quietly but firmly. "You keep that. There may come a time when you'll need it to save yourself."

I swallowed hard, a lump rising in my throat. "But... I have nothing else to give," I stammered, the weight of his kindness pressing down on me. "You've risked everything for me. I can't just walk away."

He offered a wistful smile and nodded toward his children in the distance. "You already have. If they were in your shoes, I'd pray someone would do the same. That's enough for me."

I stood there, speechless. He extended his hand, and I grasped it.

"Thank you," I whispered, my voice cracking. "Thank you for everything."

He nodded, gave my hand a final squeeze, then let go. "Go on now," he said, his voice low, almost tender. "And be careful."

Just as I turned to leave, the wife reappeared and pressed a wrapped bundle into my hands—extra cheese and bread for Shlomo and Ephraim. She rested a hand on her husband's shoulder, her eyes filled with apology, sorrow, and tenderness.

I stepped outside, the package clutched to my chest. As I made my way back toward the camp, I knew I would never forget their warmth, their courage, their humanity. In a world gone mad, there were still people willing to risk everything for a Jewish boy like me.

CHAPTER 16

Trust is Risky

Ukraine-Poland border — Late November 1940

AS EXPECTED, THE PACKAGE OF FOOD was devoured minutes after I returned to camp. But as the weather turned colder, our taskmasters became more demanding. With the grueling work and inadequate nutrition, Shlomo and Ephraim were rapidly losing weight. Most troubling, Shlomo developed a deep, persistent cough. I hadn't been sick, but it was only a matter of time.

When word spread among the prisoners that a Ukrainian family nearby would sometimes offer aid, I asked around until I had enough information to find them. Yes, I knew it was risky, but what choice did I have? I would do anything to protect Shlomo, despite the risk that some Nazi collaborators would sell us out.

I waited for another blustery winter day when the guards took more breaks to warm themselves. With a nod to Shlomo, I slipped away from the work crew and melted into the forest. After an hour, I found the house that matched the description I'd received. The house was well-kept, with lights glowing in the windows. My eyes caught a movement near the barn, so I hid behind a tree and watched.

It was a young worker, about my age, wearing a plain, tattered coat. With a deep breath, I made my approach, hands raised in the

80

"I mean no harm" position.

The worker paused, narrowing his eyes as he strode toward me. "What do you want?" His Ukrainian accent was thick, but his tone wasn't hostile.

I took a deep breath. "I'm on a work detail, and they're starving us. I was hoping you might have something—anything—to spare." I prayed my sunken cheeks and pale complexion would convince him if my plea didn't.

He studied me for a few moments, then nodded. He jerked his head toward the barn, and I followed him inside. "Stay here," he grunted. "I'll bring you food."

I watched him through the crack in the barn door. He entered the house and talked to someone in the kitchen. He pointed toward the barn, and his gesture and posture made me wary. I tried to steady my nerves, but the hairs on the back of my neck prickled. Despite my internal warning system urging me to flee, desperation won out.

A few minutes later, an older man appeared, carrying a tray of bread and pea soup. He had a crown of gray hair and wore spectacles, his demeanor calm. "Here," he said, setting the tray on a nearby workbench. "It's not much, but you're welcome to it."

My empty stomach made me throw caution to the wind, and I tore into the bread and shoveled the soup into my mouth. The man watched, his expression unreadable.

"Stay as long as you need," he said, his tone soothing. *Too soothing,* a part of my brain warned, but I still ignored it.

I realized I'd been so ravenous and nervous, I didn't leave any food for Shlomo or Ephraim. I was about to ask if he could spare any more when I heard heavy, rapid footsteps approaching the barn. The man backed away from me, his eyes flickering between me and the main door.

My instincts screamed I was walking into a trap—and this time, I listened. I would have punched through a wall if I had to, but luck or God intervened. I veered from the direction of the threat and bolted through a narrow back entrance of the barn.

Outside, the cold hit me like a slap. My stomach churned violently with the meal I'd just eaten as I sprinted across an open field, the frigid air slicing my lungs. Behind me, boots pounded, and voices barked commands, growing louder with every step. The forest loomed ahead—my only chance—and I didn't dare slow down.

But just as I neared the tree line, a figure lunged out from the shadows.

The worker.

He had been lying in wait.

I tripped on a hidden root and crashed to the ground. In an instant, he was on top of me, knife drawn, the blade trembling inches from my face.

I scrambled backward, heart hammering, panic rising. He didn't speak. He just held the knife steady, eyes flicking between me and the fast-approaching police.

I remembered the zlotys I had in the hem of my cap. With shaking hands, I ripped the seam open and thrust the crumpled bills toward him.

"It's all yours," I gasped. "Just… please… let me go."

His eyes darted to the money, then back to me. For a moment, his face twisted in hesitation, the conflict plain. Then he clenched his jaw, lowered the knife, and pocketed the cash.

I didn't wait. I scrambled to my feet and ran, tuning out the shouts and pounding footsteps behind me. I knew if I kept to a straight line, they'd catch me, so I zigzagged through the trees, ducking and weaving, until I reached the deepest, darkest part of the forest.

Branches whipped my arms and face, tearing at my clothes, but I didn't stop—not until the only sounds were my own ragged breaths and the snapping of twigs beneath my feet.

Only then did I collapse, my lungs searing. I dropped to my knees and vomited everything I'd eaten. But it wasn't just the food I was purging—it was the weight of failure. I had nothing for Shlomo or Ephraim. No food. No plan. No more kindness left to count on.

Trust had become a luxury I could no longer afford.

As the adrenaline wore off, I realized something worse: I was lost. The dense forest all around me felt like a cage, the trees and bushes blending together as if mocking me. I tried to retrace my steps, heading in what I thought was the right direction. My panic rose with each turn until, after what felt like an eternity, some of the landscape seemed familiar. I pushed through the underbrush, hoping and praying I was close to camp.

When I spied the work detail, I felt an immense sense of relief. But dread washed over me as I took in the scene. The laborers lined up for roll call—I'd been gone too long. If I ambled out of the woods now, they would punish everyone for my disobedience. If they suspected I'd been foraging or, worse, trying to escape, the punishment would be severe. My mind raced through every possible outcome as I crouched behind a tree, watching them from a distance.

Then I spotted Shlomo and Ephraim, standing in their assigned positions. The guard was calling out names, moving down the line, drawing ever closer to the moment of truth.

"Kantor, Ephraim!" the guard shouted. Ephraim stepped forward.

"Kantor, Shlomo!" Shlomo hesitated for a beat, but stepped forward, too.

"Kantor, Rafal!"

Silence.

"Kantor, Rafal!" the guard called again, his head on swivel.

I was out of time. In desperation, I crept to the edge of the woods, slid off my pants, and squatted down, baring myself in the icy wind. After a deep breath, I shouted at the top of my lungs. "Oy! Sorry! Sorry!!"

The guard's head snapped in my direction, and I saw the other prisoners turning to see what the commotion was. Feigning embarrassment—like someone caught mid-sprint by a sudden wave of loose bowels—I yanked up my pants. "I'm done, I'm done!" I called out, waving one hand in the air, as if trying to salvage a shred of dignity.

The guard narrowed his eyes and called me back into line with an annoyed grunt. "Get back here, Kantor, before I make you sorry you were ever born." I scrambled to obey.

I took my place next to Shlomo, still catching my breath. I kept my head low, flushed from the close call. The guard shot me a last glare before moving down the line.

It worked. I couldn't believe it, but it worked. No suspicion and no punishment. My only penance was a little ribbing from some of the other prisoners, which I accepted with grace. As the guard moved further down the line, Shlomo leaned over to me and whispered, "Where the heck were you?"

"Later," I mouthed. But the weight of what I had to confess made my shoulders droop. There was no more money and no more food to share, and it was all my fault.

CHAPTER 17

Released

Wereszyn/Hrubieszow, Poland — December 1940

ANOTHER MONTH CRAWLED BY, marking three months in the forced labor camp. Exhaustion had hollowed us out. Riddled with lice and worn down to shadows of ourselves, we could still work—and that was the problem. Shlomo, Ephraim, and I were dangerously malnourished, hacking with constant coughs, but not sick enough to be pulled from the ranks. Not according to the camp doctor, whose weekly examinations decided our fate. Authorities sent home anyone deemed too ill to work. Though we tried to fake our way out—exaggerating coughs or limping—the doctor waved us back to work, week after week. There were always others worse off than we were.

Our routine was comprised of gagging down our maggot-filled soup, hearing men groaning in their bunks, and thanking God for allowing us to live another day. I expected nothing to change, that we would simply work until we collapsed. But one night, a guard entered the barracks and barked, "Shlomo Kantor! Rafal Kantor! Get up and follow me!"

Perplexed by the summons, Shlomo and I followed the guard with cautious steps to the small room where the Polish doctor held his health evaluations. We sat stiffly on the edge of the cot as he examined us in silence, never uttering a single word.

85

When the examination was over, he exited the room. The guard escorted us back, refusing to answer any questions.

In our beds, Shlomo whispered, "That was crazy."

"I know," I replied. "Why just us? It's making me nervous. What if they transfer us to a different work site that's even worse?"

Shlomo yawned. "Maybe it's nothing, so don't sweat it. Let's try to rest."

Official release papers arrived a few days later, much to our shock. I held the slip of paper in my hands, staring at it as if it might disappear. We lay on the thin mattresses that night, too wired to sleep. "Is this real?" Shlomo asked.

"I don't know," I murmured. "It seems like a dream."

We received news of our imminent release during the morning lineup, and it was nearly impossible to hide the smiles breaking through our exhaustion. The cold bit at our ankles as we stood in the yard, but for the first time in months, hope stirred beneath the surface. A few men muttered quiet congratulations, but Ephraim stood beside us, pale and still, his breath curling in the morning air.

That's when it hit me—he wasn't coming with us. "You'll be next," I said, forcing optimism into my voice as I pulled him into a hug.

Shlomo nodded, too choked up to speak.

We stood there in a hush, broken only by the low groan of the idling truck engine. Then Ephraim straightened his thin shoulders and reached for our hands. "Safe travels," he said, his voice barely above a whisper. "We'll be together again soon."

"Yes," I said, though the word felt empty in my mouth. Ephraim had been more than a cousin—he was our brother in every way that mattered. Leaving him behind felt like the deepest betrayal yet.

Shlomo gripped his shoulder, his voice rough. "Take care,

Ephraim. Don't give up. You'll get out, too."

Ephraim nodded, eyes glistening. "I'll try."

A guard shouted impatiently, and the truck gave a short, sharp honk. We climbed aboard, the wooden slats cold beneath our hands. But even as the truck jolted forward, we turned in our seats, refusing to take our eyes off him. He raised a hand in a last wave, the wind tugging at the hem of his coat.

As the camp faded behind us, I etched Ephraim's face into my memory—his sunken cheeks, the way his lips pressed together to hold back emotion. I feared that without our support, he wouldn't survive.

AN ICY WIND KNIFED THROUGH our thin clothes as the truck jolted along the rutted road. We had left in such haste, there'd been no time to grab our blankets—the only possessions we still held onto. But even as we braced against the cold air, a quiet warmth flickered inside us at the thought of being reunited soon with Tatte, Mama, and Rivka.

As we neared the train station on the outskirts of Hrubieszow, Shlomo leaned close. "You think they'll pay for our train tickets?"

I frowned. "I doubt it. And unfortunately, we're completely out of money."

Shlomo stared at the ground, his shoulders trembling ever so slightly. I could see the tears welling, though he blinked hard, trying to keep them at bay. I knocked him lightly on the shoulder. "There's no way we're missing that train. We've come too far. We'll think of something."

THE STREETS SWARMED with black-uniformed SS storm troopers and the German Wehrmacht army. Seeing them was a harsh dose of reality. Although we escaped the terrible work camp, we were far from free.

The truck rolled to a stop in front of a narrow brick home in the heart of the Jewish quarter, instead of at the train station as we had expected. The peeling paint on the front door and the iron-barred windows gave it an unwelcoming vibe. As our driver gestured for us to get out, a pang of doubt crept over me as I stepped onto the street. Why were they dumping us here?

Shlomo and I hesitated, unsure whether to knock on the door or turn and bolt. As we edged closer, we noticed the front door was slightly ajar. I glanced at Shlomo for support, but he stepped behind me.

"You're older," he said, and I couldn't argue with that.

I took a deep breath and pushed, revealing a large, open room crammed with people—sitting, standing, and leaning against the walls. But no one seemed to mind. Maybe they were simply grateful to have a roof over their heads.

And then I spotted him.

"Tatte!" I shrieked. Shlomo echoed me as we edged our way toward him.

His arms opened wide, and his face lit with a smile that rivaled the sun. Shlomo and I crashed into his embrace, tears streaming freely. A flood of relief and joy washed over us after months of uncertainty and deprivation. Tatte kissed our cheeks, our foreheads, over and over. We cried, all three of us, without shame. "I missed you both so much," he said, his voice thick with feeling.

Tatte took a step back, his eyes scanning over us. His expression sagged when he took in the clothes hanging off our thin bodies like rags. His pain reflected back at us, the wish that he could have taken all our suffering upon himself.

Shlomo and I drank in the changes in him, too, the dark circles under his eyes that hadn't been there before. Whatever he had endured while we were gone, it had aged him further.

Tatte cupped our chins. "I'm so glad it worked."

"What worked?" Shlomo asked in confusion. Tatte's eyes sparkled, and for the first time since our reunion, he resembled his old self.

"I traveled to Hrubieszow to secure your release by any means necessary, ready to take the place of one of you if required. When I found out which doctor controlled the release process, I offered him a bribe. He accepted it, thank God, and I hoped he would be faithful to his word."

I stared at him, my gratitude immeasurable. Tatte had risked everything for us, and now we were here because of him. And yet... not everyone was here.

"Tatte, what about Ephraim?" I asked. "We left him behind in that awful place."

His silence told us everything. Sadly, we never saw our dear cousin Ephraim again.

CHAPTER 18

Encounter

Hrubieszow, Poland — December 1940

WE PLANNED TO SLEEP at the Jewish "hostel" for one evening and take the train home the next day. But after observing our condition, Tatte declared that finding food was a priority. Shlomo lay passed out in a corner, and I begged to come along on the mission.

"No, it's too dangerous for you," he warned. But I kept pestering him until he relented.

The presence of so many SS soldiers made it unsafe for Jews to be out in the streets. Tatte opened the front door and looked in all directions. Seeing no danger, he waved for me to come with him.

"If we see any Nazis, keep your eyes down and don't draw attention to yourself," he cautioned. "This bootlegger we're visiting sells to Jews, but he's discreet in his dealings."

When we arrived at a four-corner intersection, a single Nazi SS officer appeared around the bend. He was tall, his reddish hair cropped into a crew cut. His chiseled physique filled the contours of a perfectly tailored black uniform, and his square jaw and sharp cheekbones made him appear more like an Olympic swimmer than a soldier. I held my breath as he went by, hoping he wouldn't notice us.

I exhaled in relief, but my relief was short-lived. "Get back here, Jew scum!" the officer shouted.

My father and I turned, like sheep facing a wolf. My legs turned to rubber beneath me. Step by wobbly step, we approached the officer, stopping just a meter away. Without warning, his left fist shot out and slammed into Tatte's cheek, followed by a right hook to the jaw. The sickening thud of flesh and bone echoed in the cold air. Tatte collapsed like a sack of cement.

"You damn Jew! Don't you know to salute a German officer by taking off your hat?" His voice was a harsh growl. "Get up! Take five paces forward, turn around, and salute me properly—or I'll shoot you right between the eyes!" He tapped the pistol holstered at his side, his threat unmistakable.

I helped Tatte to his feet, holding my breath as he staggered forward. He turned, removed his hat, and gave a perfect salute. Relief flooded me, and I exhaled softly—he did it!

But the officer just smirked, clamping a heavy hand on Tatte's shoulder before driving a brutal punch into his abdomen. Tatte folded in half and collapsed again.

"How dare you salute me like that, you filthy Jew!" The officer's face flushed as red as his hair, his voice rising with fury. "Get up and do it right!"

But Tatte couldn't move. He lay there, gasping for air.

"I said, get up!" The officer loomed over him, a dark silhouette swallowing my father's prone form. "If you don't, your boy's next!" He jabbed a thumb in my direction.

For a fleeting moment, rage eclipsed my fear. My mind screamed to act—to lunge, seize his pistol, and end this. My eyes locked on the weapon, then on Tatte. His gaze met mine, raw with pain but steady enough to deliver an unspoken command. A subtle twitch of his index finger said everything: No.

The officer made good on his threat. He grabbed a fistful of my shirt collar and yanked me forward. My breath caught as he pulled me closer—then he recoiled with a strangled cry of disgust. Tiny white specks and small dark shapes—lice and nits—scattered from my clothes and hair, crawling over his fingers.

"You filthy swine!" he spat, shaking his hand violently. His revulsion turned quickly into fury as he delivered a vicious kick to Tatte's ribs.

"You're parasites—the scourge of the Earth!" he roared, pointing at us as if we were less than human. I held my breath, certain he'd draw his pistol this time.

Instead, he reached into his back pocket and pulled out a swastika-adorned handkerchief. Methodically, he wiped the blood from his hands, then let the handkerchief slip from his fingers and fall to the ground. Straightening his uniform, smoothing his sleeves, he inhaled deeply and marched away as if the entire encounter had been nothing but a minor inconvenience.

I dropped to my knees beside my father. "Tatte, I'm so sorry." My hands trembled as I helped him to sit up. Blood trickled from his face and ear, and I was worried his ribs might be broken. Hatred burned inside me like never before, toward the Nazis and those who followed them with blind devotion.

When Tatte was steady enough to walk, I guided him back to our sleeping quarters, forgetting all about my hunger. When we arrived back at the house, people sprang into action. A woman guided Tatte to a chair and instructed others to fetch fresh water and towels.

The owner told us that harassment of Jews was a daily occurrence in Hrubieszow. "Your father was lucky the SS officer didn't murder him."

I kept replaying the image of Tatte being beaten over and over. Why did I stand there, paralyzed, instead of stepping forward to take his place? Shouldn't a son be willing to risk his life to help his father? How much pain and humiliation does one witness before risking it all? But what plagued me the most was how I *might have* reacted if Tatte had begged for my help. My greatest fear was that I still might have lacked the courage to do anything.

CHAPTER 19

Protection

Czestochowa, Poland — January 1941

TATTE HANDED US NEW STAR OF DAVID armbands and though he winced with every step, we set off for the train station the following morning. Call it superstition, but neither Shlomo nor I could bring ourselves to ask how Mama and Rivka were before seeing them with our own eyes.

We boarded a horse-driven buggy to the Hrubieszow train terminal. The bumpy ride didn't distract me from my thoughts of home. I hadn't dared to imagine I would ever see it again, and now we were on our way. The ordinary things I had once taken for granted, like ruffling Rivka's hair, or hugging Mama, or sleeping in my bed, I now craved.

At the terminal, Tatte handed over money for our tickets, and since we had time before the train arrived, we found a bench and rested. From there, we observed people milling about, some waiting for the same train to Czestochowa, others to places unknown. It was a small station, with people gathered in groups, speaking mostly in Polish and Ukrainian. They spoke of ordinary things with a natural ease, their gestures familiar and unguarded. I envied them, the normalcy of it all.

When our train arrived, people gave us a wide berth as we boarded. I sensed their judgment—they didn't need to say anything.

We were filthy, mangy, and ragged, while they were neat and clean. Settling into seats, my gaze fixed on Tatte. A reddish-purple cut marred his cheek, and he held his hands below his ribs, where he'd been viciously kicked. Time and again, he had protected our family without care for himself. I winced to see the toll it was taking on him.

As the train lurched forward, I observed just how normal life seemed for the other riders. Despite the war and the food shortages, non-Jews appeared to live their lives freely. Some were commuters on their way to work, and others were traveling for the pleasure of it. Before long, with the steady chugging of the train, Tatte had fallen asleep. Both Shlomo and I watched the countryside roll by through the window.

A conductor came through our car, accompanied by a German military police officer. They checked everyone's tickets and papers. The officer didn't scrutinize us any differently than anyone else. I felt surprised and relieved.

Another station passed, and the voices on board shifted, with Polish and German the only languages spoken. No Ukrainians remained on this train as it moved westward, closer to Czestochowa, into a region almost entirely populated by Poles. As we drew closer to home, Shlomo grabbed my hand, and we both sighed with exhausted relief.

After arriving at our station, we had to fill out paperwork with the local Polish authorities. I feared they would deny us entry, or at least, give us a hard time, but happily, they rubber-stamped our return to Czestochowa. It was only a fifteen-minute walk home. Shlomo, always the energetic one, darted ahead like an excited puppy. But he kept turning back, reluctant to leave Tatte behind.

"Go ahead, I'll stay with Tatte," I said. He deserved our support after all he had done to save us.

Shlomo jogged back to us. "We'll all walk home together."

As we approached our building, we caught sight of Mama peering out the front window and waving at us. In a flash, she was out the door, running in our direction. When she saw Tatte, her shock cut through the air.

"Don't worry about me, Chava. Look who I brought with me!" Tatte said.

"My beautiful sons!" Mama cried, throwing her arms around both of us, squeezing so hard, I thought our ribs would break. "You're both too skinny!" she shrieked, releasing us.

"And ugly!" Rivka chimed in as she slammed into me with a big-time hug.

But then Mama's eyes narrowed as she noticed us scratching. Her expression shifted, and she was back in mother mode. "Out back, now! Both of you!" When we complied, she commanded, "Now strip!" As our wretched, raggedy clothing fell into a pile, Mama said, "Leave them. I'll burn them later."

"Good riddance," I muttered under my breath.

Mama ushered us inside, where she boiled water with lye for our baths. One great perk of being the eldest was that I got the first bath. Words can't describe how luxurious it was to wash away months of grime. Shlomo didn't even complain about going second. When he was done, the water had turned black, and we both said a cheery goodbye to the tiny critters who had plagued us endlessly. Clean and dressed in fresh clothes, we were new men.

Over the next few weeks, Mama made it her mission to rebuild our strength, providing us with whatever healthy food she was able to scrounge. How she managed it, she refused to say, but I suspected she bartered with our neighbors. For a brief time, the Judenrat protected Shlomo and me from being assigned to another physical labor detail, which we truly appreciated. This enabled us to rest and recover from the horrors we had endured.

As our health returned, so did our risk of being selected for forced labor again. One evening after dinner, the five of us sat down to strategize. Avoiding the worst assignments wasn't a matter of luck—it took careful planning and, often, bribery. Our best hope was to find local jobs that made us valuable to the Germans, so valuable they wouldn't consider transferring us elsewhere.

Tatte spoke first, clearing his throat. "Factory jobs will afford the best protection."

Mama scoffed. "Tovya, the only jobs available are at the Pelcery and Rakow plants, and they've both been acquired by the German company HASAG. I've heard that the work is brutal!"

I warmed to the idea. "Mama, it can't be worse than what Shlomo and I endured at the Wereszyn labor camp. Plus, the factory work is right here in Czestochowa, so we might be able to come home after work."

"I'm with Raf," Shlomo nodded, lacing his fingers behind his head. I grimaced to see how his collarbone protruded through his shirt.

Mama's face softened. "I just want my boys to be safe. I can't bear losing you two again." She pushed a piece of bread toward each of us.

Tatte patted her hand. The Nazi invasion had been brutal for all of us. My gaze turned to Rivka, taller but thinner than I remembered. It was apparent she wanted to join the conversation, but she bit her lip to remain silent.

"I'll be careful," I said, grinning at Shlomo. "We both will."

Shlomo gave the thumbs up sign. "You can always count on me! And who knows, we might pick up some dirt on the Nazis while we're working in the factories." Mama swatted him playfully, and I marveled how, once again, Shlomo had defused the tension with his wit.

Mama's eyes drilled into our souls, still serious. "Every day, I worry about all my children. Just promise me, no matter what, you won't push your luck." She dabbed her eyes with a dish towel.

"Agreed!" I nodded.

"So, what's our next step? Do we just knock on the door and tell them we're here to work?" Shlomo blurted.

Tatte sighed. "If only it were that easy. We'll need to convince the Judenrat."

CHAPTER 20

Mr. Kaplan

Czestochowa, Poland — January 1941

A FEW DAYS LATER, I watched Tatte darting around our cramped apartment. He had a gift for being clever, but in times like these, cleverness was more than a talent—it was our lifeline. There was no doubt he was aware I was watching him. Perhaps he waited until this moment so I would learn his secrets.

He pushed his kitchen chair aside, pulled up a floorboard I didn't know was loose, and reached beneath. Then he pulled out a small cloth pouch. I moved in closer as he emptied its contents— a rubber band full of zloty notes, several silver coins, and a worn gold ring that had once belonged to his father.

I crouched beside him as Papa rubbed the gold ring between his fingers. "I thought you used all our valuables to save us."

"I understand you might be thinking that I could have used some of this money to save Ephraim."

I nodded, too choked up to reply.

He put the ring down and clasped my hands. "My priority must be to protect my immediate family. Without money, we can't buy the food and supplies we need to survive. I face hard decisions every day, like how much to spend, how much to save, and who to bribe. If I trust the wrong person…"

"I understand, more than you know." Nothing about our wartime existence made any sense, but my father's devotion to us was beyond reproach.

Tatte slid the coins and the ring back into the pouch, tucking it back under the floorboard. After smoothing and folding the zlotys, he retrieved an envelope, paper, a pencil, a needle, and a spool of thread. I watched in awed silence as he worked, his hands moving with the precision of someone who knew that even the slightest error might cause his death.

"Tomorrow afternoon, you and I will go to the job placement office. Kaplan is the official in charge." Even I had heard that Kaplan did favors for those who paid. "I'll do everything I can to convince him to assign you and Shlomo to one of the factories."

The plan was risky, but I didn't have any better ideas. Tatte motioned for me to come closer.

"Raf, these talks are delicate. Wait outside the office. If anything feels wrong, knock and say, 'Excuse me, my mother is waiting for us.' Understand?"

I nodded and prayed I wouldn't have to say the words.

CRAMPED AND DIMLY LIT, the Judenrat office hummed with activity. Desperate Jews filled the space, and I winced as I listened to people's pleas for help. When we approached the reception counter, a man with thinning hair and a permanent scowl received us.

Tatte displayed his 'Important Jew' card. "I'm here to speak with the official in charge of factory placements."

The clerk's beady eyes flickered with suspicion. "You again," he muttered. He pointed down the hall to Kaplan's office.

Tatte thanked him and led the way, his hand pressed against

the coat pocket that held the precious envelope. Whenever someone passed us, I cringed. If they found the bribe money, the punishment would be a swift and terrible death.

Tatte addressed the attendant outside the door. "We're here to see Kaplan." The man, his clothes hanging off his frame, knocked. When the door opened, Kaplan's bulk filled the frame.

"Peter, take a long break," he ordered. Kaplan's beady eyes narrowed at us. "Come in, quickly."

I sat in the attendant's vacated seat, as Tatte had instructed. I jammed my foot inside the door frame so the door wouldn't fully close, enabling me to eavesdrop on the conversation.

"This is for my sons," I heard Tatte say. "For them to get good jobs in one of the HASAG plants."

"There's a waiting list," Kaplan replied. "I don't think your sons have the proper qualifications." *What a lying snake.*

Tatte cleared his throat, and I assumed he slid the envelope across the desk. "This shows they are both fully qualified."

I was so absorbed in the conversation that a sudden eruption at the reception desk almost made me jump out of my chair.

"Inspection!" a loud German voice boomed.

A tall, broad-shouldered SS officer stormed down the hallway, followed by four other Nazi soldiers. One of them grabbed me by the coat and threw me into Kaplan's office. My hipbone bashed against the edge of Kaplan's metal desk, and man, did that hurt.

"Nobody moves!" the officer spat. "Hands behind your heads!"

I froze as he searched me, but there was nothing to find. Then he moved to Tatte, kicking apart his legs and patting him down, his hands invasive and thorough. I held my breath, praying they wouldn't find anything.

When the officer finished with Tatte, he turned to Kaplan and searched him, too. Kaplan's cheeks flushed as he objected.

"This is an outrage. I have a job to do."

The Nazi officer scoffed as he rifled through Kaplan's desk, dumping the contents of each drawer onto the floor and rifling through it. I was surprised the Nazi didn't find any incriminating evidence. Then his eyes landed on the envelope.

"What's this?" he demanded, snatching it from the desk.

"It's his," Kaplan blurted, pointing a chubby finger at Tatte. A wave of dread washed over me. The officer marched around the desk and grabbed Tatte's collar.

"What are you trying to pull here?" he growled.

Tatte remained calm. "It's a letter, sir. An application for factory work."

The Nazi pushed Tatte away and tore open the envelope, lips curled into a sneer. I knew he expected to find money, and I was terrified that he would. "What is this?" he barked, his sneer turning into a frown as he pushed the letter into Tatte's face.

"My job application," Tatte repeated, his voice steady. "Listing my work experience."

The Nazi crumpled the paper in his fist and threw it on the floor, glaring at Tatte with vicious contempt. Then he fingered his pocket, the one holding a gun. *Was he going to shoot us anyway?* With a disgusted snarl, he clicked his heels together and faced Kaplan.

"Pathetic! If I get called here again, your head will roll." The pressure remained in Kaplan's office for a few minutes after the officer stormed out. Finally, like a pin popping a balloon, we exhaled.

"You…" Kaplan pointed at Tatte. "You need to leave."

Tatte nodded and shook Kaplan's hand. As their palms met, something passed between them. So subtle, so quick, I wondered if I imagined it.

That evening, after dinner, I cornered Tatte as he was resting in his armchair. "Tatte, stop risking your life for us," I demanded.

"If that Nazi had found money, you might be dead!" I couldn't even whisper, I was so upset. Fortunately, our other family members were too preoccupied to notice.

"Sit." Tatte tapped the ottoman and leaned forward so only I could hear him. "Never carry money where they can find it."

"Where did you hide it?" I was still reeling from the close call.

He whispered into my ear. "That was a decoy. I sewed the zlotys inside the collar of my shirt. When the Nazi searched me, I kept my hands interlaced behind my head to obscure the slight bulge. The officer missed it during the pat down."

I was speechless, a mix of wonder and apprehension swirling inside me. Tatte had outsmarted them. He waved me closer, knowing what I might be thinking.

"Raf, always plan for the worst and hope it never comes to pass. That's how we live to fight another day. I think this is an appropriate time to pray. Don't you?"

As I recited the Shema, I prayed to God Almighty that Tatte's luck would never run out.

▽ ▽ ▽

I EXPECTED KAPLAN TO RENEGE, but he came through for both Shlomo and me. He found Shlomo a decent job with the German Air Force, working in a repair factory. Though it wasn't what we asked for, the Jewish workers there weren't as vulnerable to being randomly snatched for forced labor. Each assigned worker carried an identification card, a shield against being poached by other German work groups. For now, Shlomo was safe and nearby.

A few days later, I started at the Rakow foundry. The place was massive, with machines rumbling constantly. Work at the foundry included unloading raw ore, smelting it down, and making steel for the war effort. But compared to what I'd already endured, it was almost a relief.

Inside the factory, there was this strange sense of freedom. I learned quickly that the Polish employees, all non-Jews, were open to trading extra food for other necessities. This was an opportunity to help shoulder Tatte's burden, to augment our meager rations.

And the best part was they served a hearty chicken soup for lunch, with actual meat and identifiable vegetables. The better diet gave me the energy to be productive, and for the first time in months, stomach pains didn't keep me awake at night.

CHAPTER 21

The Jewish Ghetto

Czestochowa, Poland — April 1941

THE NAZIS WERE WORKING to separate the Jewish quarter from the rest of the city. Each day after work, Shlomo and I met to check the progress of the construction. Our routine involved sneaking around the edges while trying to piece together what was happening. They penned us in, herding us like animals—but for the moment, it seemed we might be allowed to stay in our apartment.

Barbed wire now snaked its way around the streets like a monstrous, twisting, thorny vine. Authorities posted fresh signs in German and Polish at the entrances. The one on the Aryan side warned, "Contagious diseases. Do not enter." It was a blatant lie to keep the rest of the city from aiding us.

The sign posted on our side was more chilling. "Death penalty for leaving the ghetto."

We crouched behind crumbling walls, watching the Germans and their Polish collaborators hammer in more stakes to string up more barbed wire. The checkpoint at Aleje Boulevard had grown more menacing, with armed guards stationed at all hours, and guard dogs, too.

"I can't believe how fast this is happening," Shlomo exclaimed in the privacy of our shared bedroom. The ghetto represented more than barbed wire and guards. It served as a prison, built to contain us, to strip away whatever freedom we still had. Every time we left for our jobs and returned, they studied our armbands with vigor. We lived under a microscope, the stress becoming more unbearable each day.

Soon after the ghetto's establishment, authorities forced Moshe Janowiez, a Jew caught outside the boundary, to run back toward the entrance. When he did, a Gestapo soldier shot him in the back. He became the first victim under the new law, a warning to us all.

The news coming from outside the ghetto was horrifying. Who could prevail against the might of the Nazis, who were steamrolling through Eastern Europe unchecked? We clung together, reminding ourselves that despite everything, we remained luckier than most.

A FEW DAYS LATER, before dinner, Tatte gathered the family around our kitchen table. I could see the heaviness in his shoulders before he spoke. Mama sat beside him, her hands folded in her lap, worry lines etched between her eyebrows. Tatte didn't call these family meetings often, but when he did, we knew something important was happening.

Tatte cleared his throat and rubbed his hands together. "There are new regulations. Tomorrow, the Nazis will be further restricting our rations. Our food cards won't be enough to sustain us."

I gulped. "Tatte, I can barter for food with the Polish workers. Is there anything we can spare?"

Tatte's brow furrowed in frustration. "The SS have set up mandatory inspections at every entrance and exit. It's difficult to bring anything in. God only knows what they might do to you if they found you smuggling food. Leave the bartering up to me. My 'Important Jew' card affords me a modicum of protection."

Mama opened her mouth, then closed it. It was clear how much she wanted to object to Tatte shouldering all the risk. My father leaned back in his chair and massaged his temple.

"The Jewish hospital outside the Ghetto isn't available to us anymore. The Nazis have taken it over for their own use. They've turned an old school on Vlica Krotka into a hospital for Jews, but it's nothing like what we had. Medicine is scarce. The doctors do what they can, but they don't have the supplies or manpower to handle the hundreds of new Jews from other cities being resettled into the Ghetto.

Rivka, sitting at the end of the table, raised her hand as if she remained in school. "Won't God help us? Can't he see we're suffering?"

Silence permeated our kitchen. In a matter of months, Rivka had gone from a bold, innocent child begging to see the Holy Madonna to a quiet, introspective girl who had learned firsthand how unfair the world can be.

"Ah, my little Rivka," Tatte soothed. "Praying to our Almighty God gives us solace when life is difficult. The miracle God has given us is life. It's up to us what we do with it. Let us bow our heads and say the words of the Shema together."

After the blessing, Mama reached into a canister that used to hold sugar and took out a square of chocolate. "I was saving this for a special occasion, and I feel like this qualifies. Raf, please cut it into four pieces so you can all share."

Tatte patted his tummy. "I'll pass. Cut it into three pieces."

I gazed at my brother and sister, realizing they needed this treat more than I did. Bringing the square to the counter, I cut it into two equal pieces and made a show of handing one to each of them. The sparkle in Rivka's eyes and Shlomo's exaggerated moans made all of us crack up, as much a balm to our souls as the chocolate itself.

Later, after Shlomo and Rivka were sleeping, I heard Tatte and Mama talking. "Conditions are only getting worse. It's going to be harder, but we'll survive, won't we?" I heard Mama ask.

"Chava, we must hold on to hope. For our sake and for our children's sakes. Someday, the rest of the world will wake up and fight against the tyranny of the Nazi regime." Tatte reckoned.

I rolled over and faced the wall, too wired to sleep. Hope proved elusive when Nazi newspapers touted their victories. I'd seen the German propaganda littering the streets, calling us their number one enemy and depicting Jews with ridiculous bulbous noses. Someday, perhaps, the world would wake up and crush the Nazis. I just didn't know if any of us, even sweet Rivka, would be alive to see it.

CHAPTER 22

Our Last Yom Kippur

Czestochowa, Poland — September 1942

MY 19TH BIRTHDAY ROLLED PAST without fanfare and by this point, we'd suffered through Nazi occupation for three whole years. Illness, starvation, and hopelessness ruled the ghetto, and as we gathered for Rosh Hashanah in 1942, our spirits were low.

By Yom Kippur, the Day of Atonement, our holiest day of the year, the rumors circulating throughout the entire ghetto chilled us to the core. Train cars piled into our stations, and the threat of "Selections" or "Deportations" hung over our heads like a shroud. Which one meant possible survival, and which one meant death? Nobody knew.

I spent the morning of Yom Kippur praying in the attic with my family and others, the familiar rhythm of the words offering a modicum of comfort in our unraveling world. For services held in our Orthodox synagogue, women and men had been separated, but now we always kept our families close. Some of our more devout neighbors were terrified of missing a single day of work, afraid if they did, they would lose their positions. I wasn't sure anything we did or didn't do made any difference.

We broke for a brief rest, and I slipped outside, eager to leave the confines of the stifling attic. The ghetto streets, usually crowded, had far fewer people today because of the high holiday.

"Raf," someone whispered from behind me, startling me. It was Caleb, a man I'd met at the Rakow plant. His eyes darted around as he approached, and he pulled me into a hidden corner. He peeked over his shoulder again, then leaned in close. "Did you hear? Ukrainian SS just arrived."

I'd encountered the Ukrainian SS before, at the wretched labor camp. As conscripted thugs, they carried out the Third Reich's orders with fervent zeal. That Shlomo and I had survived them once represented a miracle. I doubted we'd both be so lucky a second time.

While the Gestapo had been relentless in their efforts to root out and confine Jews, the SS troops marked a new and ominous chapter in the Nazi's plan for us.

Caleb grabbed my shoulder. "They're rounding people up! Run and hide!!"

I hyperventilated. "Where can we go? The gates are sealed." Gasping, I blurted, "I have to warn my family!"

Caleb ran off to warn others, and I flew up the attic as fast as my legs would carry me. But when I got there, I could see from the sea of deathly pale faces and haunted eyes that they already knew.

I took my place beside my father. His voice trembled as he recited the prayers, but he didn't stop. He clung to the only thing we had left—our faith.

We prayed until sunset, the official end of Yom Kippur. After the last word, a respectful silence followed. Then the tears began, and families rushed to embrace each other.

Elijah, an elder from our building, stood and wiped his face. "This is it," his voice choked with emotion. "Our last Yom Kippur together." He appraised the faces of those he had known all his life. "May God protect us all."

CHAPTER 23

Watching and Waiting

Czestochowa, Poland — September 1942

BY THE FOLLOWING DAY, the ghetto streets teemed with SS soldiers. The streetlights stayed on for 24 hours straight, bathing our surroundings in a stark yellow glow. It was as if the very air we breathed was under surveillance. I couldn't sleep. None of us could. We were prisoners in our own homes, in our own skin. A thick iron padlock secured the gate outside our building, and no Jews could leave for any reason at all. There was no food either, not a single scrap. If we needed anything, we were out of luck. All that remained was watching and waiting, and we began to feel like ghosts.

I spent hours by the window, staring out at the street, watching my breath fog up the glass. More and more, Jews shuffled past in silence, flanked by armed guards, but we were still here. We learned authorities designated Daszynskiego Square as the selection point, where we would each meet our fate.

A horse cart rolled by, carrying bodies. I saw an old man shot right in front of his door. "Too slow," I heard them sneer.

Until this point in the occupation, the Nazis had only targeted men. But now I worried more about Mama and Rivka. Would the Nazi overlords deem them able to work? If not, would the Nazis kill them?

Two days passed, and I wondered if we'd all perish from starvation. Each morning, we asked the same question—would they come for us today?

Tatte pulled me into my room. "Whatever happens, you, Shlomo, and Rivka must stay together. Promise me you'll watch out for them, no matter what." His eyes bored into mine.

I nodded, unable to acknowledge what he was implying. That he didn't expect to survive the selection process. Mama either.

Shlomo walked in and flopped onto his bed. "I hate them. I really, really hate them."

Tatte faced him. "Hate will not save us, Shlomo. It will only eat away at your humanity."

"They've been stripping away our humanity for years, piece by piece," Shlomo snapped. "Why do we sit here like sheep? We should fight!"

"How can we fight them?" I asked, my voice rising. "The Nazis have machine guns, endless resources, and trained soldiers. We are powerless against their might!"

I had never raised my voice like that, and I instantly regretted doing it. Rivka, who stood in our doorway, broke down in tears, and this time, Mama joined her. Shlomo's mouth hung open, and Tatte closed his eyes, shaking his head.

A knock on the door startled us all, and Mama and Rivka composed themselves. I answered the door, and Mr. Cohn, our third-floor neighbor, stepped inside. "They've started the round-ups in our section. Be ready!"

"Now, Mama?" Rivka asked, her voice so small and scared. Mama nodded and carried her to her room. When they were gone, Mr. Cohn continued.

"They're going to liquidate the ghetto. Just like they did in Warsaw. My cousin and her family were there, and I haven't heard from them in a month."

Tatte shook Mr. Cohn's hands. "Thank you for letting us know. Godspeed."

Mr. Cohn grimaced and let himself out. Tatte, Shlomo, and I sat at the kitchen table, soaking in the news. The only sound now was the ticking of the clock, each second dragging us closer to whatever fresh Hell awaited us.

A short while later, Mama emerged again, a grim smile on her face. "Come out, Rivka. Show them."

My little sister emerged. When I saw her, I blinked at her transformation. Mama had cropped her long, dark hair into a short bob, and Rivka wore boys' clothes. It was the first time I had ever seen her in pants, and I wondered where and how Mama had gotten them.

Shlomo whooped and clapped. "You look like a boy!"

"You like it?" Rivka shook out each leg, adjusting to the feel.

Shlomo jumped up and twirled her around. "It's incredible! I always wanted a younger brother," he hooted.

Tatte put his arm around my shoulder. "Remember what we talked about?"

"Of course, Tatte." I prayed for even a shred of control over the fate that awaited us.

CHAPTER 24

Shema Yisrael

Czestochowa, Poland — September 1942

WE ALL SLEPT IN OUR CLOTHES with one eye open, and when the violent pounding on our door started, we bolted upright. In less than a minute, the five of us opened the door with our small bags in tow. SS soldiers pushed us outside to join our neighbors on the street.

Shlomo gripped my hand, Mama took Rivka's, and Tatte laid his arm around Mama. *Stay together* played on my brain on repeat as a series of gunshots rang out, so close it made the ground beneath us shake.

"Who did they…?" Shlomo's whisper broke off as an SS officer emerged, his smirk as chilling as the blood splatters on his boots. We knew who they had shot. It was Mrs. Richter, the elderly woman upstairs who had hobbled along with a cane.

"Monsters," Tatte muttered. "Absolute monsters."

They forced us into columns, five across, and we kept Rivka sandwiched in the middle. Soldiers surrounded us, pointing their guns at our backs to keep us moving. Rivka began trembling uncontrollably, and I squeezed her hand to lend her as much strength and support as I could.

As we marched, more Jewish prisoners joined us from other buildings. They were young and old, a few clutching infants.

Whenever someone stumbled, a guard struck them with a rifle, club, or pitiless shove. "Keep moving!" they barked, making young children whimper.

Every time a child cried out, I flinched. Would my ten-year-old sister pass as a boy, with her delicate features and featherlight bones? *Please, God*, I prayed. *Protect her.*

As we neared the town square, our column merged into single file. Tatte took the front, and I took the rear, with our family between us. I was the oldest son, and seeing my whole family selected before me would be my burden to bear. It was all I could do not to show my roiling emotions as the long line edged forward.

Just as my spirit dropped to its lowest ebb, the sound of low chanting drifted toward us, growing in volume as other voices joined. "Shema Yisrael…" The words gave us strength.

"Are they cursing us?" one SS soldier growled, confused.

A woman responded defiantly. "It's a peaceful prayer." The guard scoffed but allowed the prayer to continue.

My brief solace evaporated when I saw Degenhardt, a German officer I'd done my best to avoid. He always strutted around the ghetto, puffed up with his overblown sense of importance as the one in charge of our daily existence. There was a jagged scar tracing down his cheek, making his outward appearance match his ugly heart. Now he perched in the center of the square, holding power over our very lives. He clutched a riding crop in one hand, swatting it against his thigh as though this were a cattle auction.

I watched with mounting horror how a flick of the crop dictated each person's fate. Left or right. Life or death.

Next to meet Degenhardt's perverted justice was a rabbi whose beard was as white as his tallit. When the crop snapped to the left, our faithful and devout religious leader met his fate with dignity. Before responding to Degenhardt's directive, he spun around and raised his arms.

"My people," his voice rang out, "our suffering is temporary. Though we will soon meet Yahweh and find peace, we will pray for the salvation of all our brothers and sisters, regardless of their faith."

Degenhardt became incensed. "Enough!" he bellowed and gestured to his guards. "Take this old dog for special treatment!"

Soldiers grabbed the rabbi, but our spiritual leader shirked them off gracefully.

"I will not resist," he said, and the guards allowed him to walk between them without restraint. I couldn't tear my eyes away from him, a giant among men, his might born of unshakeable faith.

CHAPTER 25

Selection

Czestochowa, Poland — September 1942

"MOVE THE LINE FASTER," Degenhardt barked. The SS soldiers responded with rifle butts and clubs, smashing legs and shoulders without hesitation. He stood there, fat and smug, flicking his crop and screeching "left" or "right" without hesitation. When it came to children—even babies—his voice only grew more gleeful. That sound—that smug look—would haunt my nightmares forever.

At last, we made it to the front of the line. Degenhardt stood all powerful, and he jabbed both Tatte's and Shlomo's right shoulders. "Right!" he proclaimed, one after the other. Now it was Mama's turn.

Mama turned toward me, her eyes pleading, and gestured toward Rivka. I circled my arms around my sister's waist, then Mama turned around to meet her fate. I could barely breathe as that beast stared at my beautiful mother longer than most—licking his lips like she was edible.

"To the left!" he barked with finality. Mama spun around, her eyes sweeping over our faces. Rivka reached for her, but Mama gently pushed her away.

"Stay with Rafal. I love you all with all my heart." Without another word, Mama straightened her spine and stepped toward the group on the left, her head held high.

I wanted to shout, *I'll fight for you*, but the words stuck in my dry throat. I just stood there, drowning in helplessness.

Pushing Rivka behind me, I whispered, "Tall and strong, like a boy." She nodded and stood on her tiptoes, trying to appear taller. Degenhardt wasted no time in pronouncing me to go right. I grabbed Rivka's hand and towed her with me. But the beast was too sharp.

"That one's too skinny!" he sneered. "Left!" A guard slammed the butt of his rifle against our interlocked fingers, breaking us apart. Rivka reached for me as they dragged her away, her screams of "Rafal! Rafal!" piercing my ears.

I watched as Mama wrapped Rivka in her protective arms. Desperate for one last glimpse of Mama's warm eyes and Rivka's sweet face, I craned my neck. But guards swallowed up the entire group and marched them away. Babies wailed, children and adults sobbed, knowing their fates were sealed.

A soldier whacked my side with a rifle butt and yelled for me to start marching. My legs moved, one and then the other, like a robot. The blows and insults didn't even register, because my head was a million miles away.

There were hundreds of us, but Tatte found me and Shlomo pressed against the exterior wall of the Metallurgia plant. "Praise God. I couldn't bear to lose you, too." He kissed us both repeatedly.

I THOUGHT I KNEW GRIEF when I lost Ishak and said goodbye to Ephraim, but losing Mama and Rivka was even more devastating. When I thought of Mama, a bear came to my mind—a protective Mama bear who would lay her life down for her cubs. And brave, sweet, wonderful Rivka. She had lived her entire life in our cozy apartment, cared for and loved by her family. What were those monsters doing to them now?

The Germans gathered potential laborers in the Metallurgia factory grounds for a reason. High, rusted fences and huge, looming factory walls kept us contained like livestock, penned up for slaughter. The plant itself was no longer in operation, but even now, residues of oil and iron clung to the air.

The pebbly ground and scraggly weeds added to the eerie scene. The three of us stayed close while Tatte quizzed everyone about the fate of the other group. So far, no one knew any more than we did.

We came upon a few men huddled in the yard's corner, keeping their distance from the rest of us. Their faces were haggard, their clothes stiff with dirt and sweat. I couldn't look away from their blood-caked hands. An odor of death clung to them, faint but unmistakable.

Tatte's step faltered as he recognized one man. "Marcel Rosen!" he called out. Rosen, a former business associate, peered over, his expression shuttering.

I pulled on Tatte's shirt, not wanting to listen to what Rosen would say. But Tatte, resolute, wouldn't budge. "Marcel, what happened to you?"

Rosen sighed, his chest heaving. "They took us to the cemetery to bury the dead." The other men with him bowed their heads and closed their eyes.

"The fiends forced us to dig deep pits, which they filled with corpses. They tossed the bodies on top of each other like discarded rags. It was unspeakable." He choked up and took a few seconds to gather himself.

"Some weren't even gone yet. Anyone who tried to help them was shot dead on the spot and tossed right into the pit."

Shlomo staggered back, hand pressed against his heart. "You buried them alive?"

I turned around. I couldn't face any more horror. But Tatte had the courage to ask the unthinkable. "My wife Chava and daughter Rivka. Were they among those you buried?"

"No," Rosen said. "They forced old people, women, and children onto cattle cars to be taken away." He put his hand over his mouth and wept.

"Where are they taking them? Do you know?" Tatte's voice was desperate.

"Treblinka," one of the other men said, as Rosen could no longer speak.

My knees buckled like I'd been physically struck. Treblinka was a Nazi death camp. A place no one returned from. Tatte fell to his knees beside me, his strength totally gone. I wrapped one arm around him and another around Shlomo. Now we were three.

Chapter 26

Labor Selection

Czestochowa, Poland — September 1942

Throughout that same horror-filled day, German employers came to select Jewish workers. They called for any Jews who had previously worked in various organizations, looking for specific skill sets.

Shlomo, Tatte, and I knew our lives were about to splinter in three different directions. For a moment, I considered telling the authorities that we had worked together before. But the Nazis maintained excellent records, and they punished Jews who falsified information. Once again, though it sickened me, our fate was in their despicable hands.

When the liaison called for anyone who had worked for the German Air Force, Shlomo volunteered, his jaw locked in resolve. He believed he was making the right choice. Tatte and I hugged him hard, praying he was right.

Before he left, I grabbed the back of his shirt. "Do whatever you can to survive, do you hear me? Someday, I swear we will reunite." With a quick nod, he walked toward his group, and Tatte and I craned our necks, watching him fade into the crowd. Then came the next call, for workers from the HASAG organization. I hesitated, but Tatte gripped my arm.

"Take the job, Rafal," he urged. "A bird in the hand…"

His eyes glistened, but I could see his determination in the set of his chin. We embraced, and I didn't want to let go.

"I'll send word as soon as I can," I promised, clinging to him like a child instead of a nineteen-year-old man. He kissed each cheek and pushed me away. I was about to leave him when he pulled me back to him.

"Rafal, promise me you'll persevere." His grip on my arm was firmer now, as if transferring the last of his strength to me. "Hold on to hope, no matter what."

I nodded, unable to speak, as I memorized every inch of my brave father. His clothes hung loosely on his diminished frame; he was more stooped and fragile than I had ever seen him. How could I leave him in this condition, after all he'd done for me? I took a step forward and stopped, guilt weighing me down. *God. Where are you? Please tell me what to do!*

"Go," Tatte ordered. And like a dutiful son, I did.

$$\triangledown \quad \triangledown \quad \triangledown$$

HASAG WAS A GERMAN CONGLOMERATE, and I was assigned to work at their Pelcery factory, a former leather plant that had been converted to manufacture generators, small arms, and munitions.

As I waited for our group to assemble, I questioned how I could possibly help the Nazis kill more soldiers and civilians, but a booming command for a final count interrupted my thoughts. They introduced us to a new group of overseers. The HASAG factory police called the Werkschutz.

The Werkschutz were German nationals who supervised the forced laborers. Unfortunately for us, the Werkschutz fully embraced the Nazi regime's hatred and abuse of the Jews.

The gates of the Metallurgia factory grounds opened, and our Werkschutz overseers guided us through the deserted streets of the ghetto. My heart ached to see shells of houses and prayer books and other personal effects littering the sidewalk. I hadn't expected to return, and by the shocked expressions of the other workers, neither did they.

I felt a visceral need to pick up the personal effects, to fall to my knees and honor our dead. But the Werkschutz kept us marching at a fast clip, with rifles and billy clubs trained at our backs.

We kept marching until we exited the main ghetto gate and entered Aleje Boulevard, where the non-Jewish Poles lived a "normal" life. We passed people freely strolling the street with friends. It was shocking to see the restaurants and cafes, which were open and serving patrons. The smell of meats and pastries made my stomach whine piteously.

Some patrons glanced at us, but most turned away. If they ignored us, they might live their lives without the burden of guilt. But if our own countrymen and women were unmoved by our plight, who outside Poland would rise to our aid? Hopelessness washed over me, the idea of equality and respect for all dissolving into the realm of fantasy.

Upon reaching the front gate of the Pelcery plant, we were met by snarling police dogs and SS officers. As if that weren't frightening enough, the SS captain came striding toward us, menace and purpose in his bearing. His uniform was immaculate, and a patch covered his left eye. His right eye locked onto each one of us, unfeeling, assessing.

As he approached the lineup, a glint flashed from the metal toe plate of his boots. If his purpose was intimidation, he succeeded.

Chapter 27

Becker

Czestochowa, Poland — September 1942

"My name is Captain Heinrich Becker. You are here to work. If you fail to work, the penalty is death. If you steal, the penalty is death. If you lack identification papers, the penalty is death. If you complain or speak above a whisper, the penalty is death. If I dislike you, the punishment is death." I suspected that breathing the air might also be punishable by death.

"Now let's see what you're made of," Becker announced with a vicious smirk. He moved down the line, spewing insults and profanities in our weary faces, whacking men on the kneecaps if they flinched.

Then he was peering at me. "Stand up straight, you Goddamn Jew," he raged, positioning his billy club beneath my chin and forcibly lifting my head. "Dreckfass!" (*barrel of shit*) he barked. He jabbed the club into my belly before moving on to the next victim.

Following the evaluation, Becker's face twisted into something unrecognizable—gleeful, unhinged. "I'm in the mood for a game of *Hats!*" he shouted. "We'll play until every one of you rats moves in perfect synch." He climbed onto a raised platform like a deranged conductor, barking orders with sadistic relish. "Hats on! Hats off! Hats on!"

It sounded simple enough, a game of reflex, but that was the cruelty of it. If there had been a rhythm, more of us would have survived unscathed. But he varied the pace of his commands, faster, slower, faster again, with no discernible pattern. Making it impossible to follow his instructions as flawlessly as he demanded.

My hands trembled, clumsy with exhaustion, as the game dragged on—some men began to weaken—dropping their hats or stumbling out of formation. Becker's eyes zeroed in on every falter like a wolf tracking prey.

"Out of line!" he roared, his finger pointing through the air like a knife blade. He singled out a trembling inmate. "Guards!"

That's when the real horror began.

SS guards descended like jackals, yanking the weakest from the line. Boots pounded flesh with a sickening rhythm. The guards beat the men to the ground, leaving them groaning or unconscious. They then dragged them up, shoved them back into line, and forced them to continue, blood dripping from their faces and fingers.

I kept my gaze fixed on Becker, willing my limbs to obey his chaotic commands. He paced like a madman drunk on power, eyes gleaming with menace, scanning for his next victim.

Beside me stood an older man, worn out and hunched over. His name was Hirsch. We'd marched together to Pelcery—silent companions in suffering. He had lost everything. They had sent his wife and four daughters to Treblinka. He told me only once, in a voice already breaking. During the march, he collapsed, and guards beat him nearly senseless. And still, he marched on.

And now, here he was, forced into this nightmare—playing Becker's deadly game.

Becker barked another round. "Hats on! Hats off! Hats on!"

We moved like puppets yanked by fraying strings. My arms burned. My breath rasped in my throat. Around us, men flailed in desperation, hoping to stay alive one more minute.

Then it happened.

A jolt against my elbow. A blur of motion.

A hat hit the ground.

Not mine—Hirsch's.

He froze—his eyes locked onto mine, wide and unblinking. The hat lay between us like a live grenade. Without thinking, I stooped, snatched it up, and shoved it hard into his chest. "Hold it," I whispered. "Don't let go."

His hands wrapped around it like it was the last piece of his soul. But it was already too late.

Becker had seen.

He turned with slow, theatrical delight. His steel-toed boots clicked as he strode toward us, two guards falling into step behind him, hands already twitching with anticipation.

My throat clenched. My legs locked.

He was coming straight for me.

This was it.

The guards reached us.

And then—without a word—they grabbed *him*.

"No!" I cried, my voice cracking.

But Hirsch didn't flinch. His eyes found mine, battered and bloodied, yet eerily calm. He mouthed the words: *I'm ready. It's okay. Live.*

They dragged Hirsch from the line.

He didn't fight. He didn't scream. He simply let go.

Clubs. Boots. Shouts— he disappeared beneath them.

I couldn't move. I just stood there, choking on helplessness.

"Hats off! Hats on! Hats off!" Becker's voice thundered over the carnage, demanding we continue. So, we did—three hours later, it was over.

Those of us who survived Becker's twisted game were given a crust of bread and lukewarm coffee. I choked down my rations without a word. Complaining wasn't an option. Becker would've shot me where I stood.

We were led by the Werkschutz to the second floor of a vacant building. It was cold, dusty, silent. They barked at us to settle in, then left.

Somehow, through everything, I'd kept hold of my bag. During the drill, I'd tucked it between my feet—its weight an anchor. I opened it now and pulled out two thin blankets. They wouldn't keep me warm, but they were better than nothing.

I spread one blanket on the bare floor, lay down, and pulled the other over my aching body. My bag—stuffed with a single change of clothes and four sets of underwear and socks—became my makeshift pillow. I adjusted it beneath my head and closed my eyes, desperate for rest.

But sleep didn't come. Not because of the cold. Not even the pain.

It was the voices—two quiet whispers beside me, carrying just enough to reach my ears. I didn't know it then, but those hushed voices would soon become the closest thing I had to family.

CHAPTER 28

Brothers from Klobucko

Czestochowa, Poland — September 1942

LYING NEXT TO ME were two brothers from Klobucko, Jacob and Josef. Like me, they couldn't sleep that first night. The floor was cold and dusty, our bodies aching from Becker's sadistic drill.

Jacob was tall, with olive skin and deliberate movements, always cautious, always scanning. Josef, his younger brother, was smaller—at least a foot shorter—but he had a fire in him that reminded me of Shlomo. Josef's skin was lighter, his temper quicker, and his voice carried a weight that made you listen.

They told me they'd lost their parents in Treblinka. Just like that—one transport, and everything gone. The way they spoke about it—not in words, but in the spaces between them—told me all I needed to know. They were as close as brothers could be, and the grief had only made them tighter.

That night, we barely knew one another. But somehow, their presence settled something in me. I missed Shlomo so badly my chest hurt. Being near them—especially the way they leaned on each other—helped keep the ache from pulling me under.

"Do you think the depravity will ever end? Will anyone have the guts or power to destroy the Nazis?" Josef stared up at the ceiling like he was waiting for the universe to answer.

"Be careful," Jacob urged. "You can't say things like that here."

"I don't care," Josef hissed. "If I'm going to die, I'm taking Becker with me."

"Shhh!" Jacob whispered. "Enough!"

The Werkschutz guards shouted for lights out and no talking. Josef was lucky they hadn't heard him. We all knew what Becker would do if he had.

I closed my eyes and willed sleep to come. I don't know how long I drifted before the yelling began.

"Get up! Now, you swine!" Werkschutz guards stormed into the room, kicking anyone too slow to rise. We scrambled into a rough line, yawning, blinking, hearts pounding. They announced that a freight train had arrived and needed unloading.

Guards marched us into the cold night, their lanterns bobbing ahead. We huddled close, trying to fight the chill. At the railcars, cement bags towered in endless stacks. My arms already felt like lead, but participation wasn't optional. One after another, we lifted the bags, our muscles screaming with every load.

"Move faster!" the supervisor shouted, swinging his billy club at our legs and backs. Every time I heard the crack—whether it landed on me or not—I stumbled. We worked until the last bag was gone.

Back at our sleeping quarters, the clock showed 3 a.m. I collapsed into the same corner, groping for my blankets, too tired to think. My body hit the floor like a sack of rocks, and sleep swallowed me whole.

Only three hours later, the Werkschutz shouting dragged us upright again.

"Get up! To the latrine!" they barked. They marched us downstairs to relieve ourselves. Toilet paper was a luxury we didn't have, so I tore off a strip from the bottom of my pants. The thought of reusing the rag turned my stomach, but there was no other option.

A slice of stale bread and a cup of bitter, burnt liquid they called coffee awaited us upstairs. At 7 a.m. sharp, the supervisors returned. The choice was simple: slave labor or death.

That was how life began at Pelcery.

But over the days and weeks that followed, something happened—something that kept me from losing myself completely. Josef, Jacob, and I became fast friends. We worked shoulder to shoulder, and between shifts we shared whatever fragments of conversation or bits of humor we could scavenge. The weight of Pelcery didn't disappear, but it pressed less as we bore it together.

I trusted them.

In the darkest moments, when faith felt like a trick my mind played to keep me from giving up, it was our quiet solidarity that kept me going. In their presence, I didn't feel entirely alone. And in a place like this, that was everything.

CHAPTER 29

Potato Caper

Czestochowa, Poland — December 1942

IT WAS GRUELING WORK to create the munitions for the Nazi war machine. Every night, after a day of hard labor, we would assemble in the large hall, waiting for Becker to enter. We didn't need to see him to know he was coming. The clicking of his steel-tipped jackboots against the cement floor was enough to send a wave of terror through the group. Every step louder, more menacing, chilling the blood in our veins.

We stood ramrod straight as he examined us with his hypercritical eye. No one dared breathe too loud, or God forbid, cough. We all knew that even the smallest sound might draw his attention.

Roll call came next. The numbers had to match, or we would all suffer. Then came Becker's favorite game. We must have appeared ridiculous, but none of us had the strength to care. We'd turned into zombies, brains switched off, self-preservation in high gear. Three hours of this. Every single night. Our numbers dwindled as he singled men out with his cold, calculating eyes.

"Not good sports," he sneered. That was his phrase for those he thought weren't taking part in his game with enough enthusiasm. The guards dragged them off, silencing their screams and pleas for mercy. Every senseless death broke the rest of us down, piece by piece.

Back in our quarters, my arms were dead weight. It was impossible to keep my spoon steady, so I slurped my nightly soup ration instead, down to the last drop.

After a day of strenuous work and a night filled with depravity, I passed out instantly, falling into a deeper sleep each time. Whenever trucks arrived in the dead of night, it became harder and harder to rouse me. As a result, my ribs became permanently bruised by heavy boots battering me until I woke.

The roughest was unloading steel sheets, wafer-thin and sharp as knives, in the darkness and without gloves. The metal sliced through my hands, but I became numb to the pain.

Another aspect of the miserable life we all endured was escalating hunger from the relentless toll on our bodies and souls. The rations didn't come close to filling the growing void in our bellies. Some prisoners risked sneaking a second helping of soup, but those caught by the Werkschutz received lashes from their whips. Only a lucky few succeeded, and I didn't deem it worth the risk.

Somehow, I persevered. But when my brain became foggy and dull, and the simplest tasks became overwhelming, I knew I needed to act. Fast.

After we finished unloading the latest nighttime delivery, I stayed behind with Jacob and Josef. We slumped against the wall, drained and desperate.

"I know where the cooks store the potatoes for the soup," I rasped. "I'm going to steal as many as I can. Are you with me?"

Josef's eyes lit up. "I'm in. What's the plan?" he whispered, leaning in closer.

When I told them, Jacob shook his head. "This is madness. They'll kill you if they catch you. You both get that, right?"

Josef didn't balk, his jaw set. "If this is my time, so be it."

▽ ▽ ▽

JOSEF AND I MOVED LIKE SPIRITS in the wind, careful not to make a sound as we approached the supply closet. The smell of old wood and mustiness permeated the narrow corridor, but I was fixated on the potatoes. We dragged the door open slowly, just enough to slip inside. Our hands moved quickly, stuffing the bottom of our shirts with as many as they could hold.

We scurried to an empty corner of the work area. The steam pipes hissed around us, and I could feel the heat warming my neck. My plan was to cook the potatoes with the steam, eat them quickly, and return before anyone noticed we were gone.

We crouched down to start the process, but the creak of a door made me freeze. I locked eyes with Josef. *Don't move. Don't breathe.* If the guard saw us, we were dead. If we retaliated, innocent men would pay the ultimate price.

The guard's boots clacked against the floor, each step heavier than the last. A jolt of anxious energy amped up my heart rate as he approached our position. Josef's hand twitched, and I squeezed his arm to steady him. Would the guard pull his gun or his billy club?

I raised my hands in surrender, ready to meet death head on. Josef did the same. I thought about Becker and the nightmare that would follow. But when the footsteps rounded the corner, relief washed over me.

"Jacob!" I cried out. "You scared us half to death! How did you find us?"

He grinned, holding something small and brown. "Catch."

It was a potato. I caught it, my mouth opening in shock. "Oh my God, if the guards had found it…"

A wry smile crossed Josef's face. "I thought you weren't going to join us."

"I hid across the hall, watching for guards, but none appeared. In fact, it's strangely quiet tonight. They must have a Nazi meeting off site."

Nervous laughter spilled out of me, and soon all three of us were giggling like kids who'd raided a sweet shop. It was ridiculous, this scant moment of triumph. But as the smell of steamed potatoes invaded our nostrils, it felt like victory.

We savored every bite, groaning with relief. After satiating ourselves, we passed out in a stupor. When the first light of dawn peeked through the cracks, the three of us slipped into the arriving work group. No one ratted us out, and the guards were oddly tame.

Maybe God was watching out for us after all.

CHAPTER 30

Rakow Foundry

Czestochowa, Poland — February 1943

A FEW MONTHS AFTER OUR POTATO CAPER, the barracks door banged open, and a new guard stormed in. His scowl seemed etched onto his face, and his eyes swept over us with a mixture of disgust and boredom. He pounded a tin cup against the mess table to jerk us all to attention.

His voice grated like metal scraping stone. "Anyone who worked at Rakow, gather back here after the morning ration."

With a stiff turn, he stomped out, leaving tension in his wake. I leaned toward the two brothers from Klobucko.

"I'm going, and you should come too. It can't possibly be worse than this." They stared at me, hesitant. "You know Becker will toy with us until we all drop dead."

Jacob pushed the hair from his eyes and exhaled. "True." He turned to his brother, who nodded. "We're in."

Rakow wasn't freedom—not even close. We were still prisoners, still under Nazi rule. But it wasn't Pelcery. Gentile Poles ran the day-to-day operations, not the SS. That alone was a vast improvement. They knew the rhythms of the factory, and their orders weren't punctuated by a billy club jammed into our ribs or kneecaps.

▽ ▽ ▽

WE STILL SPENT OUR NIGHTS at Pelcery, but fortunately, we escaped Becker's sadistic games. Rakow had no sleeping quarters for its workers, so each morning, we marched from Pelcery to the steel plant and back again at dusk. Our overseers required roll call four times a day, as if we might vanish into thin air.

They always chose one unlucky man to keep the count, a task no one wanted. Any miscount, no matter how slim, would mean death, so we shared the burden by taking turns.

Rakow cracked open small windows to the outside world. The Polish workers there had their own quiet ways of getting things done, and I learned to barter with them. We traded whatever we could get our hands on—personal effects, worn-out clothes, even scraps of metal—for food.

It was on one of those frosty morning marches to Rakow that we encountered another group of Jews, their uniforms bearing insignias from the Luftwaffe—the German Air Force.

My brain jolted awake. Shlomo worked for the Luftwaffe, and I hadn't seen him since we were torn apart on the grounds of the Metallurgia plant.

As our two groups converged, I craned my neck, scanning every person. He found me first, rubbing my face to make sure I was real. Then he crushed me in an embrace, kissing my cheeks like he used to when we were boys.

The Luftwaffe guards, more lenient than the Werkschutz, allowed us a few minutes to catch up.

"You look like death warmed over, but I'm so excited to see you!" Shlomo beamed. He had filled out a bit and had a touch of color in his cheeks—more than I could say for myself.

"I told you we'd see each other again," I said breathlessly.

His next words tumbled out in a rush. "Our labor group is being transferred back to the ghetto."

That made me think about our apartment and our family. "Do you have any news about Tatte?"

Shlomo's shoulders slumped. His gaze dropped, avoiding mine. I grabbed him by the arms. "Please, tell me!"

His voice came out hoarse, broken. "Treblinka. Just like Mama and Rivka. They never assigned him work, so they took him and others straight from Metallurgia.

The blood drained from my head. The world tipped sideways.

"One of my fellow workers saw it happen," Shlomo whispered. "They're all gone, Raf. Now it's just you and me."

We clung to each other, swallowing the reality that our family of five was now reduced to two.

"Back to your group, Dreckfess!"

The bark of a Werkschutz guard shattered our reunion. Shlomo pulled away, his hands lingering on my arms before he stepped back. His eyes flicked to my cap—thin, frayed, barely holding together. Without hesitation, he plucked it from my head and replaced it with his own—a newer, thicker winter hat.

"Stay warm, brother!" He playfully punched my arm before jogging back to his group.

That night, I wept over the loss of my father, and now terror consumed me at the thought of losing Shlomo, too. No matter how hard I tried to push these feelings away, they always returned. I vowed to myself that if it came down to the two of us, I would sacrifice myself for Shlomo or die by his side.

CHAPTER 31

Nights at Pelcery

Czestochowa, Poland — February 1943

RAKOW WAS GRIMY AND EXHAUSTING, but comparatively, it was pleasant and predictable. Pelcery at night—that was another story. The guards beat, kicked, and verbally abused us whenever they felt like it. Which was almost always.

One night, after an especially tedious day, I was curled up on the barracks floor, my body grateful for even the thinnest sliver of rest. I wasn't the only one—we were all bone-weary, unable to converse. I was just slipping into the relief of sleep when I heard the crack of a gunshot.

I bolted upright. Another shot rang out. Then another. Strubel, the new young Werkschutz guard, was firing indiscriminately into the barracks, his face gleaming with sick excitement. It didn't matter to him who he struck. Aron, a fellow prisoner resting a few rows over, cried out as a bullet pierced him in an artery. Blood squirted all over the place.

"Got one!" Strubel called from his perch, braying like a hyena. None of us dared to move as Aron's blood continued to spread. Strubel strutted around, boasting about his kill. Murder was sport here, and we were the hunted.

Dread filled me the following morning, and I couldn't shake it during our shift at Rakow. Anxiety built during our nightly march back to Pelcery. Usually, we went straight into roll call, but this time, guards with snarling dogs awaited our arrival, and we were lined up in rows. I stood at attention, expecting the worst. When I heard the sharp click of metal-toed jackboots on concrete, I knew that the worst had arrived.

"I was told there was an inmate insurrection last night, and one of you pigs tried to escape." Becker clapped our new guard on the shoulder. "Thanks to the vigilance of Herr Strubel, the escape plot was thwarted."

Escape plot? Aron hadn't tried to escape. He'd been sleeping, just like the rest of us. This was just a show, a sick lie Strubel had spun to justify his bloodlust. If I had a gun, I would have shot the sneer off his despicable face.

"I will show mercy to anyone who confesses to plotting with the dead escapee," Becker continued, his tone dripping with mock benevolence. "Accept your punishment with dignity, or I'll start picking you off at random."

We all stood rigidly still, trying not to call attention to ourselves. Could we possibly implicate Strubel? I lacked the courage, and I wasn't the only one. When no one spoke up, Becker's expression darkened.

"Cowards," he spat, and then he started moving through the line. "To the left!" he ordered as he jabbed his crop into one man's gut. He continued striking men at random, and I held my breath as he approached my place in line. He passed me, but to my horror, he plunged his crop into Josef's belly. "To the left!"

Jacob was standing beside Josef, and his face twitched in indecision. Josef's eyes pleaded for him to remain in line, but Jacob's resolve hardened. I knew what he was thinking, as I would have done the same for Shlomo. He broke from the line and crossed over to his brother's side. A burly guard raised his club, ready to crack it down on Jacob's head. "Back in line, swine!"

"I'm staying with my brother." Jacob braced himself.

I waited for the guard to strike with his club, but Becker stopped him. "Let him go to his brother. I am merciful." His voice dripped with feigned kindness, and I didn't trust it one bit.

Which was the safe group, us or them? I dug my nails into my palms, desperate to join the brothers. But I couldn't shake the feeling that I should stay put as the selection continued row by row.

When it was over, they sent my group back to the barracks, half the number we had been before. I couldn't sleep, hoping beyond reason that Jacob, Josef, and the others would soon return. But they never did. The next morning, before roll call, I overheard the whispers. They loaded the entire group into a cattle car headed for Treblinka.

Once again, by the narrowest twist of fate, I was spared.

The weight of survival pressed heavy on me, but the only thing keeping me from sinking into hopelessness was knowing that Shlomo was still alive. I had a reason to keep going—to endure the unimaginable, to press on when every part of me wanted to collapse. He was my tether to the world of the living, the last thread connecting me to my family and sense of self.

CHAPTER 32

Albert

Pelcery plant, Czestochowa — Spring 1943

I HAD BEEN WORKING alongside Albert in the Rakow foundry ovens for three months. At first, reeling from the loss of Josef and Jacob, I tried to remain distant. I told myself that getting close to anyone was just another wound waiting to be ripped open, but Albert was determined to break through my defenses. He was always so hopeful, even in these awful circumstances.

Though quite tall, Albert walked with a slight bounce and talked with a lisp. He was an optimist, always coming up with reasons we'd make it through. "The Germans will turn on Hitler. The Allies have more soldiers, better weapons. They'll trounce the Nazis." He had a way of making it sound like our freedom was within reach.

"They're more interested in killing us than fighting the war," he'd pronounce. When I asked him once how he could stay so positive, he grinned. "The only thing I can control is my mind. I won't let them take that from me."

Albert had a fondness for jokes, particularly those that mocked our uptight oppressors. "What do you call an unhappy German?" he asked with a mischievous grin. When I shrugged, he gleefully answered, "A sour kraut!" Then his signature laugh—

"*Heesh, heesh, heesh!*"—bubbled up, making me crack up.

Whenever I got nervous about being overheard, he'd clap me on the shoulder. "You worry too much. The noise of the foundry gives us the perfect cover."

But Albert had one enemy—Strubel. Aron had been his close friend, and Strubel knew it. He constantly razzed Albert that he would be next, and Albert had the audacity to threaten to report him. One morning, Strubel finally gained the upper hand. He sauntered over to Albert, eyes full of malice. "Today, you will lead the prisoner count. The numbers better match, or your head will roll."

Albert's eyes widened in panic. We all understood what it meant if the count didn't add up. For each missing man, they would kill five others. It had happened before. Prisoners would stop others from escaping just to prevent that nightmare from repeating.

At the end of the day, Albert's count matched the morning count. As we left Rakow, I saw the relief in his eyes as he reported the number to the guard. But when we arrived at Pelcery, he counted again, and it was off by one. Albert panicked, pleading with us to help him find the missing man. We tried, but his identity and whereabouts remained a mystery to all.

The news spread through Pelcery like wildfire. The Werkschutz guard reported the miscount, and they marched us to the center of the camp, where we waited for the inevitable.

Becker came, his face contorted in disgust as he towered over Albert. "Where is the escapee?" he demanded.

Albert trembled, his explanation tumbling out. "The count matched when we left Rakow, I swear to Almighty God. Someone must have escaped on the march back, but we don't know who. Please, sir, I'm telling the truth."

An evil grin crossed Becker's face. He needed a scapegoat, and Albert was it. "Do you want to live, filthy Jew?"

Albert collapsed to his knees, grabbing Becker's boots and kissing them, tears streaming down his face. "Yes! Please! I'm begging you!"

I wished I had the courage to rush to Albert's defense, to lift him to his feet, to make him stop groveling. But to do so would have painted a target on my forehead.

Becker watched him squirm, relishing every second of Albert's degradation. He kicked Albert away, pulled a red handkerchief from his pocket, and wiped his boots clean. He flung the hanky to the guard. "Burn this and shoot the pig. Or burn the pig and shoot this," he snarled.

Albert screamed as they dragged him away by his hair. They slammed his head into the wall until the blood ran thick, until his face was a broken, pulpy mess. I wobbled, ready to pass out, and would have collapsed had the man next to me not steadied me. Somehow, Albert remained dazed and alive, though no doubt brain damaged.

Becker gave Albert his last order. "Pick five others to die with you."

Albert, bloody and barely coherent, refused. "No," he boomed with surprising strength.

One gunshot echoed, followed by a second, and a third. Becker riddled Albert's body with bullets, and when it was over, selected five more from our group at random and shot them, too. Somehow, despite my connection to Albert, I was spared again.

The next morning, we learned that the SS and their dogs had captured, mauled, and shot the missing prisoner. Strubel delivered the news, grinning from ear to ear. "Go ahead, try to escape," he taunted. "We'll give you a head start." I couldn't stop thinking that Strubel had orchestrated the prisoner's escape, using it to settle his vendetta against Albert.

That same morning, Becker appeared again, a snap of his steel-toed boots bringing us all to attention. "Take your belongings, as you're not coming back here after work. Tonight, you'll be marching all the way to Palestine."

CHAPTER 33

Small Ghetto

Czestochowa, Poland — Summer/Fall 1943

NO ONE BELIEVED HIS PRONOUNCEMENT, but our true destination remained a mystery. We marched for about an hour, passing once again through the ruins of our old ghetto. The streets were as silent as a graveyard, and when I saw the hollow shell of my former apartment building, memories surged through me. For a moment, I could see their faces—Mama, Tatte, Rivka—hear their voices, feel their arms wrapped around me. But as we kept moving, the warmth of those visions faded, and the weight of their absence clawed at my already broken soul.

My biggest regrets centered on Rivka, how I wished I had seized upon every possible opportunity to cherish her. She was so young, so full of life and vitality. I had promised Tatte I would protect her, and I failed miserably. But I saved my hatred for the Nazis, the evil behind Rivka's senseless death, and so many others.

I addressed God. *How could you let them kill children? What threat did they pose?* As always, my burning questions remained unanswered.

The column halted, jolting me from my thoughts. We stood in front of a large gate, and a Werkschutz guard handed us over to an SS officer. "This is where you will live when you are not working," he announced. "We will house all Jewish labor groups here."

As I stood there, dog-tired, a familiar sound like a cricket chirp turned me instantly alert. It was the same sound Shlomo made when we were younger, and my eyes darted to the side, scanning faces pressed behind the barbed wire. When I spotted him, fingers pressed to his lips, my heart grew wings.

Shlomo grinned at me, his eyes twinkling with their trademark mischievous spark. I didn't dare show my joy while the guards still milled around, fearing they might steal it away for kicks, and Shlomo must have shared my concern. The second the guards left, we sprinted toward each other.

"Are you real?" I grabbed his head and rubbed it with my knuckles. So much had happened in the past month, I truly couldn't believe it.

"In the flesh! If you stop mauling me, I'll show you my barracks and fill you in on everything that's been happening."

I took in every detail of my brother, trying to reconcile the boy I'd known with the confident man he had become. His face was thinner, his cheeks sunken, but his eyes were the same. When I noticed his earlobes, darkened and swollen, I gasped. "Is that frostbite?"

Shlomo gave a half-smile, nodding. "Yeah, we work outside all day, no matter the weather."

I pulled off my cap, the one he'd given me at our last meeting, and yanked it over his head, partially covering his eyes.

"Hey!" he protested, pushing it back up to see. "I missed that hat! Remind me to never let you *borrow* anything of mine ever again." He elbowed me in the shoulder.

"Ouch!" I winced, rubbing my arm, then snatched the cap back and sprinted toward the closest barrack. I heard his laughter as he chased after me, and for a brief, wonderful time, we were still just two brothers messing around. Not two desperate prisoners bounced from pillar to post at the Nazi's whim.

Shlomo and I talked for hours, and being together again, it seemed like life might be okay—at least, as okay as they could be in this nightmare. He begged me to stay with him when night fell, but the Jewish overseers wouldn't allow it. They assigned me quarters with my labor group, promising, much to my amazement, that they would arrange for Shlomo and me to be in the same lodging later. I didn't know whether to believe them, but I crossed my fingers and toes and prayed they would follow through.

They placed me in an empty apartment building with three other inmates. I knew this building like I knew my own. It was Ishak's building, the blown-out windows now covered with wood. Our families had spent so many Sabbaths with Ishak and his extended family. We enjoyed so many carefree days here, before the Nazis stole everything from us.

I walked up to the third floor, and finding the door to his apartment unlocked, went straight to Ishak's bedroom. The room was stripped bare, nothing but a filthy mattress remaining. Ishak's absence was devastating, but my memories swirled with all the good times we had together. He always enjoyed sleeping by an open window, so to honor him, I dragged a mattress there, collapsed on top, and let the tears flow.

FOR THE FIRST TIME since the liquidation of the ghetto, I wasn't walking around on eggshells, waiting for the next blow, scream, or shot. The new Werkschutz guard in charge of our escort showed surprising empathy toward our labor group. Each morning on our hike to Rakow, he allowed a few Jews to leave formation when we passed through the non-Jewish side of the city. We could barter for provisions or seek information about a loved one, and never once did he strike anyone. For the first time since the Nazi invasion, it made me consider that not all Germans were evil.

Of course, the fear never went away, but best of all, I had Shlomo by my side. After his transfer to what we named the Small Ghetto, Shlomo no longer worked for the German Luftwaffe. Instead, he returned to his old job on the railroad, and we spent all our free time together. We shared everything, from bread to the nightmares that kept us awake at night. Life without him? I couldn't imagine it.

"Have you heard any news about the war?" I asked him one night, lying on a mattress that had seen many bodies before mine.

Shlomo leaned in close, his face lit by moonlight filtering into the bedroom window. "Now that the Americans have joined the fight, the tide has turned. The Nazis are getting desperate."

I bit my lip. "Yeah, but if they get desperate, they might turn on us. We're witnesses to their atrocities. Once they don't need us for their labor..."

"That's why we stick together," Shlomo whispered with conviction. "We're stronger that way. Not just you and me, but all of us."

We both felt the shift, subtle but undeniable. Demands on the factories had increased, and the Germans needed Jewish laborers now more than ever. That gave us a sense of relief, but everyone knew their attitude toward us could change with the wind.

▽ ▽ ▽

THE GHETTO KITCHEN had become more than just a place to eat—it became the heart of our fragile community. Each evening, friends gathered in small groups, huddling over thin bowls of potato soup and exchanging news of the day. A tense undercurrent always ran through our conversations, a sense that every piece of information could mean the difference between life and death. We scrutinized everything the Germans did, whether here or in our workplaces, for clues about their true intentions. We all understood our survival hinged on being one step ahead.

We always spoke in whispers and never of anything important near the SS guards. Rumors of the Allied forces circulated like precious currency. Would they defeat Hitler? Would they come for us before time ran out? Prayers followed every whispered hope. We longed for a miracle, that we might live to see the downfall of the regime that had torn our world apart.

But not everyone shared that optimism.

"They've crammed us into this hellhole for a reason. We're witnesses to their crimes. They'll wipe us out before they surrender," one prisoner said, and many heads nodded their agreement.

Another man, eyes darting around to check for guards, bent in closer. "Some of us aren't waiting to be led to the slaughter," he whispered. "We're getting ready."

A group of Jews had organized, gathering arms, training volunteers in secret. They even somehow dug underground bunkers right beneath the noses of our Nazi overseers. The sheer courage it took astounded me. They didn't harbor illusions of escape. Instead, they aimed to make a last stand, to exact revenge, when the Nazis came to finish us.

Contact with the Polish underground proved crucial for this mission, yet dangerous. Snitches lurked everywhere, and a mere whisper of rebellion risked torture or execution. Every gun, every bullet, had to be paid for, smuggled in under the most perilous conditions. I respected these martyrs beyond description, but I wasn't one of them. I wasn't a fighter. At least, that's what I told myself. Truthfully, I wasn't ready to throw away my life like that.

Later that night, Shlomo and I sat under a sky littered with stars, too restless to sleep. We were both lost in thought, but I gathered from his constant fidgeting that he felt as unsettled as I did.

"Do you suppose they'll really go through with it?" I asked, breaking the quiet.

Shlomo let out a long sigh. "They will." He paused for a moment, then muttered softly, "We should do more."

I sat up straight. "More? Like what?"

"I don't know," he said, his frustration seeping through. "Something. Anything. I just… I just don't want to die here after all we've been through, Raf."

I didn't want to die either. But fighting the Nazis was futile. "What if they don't plan on killing us? What if they send us away instead? If so, we might survive this war after all."

Shlomo's lack of a retort spoke volumes, and my heart rat-a-tatted in my chest. "You're not going to join them, are you?"

He didn't meet my gaze. "No, of course not."

CHAPTER 34

Visitor

Czestochowa, Poland — March 1943

ONE NIGHT AFTER MONTHS in the Small Ghetto, Shlomo and I were in the kitchen, surrounded by the regulars, when an unexpected visitor entered. He was a local Jew who, against all odds, had escaped from Treblinka. He was filthy and emaciated, a walking skeleton. We did all we could to make him comfortable, but he waved us off, his eyes burning with purpose.

"Treblinka," he began, his voice ragged, "is a small village between Warsaw and Bialystok, surrounded by a dense forest. Or at least it used to be, before the Nazis took it over in 1941. They cleared the trees, and in their place, built an extermination camp."

We had all heard rumors. But it proved quite different to hear the truth from a survivor. The room became still, no one wanting to miss a single word.

"They left enough trees to hide the camp from the outside world, surrounding it with barbed wire to make sure no one could escape. Or stumble upon it by accident."

"How are people killed?" I blurted, desperate to understand how my mother, sister, and father had met their ends. I chewed the inside of my cheek, bracing myself to hear the awful explanation.

"There are thirteen gas chambers, and they can exterminate six to eight thousand Jews a day. Three to four transports arrive

151

daily. The Nazis murder the victims—our families—with terrifying efficiency." His words were emotionless, as though he read from a horror story.

No one spoke. The weight of his words crashed over the gathering like a tidal wave, his eyes locking onto ours one by one. We should have offered him a drink, but we were too shocked to move.

"The Nazis built a special railroad track, just for Treblinka, to bring people into the camp. The boxcars are so packed with bodies that many die of suffocation before they arrive."

Benjamin, a man who rarely spoke, asked in a trembling voice, "How do they… how do they get people into the gas chambers?"

"They separate the women and children from the men. They strip them naked, shave their heads, and tell them they're going to the showers for delousing. Within three hours of arrival, they're gassed and dead." He paused, his eyes becoming unfocused. "It's an efficient operation. The Nazis don't waste resources on food or shelter—they kill prisoners as soon as they arrive."

The only way to recite this grim truth was to distance oneself, that I understood. The man—whose name none of us even knew—seemed like he might collapse any second. He looked worse than anyone I'd ever encountered, even in the ghetto, where food was scarce. How he escaped was incomprehensible.

"How did you survive?" I asked.

The survivor's lips pressed together. "I don't know myself. It wasn't some grand plan. It was madness and desperation." He rubbed a hand over his scrawny face, as if scrubbing away the terrible memories.

"They put me to work in what they call the sorting barracks. Our job was to sift through the belongings of the people they'd just murdered, to set aside clothes, shoes, anything of value. They assigned me to pull gold fillings from the corpses. You don't forget that. You can't."

The man swallowed hard, his voice cracking, but he carried on. "They kept us close to the gas chambers, but away from the main camp. The guards—there weren't as many as you'd think, probably because it's so isolated? He cleared his throat. "I couldn't do it anymore. I couldn't keep stripping the dead of their dignity, as if their lives didn't matter. Every time I yanked out a gold tooth, I pulled out pieces of my heart with it. I had to escape, even if it meant dying in the attempt. One day, as we sorted, I overheard a group planning an uprising. It wasn't much, just a few men who'd stolen tools and makeshift weapons. I didn't take part in the plan, not officially, but when the chaos started… I saw my opportunity." At this point, someone got the man a drink, but he only took a sip before continuing with his story.

"The revolt began with a few men rushing a guard, stabbing him with whatever they had. The commotion spread like wildfire, with screams, shots fired, and guards panicking. We knew it was now or never. So, when the fence closest to the woods was breached, we all ran." He paused for a second to catch his breath.

"Most of us didn't make it, gunned down as we ran. But I… I got lucky. I ran to the forest before they spotted me, and I didn't stop running until I collapsed from exhaustion."

He stared at his hands. "I hid in the woods for days, living off scraps, barely surviving. I found a group of Polish partisans—Gentiles who had been helping Jews hide. They patched me up and gave me a place to rest for a few days." He took another sip, his chest heaving from the effort of talking.

"Why did you come back here?" Benjamin whispered, his voice tense. "Why didn't you stay in the forest with the partisans?"

The visitor's face filled with conviction. "I came back to warn you. The Nazis have no intention of letting you live. Your survival… it's not part of their plan. You must believe me. If you do nothing, if you wait and hope for mercy, you will all die. Every one of you."

He watched us bear the weight of his pronouncement, then continued, "You have an obligation to your families—to the ones who were already murdered. You must rise up. If you don't, you'll die as they did, stripped of their dignity."

As he spoke, I gripped Shlomo's hand, feeling that if I didn't, the fury building inside might consume me whole. He gripped me back, both of us picturing our mother and sweet sister stripped and shaved, paraded toward their deaths. Our brave Tatte, too.

CHAPTER 35

The Plot

Czestochowa, Poland — March 1943

ON THE MORNING OF MARCH 22, 1943, Shlomo and I followed our usual routine, shuffling into the kitchen for bread and coffee. As we ate, we talked about the news over the past few days. The Gestapo had recently rounded up the Judenrat, the doctors, the teachers, everyone we once counted on for leadership. They called it a "trip to the holy land." But instead, the intelligentsia were taken to a graveyard and shot.

Shlomo's eyes glistened with fervor. "There's no hope for the rest of us. They won't stop until we're all in the ground. When the time comes, we must take as many of them out with us as we can."

I didn't ask if he had already made plans, as I couldn't handle the truth. I clung to the thin hope that maybe we'd still make it through this nightmare—together.

We walked to the manned gate, our usual parting spot. He headed for the railroad work crew, and I proceeded to my factory job. We didn't bid each other goodbye—it wasn't something we did. I turned away, telling myself I'd see him at dinner, like always.

The day wore on endlessly, worsened by my foreman's brutal mood. His wooden club struck my legs more than once, each blow accompanied by a repulsive slur. "You worthless Jew, why aren't you working faster?"

To keep my mouth shut, I bit down so hard I thought my teeth would crack. All I wished for was to get through the day. To sit down with Shlomo later and pretend, even for a moment, that we had some semblance of normalcy. But when I returned to the barracks that evening, a man from Shlomo's work group stood waiting for me by the door, his face as grim as death.

"Where's Shlomo?" I asked, panicked.

"They… they caught him," the man stammered, his eyes squeezing shut. "Caught him sabotaging the tracks."

"What?" I grabbed him by the shoulders, shaking him. "What happened? Tell me everything!"

"They caught him and the others. They… they shot them. By firing squad."

My knees buckled. "No!" I screamed. "That can't be true!"

"They tried to derail a train," he said. "Six of them tore up the tracks but were caught before the train arrived."

With mounting hysteria, I shrieked, "Where is he? Where did they take his body?"

The man wiped his eyes with his shirt sleeve. "At the cemetery. We buried them in a mass grave. The guards made us dig it ourselves. After we finished, they shot my friend and threw him in, too. I begged them to kill me, but they didn't. They told me I needed to spread the word about what happens to traitors."

I couldn't process it. *Shlomo—dead—shot—traitor*—swirled in my brain on repeat. My brother. My confidante. The last flicker of light in my rapidly dimming world. Gone.

I felt as if someone ripped my heart from my chest. In its place was a gaping void.

Someone led me to a bunk—I don't know who. I sat there, unmoving, staring into space, as the hours slipped away like water through my fingers. Footsteps passed. Voices murmured. Everything was a blur.

The sun had the audacity to rise. As the light stretched across the barracks, I expected, hoped, *needed* to see him. But he wasn't there and something inside me snapped.

"You brave, stupid boy!" I screamed. "Why didn't you tell me? Why didn't you let me stop you?"

I wailed and cried until I lost my voice. When my sobs finally dried up, determination took hold. I refused to let Shlomo's sacrifice be in vain. The only way I could honor his life was to keep going, to push through, to make it to the end. To reclaim my life after the Nazis were destroyed.

"Don't let the bastards break you. Don't let them win, Raf."

I could hear his voice, clear as if he were standing beside me. Everywhere I turned, I expected to see him—to catch a glimpse of his familiar shape, his knowing smirk. And when I didn't, I pretended. I told myself he was still here, watching, waiting. That thought kept me moving, kept me alive in my darkest hours.

In the days that followed, I maneuvered carefully, avoiding the ever-watchful SS patrols. I scavenged for scraps, bartered when I could, and stole when I had to—even a rotten piece of cheese from a trash receptacle to stretch my pitiful rations. I wasn't proud of it, but pride was a luxury none of us could afford. My factory work, though monotonous, wasn't backbreaking, and that alone felt like my greatest stroke of luck.

I took each day as it came. One foot in front of the other, one breath and then another, one prayer at sunrise, and another at dusk. Despite the growing exhaustion, I clung to faith as a lifeline, knowing others had lost belief in God entirely.

Whenever resistance members approached me, I politely declined to get involved. They were driven by revenge, while I was driven by survival. I didn't blame them for feeling the need to fight. But every time they planned an action, the Germans found out. And each time, they paid the price, in rivers of blood.

I had no illusions about heroics. No fantasies of going out in a blaze of glory. Shlomo died at eighteen years old—trying to be brave.

CHAPTER 36

Last Stand

Small Ghetto, Czestochowa — June 1943

THE LIQUIDATION OF THE SMALL GHETTO started the same way every transition did—with rumors. But on June 25, 1943, rumor became reality. The SS, led by Degenhardt, launched their assault. I wasn't there to see it. I was working at Rakow, but the aftermath clung to the survivors like a shroud.

It had been three months since Shlomo's murder. His loss still throbbed, but somehow, I found the strength to keep moving. That morning, like every other, I left for Rakow with my small labor group. Only this time, our factory supervisor told us we'd be sleeping onsite.

That's when I found Samuel, or maybe he found me. He appeared just like another kid thrown into this hell with the rest of us. His clothing hung off his scrawny frame, making him appear older, and his nose had just enough curve to give him a serious expression. He moved with purpose, always a step ahead, ducking into the shadows before the guards even knew he was there. We'd grown close. The kind of bond forged when survival depends on having someone to watch your back.

That night, as we huddled over our meager meal, I whispered, "What's going on?"

"I don't like it," he muttered. "Something big is happening back in the ghetto, I can feel it."

Guards marched a handful of filthy, bleary-eyed, and beaten survivors into the foundry the next day. They were fenced off in a designated area for registration and processing. Those who had secured labor cards received permission to join us for dinner. That's when we learned what had happened.

A man named Chaim collapsed at our table. His lips trembled as he mumbled the same phrase over and over. "It was a massacre. A massacre…"

"What happened?" Samuel asked.

"Degenhardt found the bunker… the one with the ammunition." Chaim's throat went dry, and someone handed him a drink. He swallowed hard and continued.

"They threw grenades inside. Our resistance fighters fought back, but they didn't stand a chance. The SS killed them all and set the barracks ablaze."

My brain wrestled with the horror. "What about the others who weren't part of the resistance?"

He shook his head. "They marched hundreds of people to the cemetery." The SS lined them up. Shot them all. Execution style." Chaim took another sip of water, his thin hands quivering. "Degenhardt *thanked* the Jewish police for their loyal service… right before he gunned them and their families down."

Samuel blinked hard and dug his fingernails into the table. "How in the world did you and the others survive?"

"We were in the hospital, mostly suffering from exhaustion and malnutrition. They beat us before they marched us here." He looked around to make sure no guards could hear him. "It's all gone. The whole ghetto. Our old neighborhoods, completely burned to the ground." *Erased.* As if we had never existed.

The Nazi goal was rapidly becoming a reality. Czestochowa was Judenrein (*Free of Jews*), as soon all of Poland would be.

How could I have survived this long? Was it sheer dumb luck or the hand of God?

After hearing the grim news, none of us slept. How could we? We had nothing but the clothes we were wearing, and no idea what the future held. The cement floor of the foundry mess hall became our sleeping quarters, but shutting our eyes and resting was the best anyone could manage.

Later, we moved into a hastily built, stripped-down barracks outside the Rakow foundry, constructed solely for our use. This is where we would live now. Or more accurately, where we were being held captive.

Our group's new members included former police officers, men who had once worked as cleaners, and a doctor—Dr. Glatter—who set up a small clinic inside the foundry. It was a shock to have a real doctor among us, his face worn with exhaustion, but his commitment to healing undiminished. He still treated wounds, still showed up for the suffering.

Outside our barracks, the Germans erected a barbed wire fence that penned us in. There was just enough space for our roll calls and a small exercise area. The entrance was a gate of razor-sharp wire, guarded around the clock by the Werkschutz. They were always watching, waiting for any excuse to strike. I dreaded the sight of them, their blank expressions, their readiness to kill.

▽ ▽ ▽

I TURNED 20 YEARS OLD on July 4th, 1943, but I didn't tell Samuel or any of my fellow inmates. It seemed unfathomable that I'd spent four years caged like an animal behind barbed wire. Surviving minute by minute, day by day, at the whim of our tormentors. I was always waiting for something worse to happen, as it continually did.

Work offered an escape from the confines of the barracks and from the constant surveillance. I looked forward to it every day. The German SS plant commander and the Werkschutz ruled over us with iron fists, but they seemed invested in keeping us alive for our labor.

We lived in a continual state of paranoia, always watching the Polish supervisors and the guards, wary of their movements. I tried to stay inside the plant, even when I wasn't working. It seemed like our best shot at survival if they ever decided we were expendable.

Over time, non-Jewish workers declined, and we became more necessary to their operations. The insults and harassment diminished, as they didn't want to distract us from meeting production quotas.

While the rations were meager, there was just enough of it to keep us going. They gave us bread and coffee for breakfast and dinner. Lunch was a bowl of soup, and it wasn't difficult to get an extra ladle full while working on day or night shifts.

It was grueling work, but it felt good to be useful, even if it was for the enemy's cause. By working alongside the Polish Gentiles, we saw a gradual change of attitude. Some of them held steadfast to the antisemitic belief that Jews couldn't do hard labor. But over time, they accepted the truth before them. We worked just as hard as they did.

A few of them even sympathized with us. There weren't many, but a few shared what little food they had and treated us with compassion. I'll never forget them. In a sea of indifference and hostility, their compassion was a rare flame—a glimpse of decency in a world gone cold.

Each day, I prayed we could remain here until the war ended, in this place of relative safety and security. Still, returning to the barracks each night, the barbed wire and watchful eyes reminded me we weren't free.

CHAPTER 37

Six Months Later

Rakow Foundry — Winter 1944

FOR WEEKS, THE TEMPERATURE PLUMMETED to below zero. The bone-chilling cold oozed through the thin barracks walls and froze us in our bunks. Literally, there were mornings when men woke up with frostbite. At least in the factory, boilers kept us from freezing during work hours. Unfortunately, inside the ovens section where I worked, massive blocks of steel burned red-hot, glowing like lava. My task, alongside Samuel, was to rotate the blistering steel blocks regularly. We used long iron rods to pry open the oven windows, but each time we did, it felt like the searing heat was stripping away a layer of our skin.

I gripped the rod, my arms weakened from another twelve-hour shift. Samuel was next to me, panting from the heat, his face streaked with sweat and soot.

"Ready?" he asked, his eyes fixed on the furnace.

"As ready as I'll ever be," I replied.

We pushed the rod into the small metal latch, and when we opened the window, a wave of heat exploded into my face. The flames singed my eyebrows and blistered my cheeks. I winced and jerked back, but Samuel steadied me, his grip firm on the tongs.

"Stay with me, Raf," he grunted through clenched teeth. "Just a few more seconds."

My arms trembled as we turned the block of steel. The heat was unbearable, and it felt like my blood was boiling. After rotating the red-hot steel block, we slammed the furnace window shut, cutting off the fire's assault. We both collapsed against the wall, panting like we'd just run a marathon.

"Every time we do that," I wheezed, wiping the sweat from my eyes, "I think it's gonna do me in."

"This time, it nearly did." Samuel chuckled, but it was dry and humorless. "Our shift is almost finished. Maybe Dr. Glatter can give you something for your blisters."

I shook my head, chuckling despite the pain. "Some choice, huh? Boiled alive during the day, frozen solid at night."

He leaned back, eyes closed. "This work is shit, but they leave us alone. Nice to be free of guards barking orders every second."

I nodded, grateful for that small mercy. The ovens burned like hell, but they also served as our sanctuary. No one dared come near them.

After weeks of enduring the relentless heat, I finally got reassigned. The relief was so great, I almost kissed the foreman. He put me on minor jobs around the plant. Gradually, my skin healed, and I could wash my face without wincing and chew my food without pain. One afternoon, while sweeping up debris near the machines, Samuel found me. He grinned, his teeth stained with oven soot.

"Well, look at you! Living the easy life, huh?"

"Easy?" I scoffed, leaning on my broom. "I wouldn't call it that. But it sure beats the ovens."

Samuel clapped me on the back. "You don't look like you're about to melt anymore."

I shook my head, a smile tugging at my lips. "You still stuck down there?"

"Yep. But they're moving some of us around. Rumor has it

we'll both get reassigned soon." It turned out that Samuel was right. A month later, we were both moved to a small crew of four, cleaning grease and debris from under the machines between shifts. It was the job everyone wanted—no rush, no constant supervision.

"We're lucky," Samuel mused one night.

"How so?" I asked.

He kept his eyes on his broom. "We could be back at the ovens or shipped out to some concentration camp where there's hard labor and no food."

"You're right." I shuddered, but not because of the cold. "And thanks for reminding me how *lucky* we are."

"Nice zinger, Raf!"

$$\triangledown \quad \triangledown \quad \triangledown$$

BY SPRING 1944, our co-workers whispered that the Red Army was closing in on Warsaw. Samuel and I listened intently, our brains swirling. While the Russians and Germans had started on the same side, their alliance ended when Hitler tried to invade Russia. The Soviets had since aligned themselves with the United States and the other Allied powers.

"You think it's true?" Samuel asked one night while our heads were under a machine.

"I'm not sure. But there aren't as many guards around. Maybe the Germans need more soldiers on the front lines."

He wiped a greasy spot with his rag and let out a slow breath. "We can only hope."

Early in June 1944, we learned of the Allied invasion of Normandy. After our shift was over, Samuel and I hustled back to the barracks so we could talk more freely.

After shutting the door, Samuel crowed, "Did you ever think

you'd see the day? The Nazis seemed unstoppable." His eyes danced with excitement.

"I know! Maybe one day soon, we'll both walk out of here, free as birds." I clasped his shoulders in solidarity, our dreams of liberty renewed.

CHAPTER 38

Choices

Destination Unknown — January 1945.

CHANUKAH 1944 WAS A FAR CRY from my childhood celebrations. There were no candles, no chocolates, no dreidel, no loved ones to celebrate with. To mark the occasion, a small group of us huddled together in the barracks. For eight nights, we took turns talking about the past, about our families, our traditions, to keep them alive.

"My mother used to make sufganiyot every Chanukah," Samuel shared one night. "Jelly would drip all over the place, especially my face. She'd laugh and call me Piglet."

I grinned. "My Mama would always give me an extra donut, even though she knew I'd sneak them from the kitchen." I choked up for a moment, thinking back to happier days. "The last time I tasted sufganiyot was on the last birthday I celebrated with my entire family."

The Nazis didn't care about our traditions. In fact, they seemed to take pleasure in tormenting us during the holidays, choosing days of religious significance to organize deportations and massacres, to break our spirits. But in this place, the guards didn't stop us. Some even listened. It was strange, but we kept on celebrating.

BY JANUARY 1945, UNCERTAINTY hit a fever pitch. Our co-workers, just as excited as we were for the war to end, told us that the Red Army was getting closer and closer. "The Russians might liberate Warsaw any day now," one worker said breathlessly.

Samuel leaned over to me as we worked on a machine, his voice hushed. "Do you think the Nazis will kill us before the Soviets arrive?"

I scanned our surroundings before answering. "I think about that every day. They could send us to Treblinka, ship us off to Germany, or line us up right here and shoot us." A chill ran through me, and I rubbed my hands together for warmth. "All we can do is take it one day at a time."

"Agreed," he muttered. "But every time the Werkschutz calls for an assembly, I fear it could be our last."

The power failed a few nights later, plunging us into darkness across the entire plant, including our barracks. Then came the roar of planes, followed by the distant thud of bombs falling. Samuel and I huddled in our bunks, shaking and listening.

"Is this it?" I whispered.

"I hope so," Samuel replied.

We didn't sleep that night. We gripped each other, every sound jangling our nerves.

By morning, the night shift returned. Exhausted yet excited, they took turns sharing the news. "The plant was dark all night. We sat there, waiting, wondering. Some Gentile workers didn't show up for their shift. But the biggest news? Some of the Werkschutz fled!"

"They just left?" Samuel asked, incredulous.

"Seems like it," Karol, a nightshift worker, replied with a grin. "But some are still here, so we're not out of the woods yet."

"Should we stay here tonight? Or hide in the factory?" I asked the group.

"The foundry is enormous, and we know all the hiding places," Karol reasoned. "I plan on taking my chances there."

I pulled Samuel aside. "Should we risk it?"

"I'm not sure, Raf. Part of me wants to hide in the factory, but the other part…" He put his hands together, then sprung his fingers apart, mimicking an explosion.

"You think they'll blow the plant up? Or the Nazis will find us hiding in the factory before the Allied soldiers get here to save us?"

He nodded. "We've come this far. Maybe we should wait."

I was still undecided which path to take when the Werkschutz canceled our shift the next morning, preventing anyone from entering the factory. Everyone within our barracks was on edge, anxiously wondering what awaited us. By noon, the order came—pack our belongings and line up outside. The roll call we'd all been dreading was upon us.

"I don't like this," Samuel muttered as he stuffed his scant belongings into a sack. "Not one bit."

"I don't either," I said. "I think we made the wrong choice, but it's too late to change that now." I had to keep looking forward or my rising agitation would progress into a full-blown panic attack, and possibly, heart failure.

When we stood in line, they gave us double bread rations. Then the SS plant officer announced we would be marching to the Stradom railway. "We will shoot anyone who tries to escape," he announced. Under heavy guard, we began our march.

"This would be an excellent time for the Russians to show up," Samuel whispered to me.

"From your mouth to God's ears," I replied, echoing the expression my mother favored.

▽ ▽ ▽

THE COLD BIT AT MY SKIN despite the blanket I had wrapped around my shoulders. As we marched toward the main gate of the plant, I kept my head down. The anger bubbled inside me, a slow, simmering fury. Some of our group had hidden in the factory, and now freedom was within their grasp. We let it slip through our fingers like grains of sand, never to be recovered.

Samuel stepped beside me, his face shuttered. "Are you thinking about it, too?"

I nodded, biting my lip. "Yeah."

Samuel shook his head, his breath clouding the air. "Maybe they found the ones who stayed. Or maybe they'll still blow up the factory before the Russians arrive."

I still couldn't shake the heavy weight of regret. "I feel like a shaft of wheat, being blown this way and that. Here we are, marching to only God knows where. If we make it that far."

Samuel sighed but didn't argue. We trudged on in silence, watching as German tanks and artillery rolled by in a steady stream. They appeared to be evacuating Czestochowa and possibly all of Poland. Explosions echoed in the distance, the fighting moving closer.

"Look at them scamper away," Samuel muttered. "I wish they'd forget about us."

I chuckled darkly. "No chance of that." The gunfire grew louder, and for a split second, I considered sprinting toward the battle to avoid whatever awful fate awaited us on that train. But before I could act, somebody else beat me to it. A man in front of me broke formation and sprinted for all he was worth.

Retaliation happened before I could blink. Three shots rang out, and he fell to the ground. Two others dropped with him, caught in the crossfire, their bodies crumpling like rag dolls. I froze—Samuel gripped my arm to keep me from staggering.

"They won't hesitate, Raf. Don't even think about running."

"I won't," I whispered back. But I felt sick to my stomach, knowing how close to being shot I'd actually been.

After a few hours, we arrived at the Stradom train depot, where a long line of boxcars sat on the tracks. The Werkschutz handed us over to Wehrmacht soldiers and boarded a different train themselves, eager to escape.

They jammed us into the wooden cars just like the escapee from Treblinka had warned us. The train jerked forward, moving at a crawl, and the murmurs inside the car grew louder. The men around us whispered their speculations. Some thought Treblinka was our destination, others thought we'd be brought to a vacant field and shot. I closed my eyes—failing to drown them out.

Shlomo's voice echoed in my head. *How could you let them lead you like a sheep to slaughter?* I moaned and slapped myself in the head.

"Stupid idiot!" I rapped my knuckles against my skull, again and again.

Samuel's soothing voice interrupted my self-loathing exercise. "Second guessing isn't healthy, Raf. At least we're together."

Hours passed, and sleep refused to come. My mind was a storm of worst-case scenarios. Every time I drifted off, the image of the men shot earlier jolted me awake like a slap.

"Samuel," I whispered into the dark, needing to hear another living voice. "Where do you think they're sending us?"

He didn't answer right away. Eyes closed, brow furrowed, as if he were weighing the full list of horrors. Then, finally, he gave a small nod—like he'd found the perfect answer.

"The French Riviera!"

I let out something between a laugh and a cough. "Darn it," I rasped. "I forgot my bathing suit."

He grinned, just barely. It was absurd. It was ridiculous. And it saved me.

If only for a moment.

At dawn, the train stopped. When the door slid open, we were in the middle of a forest. I braced myself—would they shoot us here and bury our bodies? Surprisingly, they didn't. The guards let us stretch, drink water, even wash ourselves. It was surreal, the way they treated us like human beings, but I knew better than to trust their sudden compassion.

Samuel shuffled beside me as we drank, his eyes scanning the soldiers. "You notice something?" he asked under his breath.

"What?"

"They're nervous," he replied. "I overheard one of them talking. The Soviets took Czestochowa."

"We missed our chance," I groaned. "The ones who stayed behind—they're free now."

Anger surged through me. I slammed the side of my fist into my thigh, hard. The pain barely registered.

I knew—without a shred of doubt—I would regret that decision, or the failure to make one, for the rest of my life.

There was no judgment in Samuel's eyes, just understanding. "We couldn't have known. We did what we thought was right."

I kicked a rock. "As usual, I let fear decide for me, and now, look at us."

After the break, the soldiers forced us back into the boxcars. As the train moved westward, I could hear Shlomo ribbing me for being so weak, and Tatte's voice telling me to survive, to do whatever it took. I decided that feeling sorry for myself wouldn't help a bit. Turning to my faith, I pressed my hands together and whispered a prayer, fresh resolve washing over me.

"We'll make it, Samuel," I breathed. "We must. To honor our families by telling their stories."

Samuel laid a hand on my shoulder. "For our families."

Chapter 39

Buchenwald Concentration Camp

Weimar, Germany — January 1945

When the train doors creaked open, SS officers greeted us with snarling dogs at their sides. Their eyes, hard as stone, bore down on us as we clambered out of the boxcars, our legs stiff and our spirits dampened. They lined us up and inspected us like livestock, while the dogs snapped at our heels. No one dared to move a finger out of line.

"Keep your head down," I whispered. Samuel nodded, though neither of us could control our bodies from shaking.

A dense fog rolled in, swirling around us like a ghostly veil. I pulled my threadbare blanket tighter, but it did little to ward off the icy winds. "Halt!" the officers said, a gothic iron gate looming before us like the entrance to hell.

Buchenwald.

It had a reputation for being treacherous and depraved, worse than Treblinka, if that was possible. Even the fog seemed to warn us. *Turn back! You will not leave this place alive.*

The stench hit me before we even walked through the gate. It was suffocating, a mixture of decay, human waste, and something far more sinister. I gagged, pulling the blanket over my nose, but it was no use. The odor permeated everything.

Samuel's pale face went green, and his stomach heaved. "This awful smell… what is it?"

His question didn't require an answer. This place was death, and we both knew it.

As we marched past the electrified barbed wire, I noticed SS sharpshooters in elevated guard towers, rifles trained on us, ready to fire at the slightest provocation. My gaze flicked to the power boxes attached to the fence. If the SS didn't kill us, the electrified wire would.

The camp commander, a tall man with a pressed black uniform and an SS armband, stood on a platform overlooking the vast concrete square that stretched in front of us. His face was expressionless, the trademark Nazi appearance, as he barked orders through a bullhorn.

"This is the Appellplatz. All roll calls and inspections will take place here. Hanging or being gunned down will be your reward for any disobedience."

He waved a metal baton in the air, extending it with a twist of his wrist. Terror ripped through my body as I realized what it was—a telescopic rod, a death stick that could break bones with a single swing. I had hoped never to see one of these in person, though Nazi propaganda boasted of their power.

"They'll kill us if we step out of line." Samuel's voice was barely audible. I was afraid to respond, the horror of our situation rendering me terrified.

After the commander finished his chilling speech, guards led us to the camp bathhouse. I recalled the story of how the Nazis stripped, shaved, and gassed Jews upon their arrival at Treblinka. The prisoner tasked with shaving our heads yanked the hair from my scalp in bloody clumps, his razor rusty and dull.

When it was my turn to strip, a deep sense of humiliation

washed over me. The guards jeered at us, spewing antisemitic slurs as we stood there, naked and vulnerable. Guards then led us to a tub of foul-smelling liquid with dead lice floating on the surface.

"Immerse yourselves, you pigs!" the overseer sneered, his spit landing in the tub. I closed my eyes and dunked myself, the liquid burning my skin like acid. When I surfaced, my skin was itchy and inflamed.

Still naked and trembling, they pushed me into the line for a medical inspection. The doctors scanned us, efficient and de-tached. They pulled a few unhealthy-looking men aside and took them away for "treatment," a euphemism for cold-blooded murder.

After the inspection, they took the rest of us into a shower room. I stared at the showerhead, half-expecting gas to pour out of it, but to my relief, lukewarm water flowed instead. After the shower, they escorted us to a supply room, still dripping wet. They gave us striped uniforms and a cap—but no undergarments or socks, nothing to protect us from the biting cold.

Then a tailor sewed number 116297 onto my shirt. I was no longer Rafal Kantor. I was just a number, another faceless prison-er in this place of nightmares.

As we shuffled toward the barracks, I clung to Samuel for warmth. My body shivered, but it wasn't just from the cold. *Keep moving forward*, I told myself. *One foot in front of the other. To stop now, to give in, would be an unthinkable tragedy.*

Samuel whispered to me, "We stay together, no matter what."

As we trudged through the camp, I scanned the faces sur-rounding us—Germans, Poles, Russians, and Hungarians, not all Jewish. The diversity of misery startled me.

Daylight was fading by the time we arrived at the Quarantine barracks. It wasn't much—straw sacks for bedding, worn blankets on the bunks—but more than what I expected. We lined up for dinner, a loose term for what we received. The soup was a murky broth with a few pathetic bits of turnip floating in it. I glared at my bowl and sighed.

Samuel slumped down beside me. "I'm so hungry, Raf. We need to get more to eat than this swill. Maybe we'll get something else in the morning." I nodded, hoping he was right.

Afterward, the guards blew the whistle for lights out, and I lay on my straw mattress, staring into space. My thoughts were tangled up in the disturbing rumors I'd heard of men starving to death, their bodies devouring themselves. Was that going to be my fate?

At some point, I succumbed to sleep. I dreamed of freedom, of Allied planes flying overhead, of paratroopers dropping, and of guns blazing. I dreamed of the gates of Buchenwald being blown open, the Nazis scattering in panic. When I woke the next morning, the hard reality assaulted me like a slap to the face.

The morning inspection came next, and we lined up outside. The chill seeped through my striped uniform, the flimsy fabric doing nothing to protect against the biting wind. My shoes pinched my feet as we marched toward the latrines. Mud sloshed around my ankles, making each step more miserable than the last. The bathroom was a few feet away.

"You gonna clean up?" Samuel asked, his voice low.

"Yeah," though I wasn't sure why it mattered.

The ice-cold water stung my skin as I splashed it on my face and underarms. No soap, of course. Just a filthy community rag to wipe off the gunk.

After inspection, they gave us a slice of bread and a cup of coffee. As I sat on my bunk, chewing that hard, black bread, I knew I would need to eat everything they served, no matter how unappetizing. With the electrified fence and sharpshooters, leaving the camp to beg for food was completely out of the question.

The hours dragged by after breakfast. I expected to be assigned a job, but they left us alone. I ended up back in my bunk, and I must have dozed because when I opened my eyes, it was mid-afternoon. I decided to stretch my legs and check out the adjacent barracks.

On the way, I met a haggard, toothless man, his skin stretched thin over his bones, his eyes bulging out of their sunken sockets. His words chilled me to the core.

"You need to stay invisible," he warned, his voice only a rasp. "Keep away from the Nazi doctors. They lure you with promises of food and vitamins to make you strong. It's a lie, a vicious trick."

I frowned, confused. "How do you know this?"

"My brother, they took him, gave him a meal, a bed. Told him they were making him strong for a special work detail. He died a few weeks later from an injection filled with some horrible disease like malaria. A friend saw his body carted off to the crematorium."

On top of all our hardships, now we had to guard against medical torture. "Thank you for warning me," I murmured, though the news made me feel sick.

He hobbled away, leaving me standing there, abandoned and alone. I stuffed my hands in my pants and trudged back to my barracks. Filthy, disgusting bodies staggered past me, and I broke into a run. Back inside, I dove onto my bunk and squeezed my eyes shut.

If I could sleep through this fresh horror, I would.

CHAPTER 40

Samuel

Buchenwald, Germany — January–February 1945

WE SPENT TWO WEEKS in the quarantine barracks. Not that the Nazis cared about our health—they kept us there to make sure we didn't spread any diseases to *them*. Each day, I felt the weight dropping off, turning my limbs frail, and making my joints hurt. With no work to distract me, I vacillated between obsessing over my next meal and my limited chance for survival. The silence here was more brutal than any labor, forcing me to dwell on everything I'd lost.

After our brief two-week "vacation," an SS guard entered our quarters and ordered us to get ready to move to a new barracks. I favored the shift, hoping for a chance to work outside the camp, and barter for additional provisions.

I couldn't have been more wrong. They led Samuel and me into an already overcrowded barrack, with three-tier bunks and not a single blanket or straw mattress. Sunken-eyed prisoners, appearing more dead than alive, hissed at us when we entered the building. To make matters worse, the guards didn't assign us bunks. Every sliver of space was occupied. Row after row of prisoners crammed together on wooden boards.

"Where are we supposed to sleep?" Samuel asked the guard.

He smirked and waved his hand around the room. "That's your problem, not mine."

Not only were all the bunks taken, but there was barely any space on the floor. Apparently, if you had to sleep on the floor, the best spots were against the wall, where you were less likely to be trounced on. But bleary-eyed prisoners had already laid claim to those spots.

Samuel and I wedged ourselves between two prisoners who clearly resented surrendering an inch of their precious floor space. There was no room to lie down, so we wrapped our arms around our knees and pressed our backs together for support. I couldn't fathom how anyone slept like this.

Hours later, a guard burst in announcing, "Evening rations." Samuel and I perked up and helped each other rise. They distributed the food outside, despite the freezing temperature.

To our surprise, most of the prisoners remained in their bunks or in their personal spots on the floor. I pitied their weakness, wondering if the lack of camaraderie I'd noticed had to do with viewing death as a welcome release and not wanting to prolong the inevitable. But Samuel and I were clinging onto life, and would accept any nourishment offered, no matter the weather.

When we pushed open the door, we noticed we weren't the only ones out here. The line of shivering prisoners stretched around the corner. Two SS guards with weapons stood on either side of the Kapo as he doled out the rations.

Samuel and I stood in line, our teeth chattering, and by the time we received our meal, I was sure the food would freeze to our trembling hands. "Let's bring it inside so we can savor it," I said. Samuel nodded, and we cradled our bread with reverence as we trudged back to the building.

We were barely back inside the barrack when striped wraiths closed in around us. They salivated over the bread, their eyes glazed and feral. One of them, a tall, thin man with a swollen jaw and yellow teeth, extended a bony hand. "Give it here."

I took a step back, clutching the bread in my hands. "It's mine. Go find your own." My voice sounded weak even to me, as I realized how dangerous this moment had become.

Another prisoner, his clothes dwarfing his withered body, descended from an upper bunk. "Yours? We're all starving here. You think you're special?" With a growl, he lunged forward, ripped it from my hand, and stuffed it in his mouth.

As he licked his fingers and returned to his bunk, a profound sense of loss and helplessness overwhelmed me. I couldn't see Samuel in the swarm of grasping hands surrounding him, and a skeletal elbow poked me in my face as I pushed through the mob. I retaliated by dropping my shoulder into his ribs and bullying my way through.

When I reached Samuel, we both watched the swarm tussle over his scrap of bread, tearing it into crumbs they stuffed into their mouths with desperation. The Nazis had won. They had stripped us of all humanity, forced us to rely on our basic animal instincts to survive. Alas, I'm ashamed to admit it, but in that moment, I didn't blame the Nazis. Instead, I blamed the prisoners, the living dead, despite knowing they had endured this hellhole longer than Samuel and I had.

I stood there panting, wondering if I shouldn't just dash outside and zap myself with the electric fence. I jumped when a hand landed on my shoulder—Samuel's.

"Well, that was a valuable lesson," he said dryly. "We eat outside from now on, no matter how cold it gets."

▽ ▽ ▽

DAYS AND WEEKS BLURRED INTO ONE, every minute scraping away another piece of my humanity. Hunger gnawed at me constantly until any remaining shred of hope crumbled into the dust. Each day, Samuel and I witnessed something more depraved than the day before. It got to where we were no longer surprised by anything we saw.

The previous night, a group of men tore a prisoner from his bunk, threw him to the floor, and claimed his spot as their own. At least Samuel and I waited until someone died before claiming his bunk.

"It's a dog-eat-dog world," played in my brain on repeat, and honestly, I didn't even recall where I'd heard the expression. We took turns removing dead bodies, dragging them outside to the growing pile stacked between the buildings.

▽ ▽ ▽

DYSENTERY RAN RAMPANT in our barrack, draining every ounce of strength and dignity we had left. Each morning, I'd wake up sticky and damp from discharge dripping down from the bunk above. Some men were too weak to make it to the latrine, making them a mess of filth and suffering. The guards didn't care—to them; we were not more than the waste our bodies expelled—just trash to be shoveled away when we finally collapsed.

Samuel had it bad. For the past week, he'd been coughing up blood and phlegm, every breath rattling his sunken chest. I didn't dare leave him, not caring whether I'd catch what he had. I just wanted to keep him safe, keep the others from throwing him down and claiming his spot. We huddled together in that bunk, and I registered every rise and fall of his chest. His sharp bones poked me as he wasted away before my eyes.

"Raf," he whispered softly. "I don't think I'm going to make it."

I tried to keep it light. "Hey, we're going to set up business together, remember? You can't quit now."

He tried to laugh, but it came out as a wet, hacking cough. The heat radiated off him like a furnace when I touched his forehead.

"I'm scared," he mumbled. "Don't let anyone else touch me."

Samuel was my rock, my confidante, my brother in every way that mattered. He had always been the hopeful one, keeping the spark alive for both of us. The thought of losing another cherished person was unbearable.

"You need to fight. You're the best among us, Samuel. We need to stick together, remember?"

His brown eyes were distant, and his breaths were shallow and strained. He turned to me, his gaze flickering. "Promise me, Raf, that you'll never give up. You need to survive, for both…" His head lolled to the side, and his mouth sagged.

"Samuel! Come back!" I shrieked, but he didn't respond. I pressed my ear against his chest, hoping, praying for a whisper of a heartbeat but finding none. "No!" I grabbed his shoulders and shook him. "Don't leave me! You promised!" But it was no use.

Scrawny hands grasped for him, but I pulled Samuel's body close, cradling him, brushing my hands all over his face and hair. My heartbreak overwhelmed me until I was too exhausted to cry anymore. In my anguish, I felt someone put a thin blanket over me and a balled-up shirt under my head as a cushion. A stranger was comforting me.

A sign that compassion and humanity were hanging on by the narrowest of threads, despite the Nazi's efforts to wipe them out completely.

CHAPTER 41

The Finishing Camp

Destination Unknown — February 1945

THE NEXT MORNING, an older prisoner invited me to walk him to breakfast. I understood why—he was sparing me from witnessing Samuel's body being added to the growing pile outside. An attendant would strip Samuel of his clothes, then paint large identification numbers on his chest. Later, a wagon would come and take his body to the crematorium. It was a grim process, and one I was happy to miss.

Despite my promise to Samuel, listlessness set in. I no longer had the drive to rise each morning, my embattled mind in constant combat with my shattered heart. *Why am I fighting so hard? There's no one left who cares about me. Why not just put an end to this useless charade?*

I was wasting away. Each breath came with a persistent and painful wheeze, my body and will failing in tandem.

I WAS HANGING ON by the slimmest shred when the SS ordered our pitiful group into the forest outside of the camp. They marched us to a large pit, next to it a pile of stones. *This is it. They're going to shoot us and throw us in.*

I felt no fear, just resignation and relief that my suffering might finally end. But instead, our severely weakened group was forced to haul heavy stones from one hill to another, trudging through slushy snow, while a line of SS guards mocked our every faltering step. When a prisoner slipped, the guards beat us and doubled our load. I received blows to my back and to my skull, but somehow, I kept going, though frostbite attacked my extremities with a vengeance.

When evening fell, they ordered us back to the barracks. Guards shot any inmates too weak to walk upright. Somehow, I found the strength to carry a fellow prisoner, likely because he weighed no more than one of those damned stones.

The next day, the death toll tripled. Within my barracks, there was now plenty of room to spread out. Of the prisoners who remained, most were so downtrodden by the previous day's torture that they lost all hope and welcomed death with open arms. Even the most deeply devout Jews among us renounced their faith, unable to reconcile their intense suffering with a just God.

Miraculously, a glimmer of inner strength rose within me, reminding me to honor my pledge to my family and to Samuel, to live despite the enormous odds stacked against me. But to survive, I needed to find a way out of Buchenwald. Or else this macabre game of torture roulette would surely do me in.

Through the grapevine, I learned that Buchenwald was a replenishment center for other labor camps, and prisoners could volunteer for outside work. While I knew that men who left rarely returned, anything had to be better than staying here. With the hope of extra rations dancing in my head, I scratched my name on the labor camp registration list.

In the following days, SS doctors subjected everyone who signed up for physical exams. Somehow, we all passed and received new identification papers. On the day we left, the guards marched us to the bathhouse and gave us another "trim." Then they plunged us into the delousing tank, which was worse the second time around. After an icy shower, we sprinted to the supply room for "clean" clothing. This whole sordid ritual gave me hope that real jobs awaited us instead of more torture.

They formed us into a column and marched us to the train station and into idling freight cars. Yet another journey, destination unknown.

$$\triangledown \quad \triangledown \quad \triangledown$$

THE NEXT DAY, I awoke in agony. Each attempt to move made me light-headed and weak, my vision rapidly clouding over. My last coherent thought before darkness claimed me was *at last*.

Hours later, or perhaps only minutes, blaring sirens jolted me awake. It was a bombing raid, and the guards sprinted away, abandoning us to fend for ourselves in the locked boxcar. I reveled in the roar of the overhead planes and silently cheered as bombs whistled down. *Maybe one will land on us*, I thought. *I wouldn't mind going in a blaze of Allied glory after all. If Shlomo were here, I know he would approve wholeheartedly.*

But the explosions faded into the distance, and when all-clear sirens sounded, the guards returned to shepherd us onward. It was so anticlimactic that time lost all meaning in the days that followed. I slipped between feverish dreams and fleeting bouts of awareness. Sometimes I tasted drops of coffee trickling down my throat, which must have kept me tethered to life. Every so often, I'd hear agonized groaning, only to realize it was coming from me.

These strangers took care of me, fed me scraps of bread, and offered their precious warmth. If not for them, I'd have perished, another anonymous victim of this foul war.

The train shuddered to a halt. "Get out!" the guards barked, shoving us forward. I stumbled, disoriented, needing help to step down from the boxcar. I struggled to keep pace with the others, stumbling every few steps. Falling behind meant death, which would have been my fate if other prisoners hadn't lent their support.

As we shuffled forward, we passed a group of zombie-like men hacking at the road with pickaxes. One of them grumbled, "They'll work you to death here."

I had barely enough strength to stand, let alone swing a pick-axe. I called out, "Can you spare any food?" The men shook their heads, and their lack of a reply made me wonder if there was any food at all.

After hiking several miles, getting more worn out with each shuffled step, we arrived at the gates of the labor camp. It was a no-frills place, located in a bleak clearing, dotted with a few single-story barracks, and loosely enclosed by barbed wire. SS guards eyed us from the gate as we halted in front of a small building. I felt so insubstantial, a gust of wind could have blown me away.

The officer in charge stepped forward for inspections, and I could not take my eyes off his ridiculous blond handlebar mustache. Naturally, he looked at us as though we were trash, but I was inured to that by this time.

The camp's doctor approached, ready to examine the new arrivals. He was an older man with snow white hair, dark circles under his eyes, and a pronounced hunch. I blinked—was this another hallucination? He looked like my childhood doctor from Czestochowa.

I blinked again, and he was still there. Through the haze of my fatigue, I stammered, "Dr. Glatter?"

His eyes widened in recognition, and a flicker of warmth passed between us. "Kantorek," he said, using my childhood nickname. "We meet again."

CHAPTER 42

Dr. Glatter

Location Unknown — February 1945

HIS FAMILIAR VOICE was a chilling reminder of how far we had both fallen. But seeing someone from Czestochowa, from a time when the world made sense, was heartening.

Dr. Glatter, sensing my fragile state, leaned in close. "Rafal, I'll get you into the camp hospital. I'll explain more when we're safe." He led me out of the column, and I must have blacked out, because when I regained consciousness, I was resting on a bed with a real mattress. The softness felt so foreign, so distant from my recent experience, that tears welled up in my eyes.

"You're my guardian angel," I whispered to Dr. Glatter. As Jews, we didn't believe in Heaven, but there was no other explanation for him appearing as my savior at my most desperate hour.

The hospital was an oasis in this desolate place. He instructed an orderly to bring me a bowl of soup. Its aroma made me realize how long it had been since I'd eaten anything more than a scrap of bread. I was so weak that Dr. Glatter had to spoon it into my mouth. I didn't care how much of it dripped on my chin as the life-giving fluid coursed through my ravaged system.

After I finished, Dr. Glatter asked softly, "What of your family, Rafal?"

"Gone. All of them," I choked out.

He patted my arm, his face registering the sorrow I felt deep in my soul.

I stayed in the hospital for a second day, consuming more soup and entire pieces of bread. When others in the ward were too sick to eat solid food, I accepted their bread rations. In return, I gave them my soup.

On the third day, Dr. Glatter's news struck me hard. "Rafal, I must send you back to Buchenwald. It's your only chance to survive. The Nazis consider this a finishing camp."

"A what?" I asked.

He didn't mince words. "This hospital is only for those who get sick during transport. After a day or two of convalescence, they force prisoners to join the labor details and work you until you drop dead."

To leave the warm hospital, to return to scraps of food and disdain, and to never see Dr. Glatter again was more than I could emotionally bear. "Can I stay here one more day? Please?"

Dr. Glatter's face crumpled. "If I could keep you, I would. You must believe me."

We assembled in the labor camp square, the living dead, enduring inspection by a clipboard-carrying SS officer. I wanted to ask the camp commander why he just didn't shoot us right there—he'd probably done worse to healthier men. But I held my tongue not for my sake, but for the sake of those beside me. As depressed as I was, I hadn't sunk so low that I could disregard another man's life.

▽　▽　▽

OUR RETURN TO THE TRAIN DEPOT was a lumbering procession. Each of us dragged our feet, trying to delay our return. As I climbed into the boxcar, I chose a spot and sank down, closing my eyes.

I was more lucid during this leg of the journey, yet the trip blurred into a monotony of occasional water stops and frequent air-raid alarms. Were the Allies closing in? If so, would they come fast enough to save me and the other prisoners?

After days of travel, we arrived back at Buchenwald. The thought sickened me to the core—that somehow, my chances of survival were better in this wretched place than at the finishing camp. The boxcar doors groaned open, and the guards forcibly shoved us into a column. We trudged toward the barracks, each step rattling our ribcages and filling us with dread. A thick haze clung to the atmosphere, soot from the crematoria settling onto my skin and invading my sensory organs.

When I had first arrived here, Samuel had wondered, "What's that smell?"

I couldn't describe it then. Now, I knew.

Each breath carried the rancid odor of decomposing flesh and sulfuric miasma, making it impossible not to gag. But it was a smorgasbord of delights for black flies and maggots, who feasted with abandon.

The most repulsive parasite of them all? The Nazis, elitist sadists who delighted in exacting torture, perpetrators of the greatest evil the world had ever known.

CHAPTER 43

Graveyard of the Damned

Buchenwald, Germany — March 1945

RETURNING TO BUCHENWALD was like entering a graveyard of the damned. Everywhere I looked, I saw plodding cadavers, nothing but skin pulled taut over bones. Each day, men dropped from illness, exhaustion, or starvation—often right in front of me.

I had regained a sliver of strength, thanks to the ministrations of Dr. Glatter. But it vanished almost immediately from hours of standing for long inspections, lugging stones in the forest, and not enough food to keep a rat alive. My body felt like it was collapsing inward, my bones scraping against each other as if lined with broken glass.

The Nazis had done it. They'd stripped us down to our basest animalistic needs, turned us into skeletal versions of ourselves. I hated how Hitler's ruthless vision was materializing, so close to war's end. My only remaining hope was that someone, somewhere, would survive to tell the world about the systematic murder of countless Jews and others. I honestly didn't think it would be me or anyone else from this godforsaken camp.

Constant diarrhea made me dizzy and weak, and images of Samuel's demise plagued my every thought. Rations, slim as they were, cycled through me in minutes, and I often couldn't reach the latrine in time. I had no dignity or pride left and didn't even care when my own filth ran down my legs as I staggered under the weight of stones. The alternative was a beating from a guard, the club liable to break my brittle bones. I'd seen it happen too many times to count.

One morning, my body refused to move. I woke too depleted to pull myself out of the bunk. I tried to stand, only to black out and fall to the floor. The next thing I knew, someone was smacking my face, urging me back to consciousness.

"Get up. It's time for roll call!"

Startled, I realized it was Eli, a newer bunkmate appearing marginally healthier than the rest of us. He knelt next to me and tried to help me to my feet, but I must have blacked out again. Somehow, Eli and another prisoner dragged me to roll call, and for three agonizing hours, they propped me up to keep me from falling. When we finally made it back inside, Eli settled me onto my bunk and draped a blanket over me.

His eyes betrayed his worry. "Raf, you don't look so well."

I managed a weak smile. "You checked a mirror lately?" We shared a grim chuckle, making my head hurt.

"You're shaking." Eli frowned, adjusting the blanket over my shoulders. "I'll stay with you for a while longer, but you should see the doctor. Unfortunately, you'll need to bribe the barracks chief."

Rumors drifted through the barracks that the chief kept a daily quota of dying men for the "mercy shot." I remembered the warning I received soon after arriving in Buchenwald, but now, it seemed like the shot might be a mercy after all.

When the chief arrived, I offered him my evening portion of bread—a poor bribe, but all I had. In return, I begged him to put me on the list for the camp hospital.

The bribe worked. Inside the camp hospital, there were narrow beds with thin mattresses and worn blankets, both of which we lacked in the normal barracks. I fell asleep wondering if I'd ever wake up again.

$$\triangledown \quad \triangledown \quad \triangledown$$

IN MY WAKEFUL BOUTS, I tried to make it to the hospital latrine, but it wasn't always possible. As weak and disgusting as I felt, many men were worse off. I quickly learned that it was important to eat the paltry portions we received, no matter if it ran through my system in minutes. When someone didn't touch their food for too long, the nurses would alert the doctors, and the mercy shot would follow. Seeing so many men die, I realized that I would do anything to stay alive.

One attendant, Herr Kruger, slithered around the room, taunting us through his rotting teeth, "Today is the day I'll give you the *vaccine*. It'll end all your pain. Why fight it?"

Whenever the camp doctor was absent, he hovered over each of us, threatening to jab us. He grinned when a patient shrank in terror, and I honestly wished I had enough strength to grab the syringe and jab him with it. I was especially incensed when he targeted the patient beside me, a distinguished older gentleman who was far worse off than I was.

"Get away from him, you butcher," I shouted at the top of my diminished lungs.

The doctor turned to see the commotion, gave us a stern look, and returned to his patient.

Kruger breathed in my face. "Your time is coming too," he said with a sneer.

"You're a bully," I retorted. I'd finally reached the point

where I didn't give a damn about consequences. Kruger's eyes narrowed, but he moved on to taunt others.

The older gentleman and I had grown close, conversing in our lucid moments, and it warmed my heart when he called me son. Though life was rapidly draining from his body, his mind and spirit flickered still.

He cleared his throat. "The Allies are on German soil, advancing fast. You must see the Germans pay for their crimes. Promise me!" He broke into a coughing fit. When he recovered enough to speak again, his voice was strained. "Son, will you hold my hand? My time is up. I can feel it."

"Of course." I blinked back tears as I took his hand in mine. His skin was paper-thin and cold, and his breath was rapidly becoming shallower. I recited the Shema, and halfway through, he was gone.

Out of the corner of my eye, I saw Kruger approaching. "What are you doing!" he hissed, staring at our clasped hands.

I was furious that he'd intruded on such a sacred moment, but I forced myself to meet his gaze and act calm. "He died. Isn't that what you wanted?"

Kruger tapped a syringe on his clipboard, giving me that awful grin. As he stalked away, I lay back on my bed, mentally and spiritually shaken. I didn't even learn the old man's name, yet he'd trusted me to witness his last moments on God's green earth. I took his hand again and finished my blessing.

"I'll never forget you as long as I live," I whispered to him.

▽ ▽ ▽

MY BODY WAS STILL WEAK and riddled with dysentery, but the hospital was no sanctuary anymore. My growing paranoia convinced me that the attendant might jab me when I was sleeping.

"I'm ready to return to the barracks," I told the doctor after a restless week. A day later, they discharged me.

The moment I stepped outside, I knew I'd miscalculated. I gripped the doorpost to steady myself. Spring had arrived in this somber place, and despite the poisonous air, a few dandelions poked through the fencing. While I caught my breath, I stared at those weeds like they were the most beautiful things I'd ever seen.

As I trudged through the camp, I noticed an influx of new prisoners wandering the grounds. Upon opening the door to my dwelling, I was horribly disappointed to see that only standing room was available. There was no way I was well enough to manage that. As I weaved through the crowd, I found my bunk spot occupied and gave the person a nudge. When he turned toward me, I braced myself for a fight, afraid I would lose. I cried with relief when I realized it was Eli.

"Raf, you came back! I'm just holding your spot, pal." His eyes were yellowy, but so were mine and everyone else's.

It was a challenge to climb in next to him, but Eli gave me a hand. When he noticed my mismatched hospital uniform, his laughter turned into a coughing fit. After recovering enough to speak, he quipped, "They washed you up, eh? You're not smelling half as bad as before."

"And you, my friend, still smell like a cat's litter box." I pinched my nose. "Who are all these new *resort* guests?"

Eli sat up on his bunk and rolled his shoulders to take out the kinks. "They're evacuees from Bergen-Belsen and other camps." He hacked away some of the phlegm in his throat, and I rubbed his back. "I heard that entire towns are collapsing under the Allied advance. German soldiers, Nazi officers, they're surrendering without a fight." He punched the air in a muted victory salute.

"It looks like they're consolidating all the Jewish prisoners here," I said. "Do you think there'll be any Jews left in all of Europe after this?"

"I have to believe some European Jews will survive, even if it's not us." He scratched the stubble on his head. "Corralling us makes it easy for the Germans to barricade the gates, torch the entire camp, and take us out in one go. There would be no witnesses, no records of their crimes."

There were murmurs of assent from all present.

"There's not an ounce of mercy in their bodies. If the Nazis are going down, I'm sure they'll take us with them," another prisoner said.

Eli tapped his finger on the wooden bunk. "The guards are on edge, pacing like mad dogs. The whole place is a tinderbox and we're the kindling."

CHAPTER 44

Holding On

Buchenwald, Germany — April 1945

THE AFTERNOON OF APRIL 4TH, the SS commandant's voice crackled through the camp microphone. Most prisoners were milling about the grounds, soaking in the sunshine. Eli and I were outside, resting on the grass, when the announcement came.

"Attention! All Jews assemble at the main gate for immediate evacuation. Our enemies are approaching the camp, making it unsafe for us to remain. All those who evacuate will receive double rations."

Unsafe for us? Double rations?

The announcement cut through the camp, causing a blend of gasps and rapid-fire chatter between prisoners. To me, the decree reeked of deception, of which the Nazis were masters.

I turned to Eli. "When have the Nazis ever protected us from harm? Besides, did you notice the decree was for Jews only? Why just us, and not the non-Jewish prisoners? I don't trust them, not one bit."

Eli's brow furrowed. "Agreed. But they're offering double rations! How can we refuse?"

Anger surged through me. "Double rations? Eli, that's the bait! They're playing on our desperation. If they have extra food to spare, would they really waste it on us?"

"You're probably right. But it's so tempting, I don't think I can resist." He closed his eyes, thinking it over.

Remorse filled me head to toe, and I grabbed Eli's arm. "Please trust me. If I hadn't fallen for their lies before, I'd be a free man now and my good friend Samuel would still be alive." My pulse ratcheted upward, but I had to spit this out. "My last job was in the Rakow plant. If we'd hidden out in the plant when the Nazis left, we would have been freed by the Russians who liberated Czestochowa shortly after we left."

Eli's eyes widened at my admission, but he allowed me to continue. "I've been a sheep for too long, letting the Nazis drag me from one nightmare to the next, never questioning, always obeying. But I refuse to let them fool me again. If I die here, so be it. Are you with me?"

Eli nodded. "I'm with you, Raf. All the way to the end."

We knew the Nazis would sweep every corner of the camp searching for Jews. Our shirts, with the yellow Juden star stitched into the fabric, marked us as the hunted. I waved a hand at a nearby heap of dead bodies, non-Jewish, based on their uniforms. They hadn't carted the bodies away to the crematorium yet, a sure sign the camp leaders were losing control.

"If we change our shirts, we won't be instantly identifiable as Jews." A flicker of revulsion passed over Eli's face, but he nodded.

Together, we sorted through the stiff, lifeless bodies, gagging from the overpowering stench of decay, until we found shirts in decent condition that looked like they would fit. After removing them from the cadavers, we stripped ours off and tossed them aside. Then, with our fingers, we dug into the dirt and buried them.

Realizing it wasn't safe to remain outside and lacking ideas on where else to hide, we returned to our own barrack. As we lay in the bunk, clinging to each other for strength, the SS Commandant's voice reverberated through our eardrums as he repeated his offer again and again. One by one, men fell for the bribe, shuffling out the door, until only a handful of us remained. For hours, we kept still and quiet as the guards marched past.

I was wound tighter than a spring, waiting for the final battle to begin. And when it did, I vowed that for once in my sorry life, I'd fight with all I had.

THE ROAR OF MACHINE GUNS grew louder with each passing day, as did the steady drone of Allied planes overhead. My insides would cheer, even though my body was on the verge of collapse. Liberation was so close I could almost taste it. The SS had stopped calling for Jews to gather at the main gate. Whether they fled or were hiding themselves, no one knocked on our door, either to finish us off or give us paltry rations. But the solidarity between our fellow prisoners held, we would live or die together.

None of us had eaten in six days. Desperate for any distraction from the unbearable emptiness, I forced myself off the bunk. The cold barrack floor pressed against my bare feet, but I had to keep moving—no matter how much each step felt like trudging through quicksand.

Stumbling outside, I let the sun's warmth cut through the haze in my mind. I took a few steps, blinking against the light, when my breath caught in my throat. Standing right in front of me, as if plucked from a memory, was the older gentleman I had met in the hospital.

We hugged and kissed. He held my hand and helped me sit down on the front step of the next building. "Tell me, Raf, what's bothering you?" his voice soothing.

I began unburdening my tortured soul, the words spilling out of me. I spoke of my family and how I blamed myself for their deaths. Only thinking of my survival when it mattered the most. How I was a coward and failed everyone who ever loved me.

The older man draped a comforting arm around my shoulders. "Rafal, your family forgives you. In fact, they're right here, sitting with us. They want to hear you sing."

My family? I lifted my head, and there they were—whole, untouched by war, just as I remembered. Shlomo with his cocky grin and perpetually messy hair. Rivka, her braids neatly tied, her brown eyes shining. My parents, standing arm-in-arm, as strong and proud as ever.

I tried to speak, to sing, but my throat locked. My breath shuddered. All I could do was stare, overwhelmed by the sheer force of their presence.

The older man smiled, his eyes brimming with warmth. "Hold on to life, my son," he whispered. "You're almost home."

My eyelids grew heavy, and my family's faces faded. "No!" I cried out. "Don't leave me!"

"Wake up! Wake up!" Someone was shaking me. I blinked and blinked until I realized I was still in my bunk, with Eli looming over me.

"Raf, you were talking in your sleep. I'm sorry I had to wake you, but you must stay quiet. We don't want to draw any unwanted attention."

My eyes darted in all directions. "Eli," I croaked, "I saw my family, I swear it! Why did you take me away from them?"

"Raf, it was just a dream," he said softly.

"No," I cried. The pain of losing them again was unbearable.

CHAPTER 45

The Americans!

Buchenwald, Germany — April 11th, 1945

ASSAULTED BY ANOTHER WAVE of dysentery, I dragged myself down from my bunk. I could not, would not, befoul our hiding place, even though we'd dedicated a corner of the barrack as our latrine area. I had just made it outside when I heard a deafening *boom*, and the ground shook, followed by a barrage of gunfire and artillery. I was knocked off my feet and crawled to the side of our barrack. Unable to go any further, I squatted down there. Sneaking back inside afterward, we all cowered in our bunks as the fighting continued for hours.

When it stopped, we peered out the small, filthy windows, propping each other up. Before our eyes, an SS guard fell from a watchtower, blood blooming on his gray jacket. A wave of elation, disbelief, and nervousness filtered through our small gathering. None of us spoke, each of us terrified that doing so would shatter the miracle.

Who is fighting the Nazis? Americans? Russians? Will they blow up our building, not realizing we're inside?

The door to our barrack crashed open, making more than one man scream. We took a collective sigh of relief to see a wide-eyed prisoner instead of a gun-toting guard. "The Allies defeated

203

the Nazis! The guards are dead or captured!" He was ready to collapse, so Eli ushered him onto an open bunk. Then, with a determined expression, Eli dragged himself outside to check.

He returned moments later, panting, tears of joy coursing
down his gaunt cheeks. He leaned against the wall and cried out,
"It's the Americans! They came for us!" He fell onto the nearest
bunk, eyes closed, but a smile illuminating his face.

A short while later, our barrack door swung open again, and a
small band of American soldiers burst inside. They appeared so tall
and powerful—like heroes from the silver screen. Their eyes roved
over each of us, and one by one, they removed their helmets.

One soldier moved closer, his face drawn with horror. "My
God, they're still alive." He recoiled, afraid to touch us.

Somebody murmured "freedom" in Polish, and we all began
to chant and weep. I staggered out of my bunk and fell into the
arms of one of our liberators.

"You're safe now," the American whispered. "You're free."

The soldiers talked to each of us, embracing those capable of
lifting their heads, patting the foreheads of those unable to move,
their tears mixing with ours. Their faces washed in disbelief as they
took in our fragile husks—the living cadavers we'd become.

"We'll make them pay for this," a soldier declared.

The compassion from the Americans filled the gulf in my
soul. These generous foreigners began emptying their pockets,
giving us everything they had—nutrition bars, water, cigarettes,
and chocolate. They pressed it into my hands, their gestures so full
of kindness. If I had died in that moment, I would have gone in
peace, knowing we had lived to see liberation and Hitler's defeat.
A soldier gently lowered me back down beside Eli.

"Help is coming. Hold on," he urged. I nodded, drifting between reality and dreamland.

Eli's hand found mine, his grip steady. "We made it, Raf!"

I gripped him back. "We did it. Against all odds."

CHAPTER 46

Delirium

Buchenwald, Germany — April 13th, 1945

WORD OF OUR LIBERATION spread like wildfire. We were now free to wander the grounds, to step beyond the barbed wire, to venture into the countryside or nearby Weimar, if our bodies allowed it. The American authorities assured us they were investigating the Nazis' atrocities against the Jewish people and other groups, and that they would document their findings. They asked if we were willing to speak about our suffering—to bear witness.

I wanted to stand among those brave ex-prisoners, to make sure the world knew the truth. But my body refused to cooperate.

The fever gripped me once more, a relentless fire searing through my limbs. Someone piled blankets over me and tilted a cup to my lips, dribbling water down my throat, but I still shook uncontrollably. The simple act of opening my eyes sent waves of sharp, throbbing pain through my skull. I tried to call out, but no sound came. The room tilted, swaying and spinning as a wave of heat rushed through me. I sank beneath it—deeper, weightless.

I'm home.

Snow is piled high on the windowsill, but inside, our house in Czestochowa is warmed by the rich, yeasty scent of Mama's challah, fresh from the oven, and the sweet tang of Shabbat wine. At the worn but well-loved pine table, Tatte, Mama, Shlomo, and Rivka sit in their usual places, their faces glowing in the candlelight.

I serenade my family with *Nisim, Nisim,* about the power of miracles, and one by one, they join in, our voices lifting in harmony. After the song, Rivka, eyes shining, tells of touring castles and learning to ride horses. Shlomo, ever the storyteller, spins tales of climbing Kilimanjaro, of standing atop Everest, famous and triumphant. I talk of (mostly true) adventures with my dearest friends—Ishak, Albert, Samuel, Eli, and my cousin Ephraim.

Standing tall and proud, Tatte leads the blessing over the wine and challah and carves the juicy roast. Mama heaps our plates with food, urging us to savor our Sabbath meal.

But then the warmth vanishes, its absence radiating through every fiber of my being.

I now stand in an open pit, surrounded by faces—some angry, some resigned, all staring at me with sunken eyes. Tick… tock… tick… tock echoes through my brain, each beat pounds in my ears.

A voice calls my name, faint but unmistakable. "Rafal… Rafal… how could you leave me?"

I spin in a circle, searching every corner. "Rivka? Where are you? I'm so, so sorry!"

With a crack, the ground beneath me splits apart.

I stumble back, too horrified to scream, as I see everyone I've ever loved and disappointed bound in heavy chains, their faces streaked with tears of blood. I lunge forward, desperate to free them, but the chains wind around my arms and legs, tightening, crushing, dragging me down, down, down…

Then comes the voice, sharper, louder, more menacing than the still ticking clock.

"To the right. To the left. To the right. To the left.

You will live. You will die. You will live. You will die."

I open my eyes, and I am alone, in a sea of endless oblivion—
where I belong.

"HIS FEVER BROKE. I think he's awake now."

Are they talking about me? What's pressing against my forehead?

I blinked awake, and a nurse stepped into view. She leaned
down to take my wrist, placing her fingers over my pulse. Her
touch was careful, respectful, nothing like the rough hands I'd
known for so long. I took in her cobalt blue eyes and kind smile.

"Where am I?" I croaked. My throat felt like sandpaper.

"Welcome back to the living, Mr. Kantor. You're in an American field hospital."

"How did I get here?"

"Your friends flagged down American soldiers, who carried
you in their jeep. You've been in and out of consciousness for the
past few days but are responding well to the fluids and vitamins
we've been giving you."

"Vitamins?" I squeaked.

The nurse gave me a reassuring pat on the shoulder. "I promise, these are healthy vitamins. We're aware of what the Nazi doctors did, of the deadly injections they forced on prisoners. You are
safe with us, nurse's honor."

She pointed to the tube attached to my arm, and I was mes-
merized by the fluids dripping into me. They must have been safe,
as I was fully lucid, and I no longer burned from the inside out.

But I was still in Buchenwald, that much I gathered from the
muted voices and the faint stench lingering in the air. A Hungarian
Jewish doctor speaking Polish told me the American field hospital
was a repurposed barrack. "We gave you cold showers three times a

day to bring your fever down," he said, and I couldn't believe I didn't recall any of that.

When the doctor left, the nurse put two pills into my palm and handed me a cup of water. "Take these and rest. You've been through so much, but you're on the mend." Her soft voice was reassuring. She turned to leave, but my insides clenched.

"Nurse… wait."

My voice cracked, my throat tightening around the words. "I… I want to thank you for saving my life."

It was all I could manage. My composure slipping fast.

She swung back, her expression full of warmth. "You're very welcome, Mr. Kantor. I'm just doing my job." The nurse glanced at her clipboard, needing to see other patients.

"Please," I whispered, reaching out to her. "Wait."

"Is there something else I can do for you?" she asked, her face full of patience.

I took a deep breath, the weight of everything I'd held back spilling forward. "Thank you for calling me Mr. Kantor," I sobbed. Hearing my name—just *Mr. Kantor*—spoken with such respect was more than I could bear.

Gratitude overwhelmed me; I could barely express it. Her expression shifted to one of quiet understanding as she realized what those words meant to me. She pulled a chair up beside my bed and pressed a tissue into my palm. After I wiped my eyes, she stayed for as long as she could, holding my hand in silent respect.

▽ ▽ ▽

THEY TOLD ME I NEEDED MORE REST, and the drugs helped me get it. But when awake, my thoughts turned to Eli. The last time I saw him, we were together in the barracks, cheering the arrival of our American saviors. We hugged each other, weeping with joy. That's the last image I had of him—frail but alive.

When I remembered his last name was Schwartz, I asked the nurse if she could check on him for me.

She promised she would. But days went by without a single word. *Perhaps she's too busy to check,* I told myself. *If I made it, he must have, too.*

I asked again, and I saw the truth in her downcast eyes—she had been holding off until she was certain I was strong enough to hear it.

She gently took my hand. "Your friend Eli came to the hospital the same day you arrived. I'm so sorry, Raf. We tried everything, just as we did with you. But unfortunately, he didn't make it."

Her confession crushed the air from my lungs.

"Everyone I've ever loved is gone. How do I keep going when I'm all alone in this world?" I curled into the fetal position, too grief-stricken to face her or anyone.

The nurse laid her hand on my bony shoulder. "You can honor your loved ones by remembering them and *living* for them."

PART III

RECKONING

CHAPTER 47

Freedom

Buchenwald, Germany — May–July 1945

GERMANY OFFICIALLY SURRENDERED on May 8, 1945. The loud-speakers blared: *"The war is over! Hitler is dead!"*

Cheers erupted in the hospital ward. We whooped and hollered, tossing papers into the air, hugging everyone within reach—patients, nurses, orderlies, doctors alike. As incredible as it seemed, the nightmare had ended. But the celebration was brief. War still raged in the Pacific, and we were still housed inside Buchenwald, a place that would always reek of horror and depravity.

AFTER WEEKS OF CONVALESCENCE, the doctors declared me well enough for discharge. The news filled me with both excitement and unease. I had grown accustomed to the steady rhythm of hospital life, my needs met while my strength returned. Now the world outside awaited me—uncertain, uncharted. But it was mine to face. For the first time in years, I had a choice.

That morning, I stood alone in the hospital bathroom, staring at the sink as if it were a holy altar. Everything around me looked ordinary—so ordinary it was extraordinary.

I turned the faucet, and hot water poured into my cupped hands. Not the ice-cold spray of the camps that burned down to the bone, but warmth. I held my hands under it until they reddened, savoring the sensation. Soap waited—real soap, smooth and fragrant. I lathered my skin, worked it into my hair, and felt the filth of years dissolve.

The water closet had a door—for privacy. And toilet paper—clean, white, soft. Not the disgusting, soiled rags passed from man to man.

I spread shaving cream across my face, its scent sharp and clean. The razor was sharp too, gliding rather than tearing, nothing like the rusted blades that once scraped me bald without care or mercy. I combed my dark hair back into place, slipped deodorant under my arms, and caught myself smiling faintly at the scent.

I picked up my toothbrush—heavy with meaning, almost ceremonial. I brushed slowly, savoring the cool flavor of toothpaste as it foamed against my teeth. When I finished, I cupped my hand over my mouth and breathed in. Fresh. Clean. The sharp scent lingered, almost sweet. How different from the rank garlic and decay that once clung to me, the stench of neglect and survival. For the first time in years, my own breath didn't revolt me—it reminded me I was human again.

Next came underwear, then socks. Socks! I stared at my shirt—a blue oxford, pressed, with buttons. No star. No number. Just a shirt. I worked each button reverently, like a prayer. Then khaki trousers, with a belt snug at my waist.

I looked in the mirror. My reflection looked back—a man, not a number. A survivor. I tested a smile, and for the first time in years, it was real.

When the nurse brought my discharge papers, I folded them in my hands and walked out of the ward. Out of the place where my body had been mended, into a world where my soul might heal.

The hallway smelled of polish and disinfectant. Light streamed through the windows. Each step felt fragile, yet momentous.

I was free. Truly free. Free to be uncertain. Free to worry about tomorrow. Free to build something new, no matter how long it took.

And in that moment, freedom was in the small things: hot water, tissue, a toothbrush, and socks.

I survived it…I really survived it.

CHAPTER 48

Interpreter

Buchenwald, Germany — July 1945

WHEN I STEPPED THROUGH the hospital doors, I froze. The world outside struck me like a revelation. For so long, the world had been gray. Gray skies. Gray faces. Gray ash drifing like snow over the camp. Even the sun, when it dared to appear, seemed drained of warmth, as if light itself had surrendered.

But now—color! The sky stretched wide and impossibly blue, the kind of blue I had forgotten even existed. Sunshine spilled across the courtyard, warm and pure on my face.

I stood still, drinking it in. The breeze carried the scent of earth and budding trees, not acrid smoke. Somewhere nearby, a bird trilled—an ordinary song, yet it pierced me with its beauty. For years the only cries I had heard were those of pain and despair. This was different. This was life announcing itself.

People passed me—heads lifted, strides sure. They weren't shuffling, broken shadows. They smiled, even laughed. Their faces carried light, not fear. I had to remind myself I was one of them now.

Music drifted faintly from an open window, a tune light enough to bring me joy. I closed my eyes, letting it wash over me. Every sense came alive, as if the world was inviting me back, piece by fragile piece.

I whispered to myself: *I am free.*

Lifting my bag, I made my way toward my newly assigned barrack. Opening the door, I stopped short. Cots with mattresses, blankets, and—wonder of wonders—white fluffy pillows had replaced the wretched bunks. A water cooler with paper cups stood in the corner, offering fresh drinking water within easy reach. I had to blink to be sure it was real.

Then I spotted a familiar face—David, a freckle-faced twenty-year-old from Warsaw I had met in the hospital. We passed the time playing cards and sharing a love of books.

"I've been saving this one for you, Rafal!" he called, pointing to an empty cot beside his.

My lips lifted into a smile.

"Isn't this great?" David bounced the mattress with his hand. "After you settle in, how about we go outside and see what freedom tastes like?"

I tossed my bag onto the bed. "Let's go."

Outside, we tilted our faces toward the sun and basked in its healing warmth. Enjoying a moment like that without fear of retribution felt miraculous.

After a while, we began strolling the quiet grounds. "Is it my imagination," I asked, "or has the camp emptied out?"

David nodded. "Men are leaving daily now. There's been a steady stream of trucks."

"Where are they going?"

"The French, Belgians, Dutch—they're returning home, to whatever's left. Some of the Russians and Ukrainians who don't want to go back to Soviet territory are finding countries to take them in."

I sighed. "Poland won't welcome us back. Have you thought about where else to go?"

David shrugged. "No country seems to want us, Raf."

"So, what are we supposed to do—stay here forever?" My voice rose with every word.

David pressed his lips together. "The administrators here are sympathetic, but their governments aren't in a rush to welcome Jews."

I crossed my arms. "This isn't what I imagined freedom would be like."

"You and me—we survived for a purpose. We'll make our own place in the world, you'll see." David reached into his pocket and pulled out a glossy red apple. Tossing it in the air, he caught it with his other hand, then bit into it with a messy grin. "There's a whole bowl of them in the mess tent."

The tension broke.

As we walked toward the mess tent, I studied the buildings around us. Like us, they had been given a second chance. But while they were rooted to the ground, we were not.

▽ ▽ ▽

WITH ABUNDANT FREE TIME, I explored the camp, discovering routes unknown to me during my imprisonment. One afternoon, while I was passing the crematoria building, I saw an American soldier studying a nearby display.

"Hey," he called out. "Do you speak English?"

I had learned some English in school and was eager to improve. "Yes. Some."

He pointed to the German sign detailing the horrors the Nazis perpetrated here. "Can you translate this?"

I stumbled to find the right English words, but he listened to my halting description. When I finished, he rubbed his smooth chin. "Thank you," he said and handed me boxes of dried raisins and cigarettes for my help. "I can't imagine what you went through. Hitler was pure evil."

I took the gifts, stunned that he understood my rough translation. As I walked back to my dorm, an idea sparked in my brain. Perhaps I could do something more useful with my time.

The following day, I approached another group of soldiers lingering by the same exhibit and offered to translate. They were so appreciative of my halting English, they passed the word to other soldiers. With each conversation, my English improved. And the better I got, the more word spread. Each time I spoke of the camp's terrible purpose, its power to hurt me diminished more and more.

A soldier hailed me after I'd given a group translation and tour. "Are you Rafal?"

"Yes, sir," I replied, standing at attention.

He handed me some soap and a tin of coffee. "Take this, please. I can't thank you enough. Your translations have been invaluable. Many of us couldn't truly comprehend what the Nazis did to the Jewish people."

As my work as an interpreter thrived, I gathered an odd assortment of treasures that acted as camp currency. Tobacco products, canned meat, soap, and toothbrushes were easily bartered for other things. My biggest score was mint-flavored toothpaste. Each time I used it, it tasted like candy and made my mouth tingle!

Every tour and translation helped me find purpose in the wake of so much loss. I found peace in fulfilling my most fervent pledge—to let the world know the horrors that befell millions of innocent Jewish people who could no longer speak for themselves.

CHAPTER 49

Post-War Tour

Weimar, Germany — July 1945

ON JULY 4, 1945, I turned twenty-two years old. After nearly six years under Nazi rule, it was time to step beyond the camp gates—not as a prisoner, not under guard, but as a free man.

The midday sun blazed overhead, the sky a brilliant, endless blue. As we walked out of Buchenwald's gates, a giddy, almost reckless energy surged through us. David strode beside me, grinning wildly. Beside him, his friend Levi whooped, throwing his arms in the air as if he were shaking off invisible chains. I felt like singing, so I did, unafraid of who might hear.

Levi had entered Buchenwald with David, and like me, he was in his early twenties. He was wiry and quick with a smirk that rarely left his face. His dark hair tumbled over his forehead, and he constantly raked his fingers through it, sweeping it back behind his ears—only for it to fall forward again. As far as he knew, he was the only survivor in his family. He and David had ventured outside the camp before, but this was my first time, and I wasn't sure what to expect.

As we approached the city of Weimer, Levi glanced around and said, "Be prepared. Since they lost the war, the Germans walk with their heads down, like they're afraid to make eye contact."

I scoffed. "They should be ashamed. Of living close by and doing nothing to help us."

We passed through rubble-strewn streets, blown-out buildings, and entire blocks leveled by bombings. The destruction around us felt surreal, yet as I thought back to the devastation the Nazis wrought on Bloody Monday and the bodies buried on Buchenwald's grounds, it seemed no more than the Germans deserved.

After walking through several deserted blocks, the smell of baked bread drew us toward a small bakery. Inside, a woman stood behind the display counter, her face drawn but kindly, and she offered us bread and cabbage soup, free of charge. Her voice shook as she told us her story—her husband, a German soldier, was lost in Russia, and her fifteen-year-old son was forcibly conscripted and sent to the front lines.

She dabbed her eyes with a checkered cloth. "They took him away, and I haven't heard a single word from him since." She cursed Hitler, claiming she hadn't known about the atrocities happening all around her.

"How could you not know? Surely you saw the train cars full of Jewish prisoners, heard our cries, smelled the horror of burnt flesh!" Every word I spewed turned louder, angrier. "How could any German fail to know what was happening all around them? You'd have to be deaf or blind. Or willfully ignorant!"

The woman shrank back, cringing from my verbal assault. "I'm so sorry, from the depths of my soul," she cried. "We knew but were so scared to act, to voice our objections. Nazi spies were everywhere, waiting to pounce on the barest whisper of insurrection. You must believe me." She buried her face in her hands, sobbing.

Seeing her reaction, I was truly ashamed and apologized for blaming her. She was shattered by the same war, just trying to survive amid fear, devastation, and personal loss. In every country, Germany included, civilians were caught up in war wrought by the power-hungry appetites of the Axis leaders, Hitler and his SS cronies first among them. We finished our lunch in silence and put some coins on the counter before we left.

After lunch, we wandered deeper into Weimar. American soldiers patrolled the streets, standing guard in jeeps outside government buildings, their presence a reminder of who was now in charge. The German citizens we passed moved with slumped shoulders and downtrodden expressions, yet their sidelong glances carried a trace of resentment, as if we were somehow to blame for their misery. But unlike with the baker, none of us could feel any sympathy for their situation.

"You reap what you sow," David muttered as we passed a crowd staring blankly into the wreckage of an apartment building.

Levi nodded. "They can rebuild, still have a city they can call home. They don't care about our suffering, so I find it hard to care about theirs."

"Most people are only capable of caring for themselves," I murmured, more to myself than to them as we trudged back to Buchenwald. After seeing the extent of the destruction, I imagined the wreckage the Nazis must have left as they steamrolled across Europe. Whether or not the countries rebuilt, the scars would remain, just as they would with us.

▽ ▽ ▽

A FEW WEEKS LATER, the three of us sat cross-legged on David's cot, a deck of cards spread between us. David tapped his fingers against his knee waiting for me to play my hand, while I searched for any cards worth keeping.

Our dormitory administrator entered, wordlessly handing each of us a folded newsletter before moving on. Levi unfolded his and began reading aloud.

"A territory agreement was reached between the Allies, and effective immediately, the Soviet Union will take over administration of East Germany, and this includes Buchenwald."

I set my cards down.

Levi swallowed, then continued. "The United States military will be evacuating Buchenwald in the next 48 hours, and the administration of the camp will be turned over to the Soviets at that time."

A heavy silence settled between us. David's fingers, once drumming impatiently, now curled into fists against his knee. The Americans were leaving—and with them, our sense of peace.

CHAPTER 50

Displaced Persons (D.P.) Camp
Wildflecken, Germany — August 1945

AGAINST ALL ODDS, Buchenwald had become a home of sorts. But we all agreed on one thing—we shouldn't stay in the Russian sector of Germany. We had heard of their brutal treatment of Poles before the war and hadn't forgotten their non-aggression pact with Germany. It would be far safer to stick with the Americans.

"Anyone willing can join an American convoy headed to West Germany," Levi said, closing the newsletter.

By tacit agreement, the three of us gathered what little we'd amassed and waited for an available army truck. When one finally stopped, we climbed into the cargo area. We each had our own seats and lots of legroom. It felt like luxury after years of being transported in crammed train cars and uncomfortable trucks.

The American convoy rolled forward, passing through villages and bomb-scarred cities. We had seen destruction in Weimar, but this was devastation on an entirely different scale—neighborhood after neighborhood reduced to rubble. Hitler had gambled, and his citizens had paid the price.

At a rest stop, the American soldiers spread blankets on the grass, passed around snacks, and switched on a radio. Music drifted into the air, rich and beautiful. I closed my eyes, letting the sound wash over me.

When we arrived in Wildflecken, the trucks pulled up to an enormous camp surrounded by barbed wire. U.S. military guards stood at the gate, weapons in hand—not to imprison us, but to protect us.

While waiting in the registration line, we spotted two U.S. MPs escorting a prisoner to an unmarked building.

"He's a Nazi," the clerk at the desk explained. "Tried to escape Germany disguised as a refugee. We've caught a few, thanks to the survivors."

"Those fiends are lucky they're under guard," Levi said under his breath as he slipped an identification lanyard over his head. "There's probably an entire brigade of survivors who'd tear them apart if given the chance."

After registration, a blond-haired woman handed us a small welcome bag filled with snacks, chewing gum, and toiletries.

David grinned, shaking his bag. "What a difference, huh? To be treated like a human being again?"

I nodded, but my gaze lingered on the gate and the fence that surrounded us. No matter how different this place was, I felt uneasy about being penned in.

Red Cross volunteers walked us to our barrack, outfitted with two crisply made bunk beds. Later, we made our way to the kitchen for our rations, where our hosts greeted us warmly. We carried our food outside and sat at picnic tables, taking in the scene around us.

Families. Children playing. Couples holding hands.

The sight filled me with an unexpected mix of joy and sadness.

Levi leaned in. "The Nazis captured these families from Eastern Europe and forced them into slave labor. They don't want to go back. They feel as betrayed by their home countries as we do."

I watched two young boys tossing a ball between them. I had spent so long surrounded by men, I hadn't dared believe that any children or women still survived. I couldn't help but wonder how many young children like Rivka were orphaned by this terrible war.

After lunch with David and Levi, I visited the dispensary for my usual ailments—migraines and the periodic bouts of dysentery I suffered from as my body struggled to adjust.

Sleep still came in broken stretches, but on the upside, I had gradually regained some of the weight I'd lost. Now, I just had to deal with everything else—this fragile new normal my body still fought to accept.

$$\triangledown \ \triangledown \ \triangledown$$

DUSK SETTLED AS I STEPPED OUT of the cafeteria, my stomach feeling good after a light meal. I descended the cafeteria steps, looking forward to turning in early. As I made my way toward the barracks, I passed the dance hall, its windows glowing with warm light. Inside, people spun each other across the floor, laughing, lost in the pulse of American music. Swing dancing. Joyful, reckless movement. I barely registered it, my thoughts already shifting toward sleep, when—

I slammed into someone—hard. The force knocking him to the ground.

"I'm so sorry! Let me help you up." I extended my hand, but he ignored it, shooting up to his feet in an instant.

"Next time, watch where you're going," he snapped, in thick German accented English.

His hat lay on the ground. He turned to pick it up, and that's when I saw it—a syringe slipping from his front pocket, catching the dim light before hitting the dirt. Despite the longer hair, beard, eyeglasses, and the civilian clothes, I recognized him!

"Kruger!"

The name left my lips like a curse. His eyes widened. He shoved me and bolted.

"Stop him!" I shouted, but the music swallowed my cries. No one was near enough to hear me as I took off after him.

He turned corners, and I followed, pushing through the now dark alleys. But then—nothing. He vanished. I slowed, scanning the area all around me, cursing under my breath.

A sudden blast rammed into me from the side, knocking me off my feet. I hit the ground hard, arms pinned beneath me, Kruger's weight crushing the air from my lungs. He leaned in close, the smell rolling off his breath thick and rancid—like something had died and stayed there—syringe locked in his jaw.

"I know you too…" he hissed. "And now, I get to give you your mercy shot."

His grip locked me down, but the moment he freed one hand to grab the needle, I struck. My fist shot up, connecting with his nose, snapping his head back. Blood sprayed everywhere. It covered him, covered me—so much blood it felt like drowning. I scrambled, twisting free.

He was still conscious when I grabbed the syringe. I didn't hesitate.

Then—

A siren.

Loud. Deafening.

I gasped and shot upright.

The dance hall was gone. The night was gone. Thirty empty beds surrounded me.

My alarm clock blared on the nightstand.

What?

I gradually returned to awareness and found my blanket on the floor in a tangled heap. My skin was drenched in sweat, my heartbeat pounding like I was being chased in real life.

Another nightmare.

I remembered I set my alarm for a quick nap, just an hour, enough to rest before heading to the dance hall. Since liberation, the nightmares came in different forms, but each one felt real—too real. My conscious knew we had been liberated, but my subconscious did not.

It took me a few minutes to calm down. After my heart rate leveled off, I swung my legs over the bed, put on a clean, dry shirt, and splashed cool water on my face. I drew a deep breath and stepped outside, eager to join my friends.

CHAPTER 51

Wanderers

Frankfurt, Germany — August 1945

DAYS AND WEEKS SLIPPED into a monotonous routine. Lining up for meals. Lounging around. Trading jokes to pass the time. Night after night of restless sleep.

"I'm sick of Germany," David grumbled one afternoon. "I'm sick of living in limbo, being powerless over our lives."

Levi exhaled sharply. "What will happen when the Americans decide to pull out again? Will we follow them blindly?"

"I'm tired of feeling powerless, too," I said, throwing down a magazine. "We need to gain control over our lives, start making decisions for ourselves. I heard that many Jewish survivors are heading to Frankfurt. What do you say?"

David and Levi readily agreed, and the next day, we packed our belongings, grabbed our rations, signed our exit paperwork, and made our way to the rail station. The train ride was uneventful, and before long, we arrived in Frankfurt. We were shocked by the extensive bombing damage throughout the depot. But despite the shattered windows and crumbled walls, the place was alive with activity.

Ragged German soldiers filled much of the station, many fresh from prisoner-of-war camps. So many bore missing limbs and bandaged faces. They were just kids, some younger than us. I didn't know if I pitied them or loathed them, so I forced myself to look away.

The Red Cross had set up a station at the depot to assist former concentration camp survivors. "You can find food and shelter at a hotel across the river," one of the workers said. "The locals call it the D.P. Hotel."

With our belongings strapped to our backs, we made our way through Frankfurt's rubble-strewn streets, weaving around pedestrians and bicycles. The Germans had blown up parts of the bridge to slow the Allied advance, but enough of it remained for us to cross.

The "D.P. Hotel" stood resilient amidst Frankfurt's ruins, windows intact, a rough sign marking it as a gathering place for survivors like us. As we settled in at tables set with real linens and silverware, I kept blinking to make sure it wasn't a dream.

American Jewish soldiers joined us, listening, encouraging, trying to keep our hopes for finding a home alive. A survivor at our table brought up Palestine. "If only we could go now. That's truly our homeland."

A murmur of agreement rose, but we all knew the truth—the British wouldn't let us in. Even now, after all that had happened, they still blocked Jewish immigration to Palestine.

One of the Jewish-American soldiers leaned forward. "Some influential Jews back home are urging England to ease those restrictions. And the U.S. might allow more Jewish refugees in, outside the regular quotas." He said it with genuine optimism.

Across the table, Levi's fork tapped a restless rhythm, a sign his frustration was brewing. Finally, he let it out.

"Why are we even debating this? After surviving the worst mass murder in history—the entire world should be throwing open their doors to us! We should be able to go wherever we want, free to build lives where we choose. But here we are, stuck in Germany, the last place we want to be."

When Levi saw the crestfallen faces of the American soldiers, he deflated. Pushing back his chair, he apologized. "You're only trying to help, I understand. But it's frustrating, as we can't go back to Poland. I need some fresh air, if you'll excuse me."

We watched him go, but Levi's statement stayed with us. By that point in time, the entire world became aware of Hitler's scheme to exterminate the entire Jewish race. At last count, the death toll had reached the millions. Why were so many countries unwilling to embrace the few of us who survived?

Lying in bed that night, my thoughts drifted back to Tatte, to the strength he always exuded no matter how dark life became. He would have known what to do next. But without him, I felt like a child again, afraid of making the wrong choices.

$$\triangledown \quad \triangledown \quad \triangledown$$

FRANKFORT, WHILE ACCOMMODATING, didn't live up to its promise. Our plan was simple—keep moving, city by city, until we found a place that seemed like home. We returned to the train depot and saw a crowd of people heading to Bamberg. Without too much debate, we decided to join them.

Two days later, we arrived and were struck by the quiet charm of the town. Unlike so many other places, Bamberg stood pristine, its medieval buildings untouched by war. It was almost obscene how normal it all looked.

I caught sight of a sturdy-looking German woman in a white cap and apron, her attention turned elsewhere. "Excuse us, frau. Can you give us directions to the mayor's office?"

She spun around, her blue eyes widening as she took us in—

three unshaven, wandering Jews. To her credit, she didn't hesitate. With brisk German efficiency, she not only gave us directions but insisted on escorting us to city hall herself.

The mayor received us with strained graciousness. He checked our papers, nodding and scribbling notes. Then, with little ceremony, he provided us with money and ration cards and arranged lodging for us at a nearby church.

Despite his generosity, I caught the flicker of relief on his face as we stood to leave. His attitude rubbed me the wrong way, but I didn't want to jeopardize our lodging by speaking up.

Bamberg's streets were narrow and cobbled, just wide enough for a horse and cart. I nudged David and pointed to the street sign ahead.

He let out a wry snicker. "Of all the places they could put us, they picked a church on a street called Juden Strasse."

Juden was the German word for Jews. Whether it was fate or irony, we were yet to discover. The church was a relic of another era—thick stone walls, worn wooden beams, the lingering smells of old wax and incense. The priest, a trim man in his fifties with graying hair and kind but cautious eyes, welcomed us. He escorted us upstairs to a clean room with real beds and heavy blankets.

"You can stay as long as you need," he said. But before he left, he tossed us a bar of soap, which Levi caught in midair.

We each scrubbed away two days' worth of sweat and grime, the water turning murky in the basin. Clean at last, we slipped into the beds, breathing in the scent of fresh linen sheets. *I could get used to this*, I thought as I punched my pillow into shape, pulled the covers up, and crashed.

▽ ▽ ▽

A GENTLE TAP ON MY FOREHEAD stirred me. Blinking awake, I found the priest standing over me.

"Come, it's time for supper."

Our stomachs growling with anticipation, we made our way downstairs to the kitchen, where steaming bowls of beet soup, fresh black bread, and an array of cheeses awaited us. Maybe my thoughts were affected by our Christian surroundings, but I wondered if we'd found heaven on earth.

The priest joined us at the table, eager to hear our stories. At first, we each kept it light. But as we relived the pain of losing our family members, each of us got choked up.

Seeing our distress, the priest stiffened, as if uncomfortable. "The Nazis persecuted the Church as well—seizing funds, confiscating sacred artifacts. They even killed priests who resisted."

David shifted beside me, his cheeks reddening. I saw the storm brewing in his eyes. "And yet," he said, his voice laced with anger, "you still had a soft bed, warm meals, and clean clothing."

"I… I'm sorry," the priest stammered. "We're so isolated here, I truly didn't know the extent of your suffering." He rose from the table and began clearing plates.

I placed a hand on David's knee beneath the table, a silent plea to let it go. We heard of the suffering of some clergymen. The whispered tales of the few brave people who had risked everything to help. But for most, it was always the same refrain.

"I didn't know."

It was the standard defense—one we were tired of hearing.

WE WANDERED AROUND PICTURESQUE Bamberg for a few days, and one afternoon, ducked into a bar in the historic business district for drinks. It was packed with American soldiers reveling in their victory, and the air was thick with cigarette smoke.

I approached the bar, and the German bartender slid a drink my way without a word. As I lifted it to my lips, an inebriated American soldier stumbled onto the barstool next to me.

He pointed to the pin I wore on my collar. "What's that star mean?" he said, slurring the words together.

I stared him down. "It's a Jewish star."

His face twisted in disgust. "I hate Jews!" he bellowed, loud enough to be heard over the noise.

Ignoring the stench of whiskey that rolled off him, I spit back, "Then you're no different from the Nazis!"

His eyes narrowed as he yanked his pistol from its holster, aiming the barrel right between my eyes. I didn't move a muscle, as I had stared death in the face too many times to flinch now. The barrel wavered in front of me, his grip unsteady. "I dare you," I said, seething.

Shouts rang out as fellow soldiers lunged forward, grabbed the gun, and restrained his arms. "Jesus, Charlie!" one of them snapped. The drunk idiot let out a string of garbled obscenities as they dragged him into the street.

We waited about five minutes until we were sure he was nowhere close. Then David and Levi yanked me out of the bar, clearly afraid I might get us all in trouble if we stayed. A moment later, two more soldiers followed us.

"Hey, wait up!" one of them called.

I whirled, my fists primed for a fight. "What do you want?"

They threw up their hands in surrender. "Easy, easy," the taller soldier said, like he was talking to a skittish horse. "We're nothing like that bastard. We came here to stop Hitler, and what we saw in the camps will haunt us for the rest of our lives."

His friend nodded. "We're going to report him to our captain. He won't tolerate that kind of behavior."

After they left, David poked me, his face flushed with anger. "Are you insane? After taking years of abuse from the Nazis, you decide to go head-to-head with a drunk gun-toting Allied soldier?" He paused to calm his breathing. "You think you can back-talk every antisemitic in the world? For God's sake, Rafal, they're everywhere, even in the United States, apparently."

I didn't argue. He was right. But after everything I endured, the thought of anti-Jewish rhetoric made me sick. Especially, hearing it from the Americans.

We didn't stay in Bamberg much longer. We heard of a Jewish settlement in Feldafing—Bavarian village near Munich. The idea of being among our own was too tempting to ignore. We rushed to pack our bags and set off for the rail station.

Chapter 52

Finding Our People

Feldafing D.P. Camp, Germany — September 1945

AT THE FELDAFING STATION, we encountered cheerful music and Yiddish songs, a favorable change from our arrivals in Frankfurt and Bamberg. Young survivors like us stood in loose clusters, some dancing on the platform. My soul leaped to join them, though my feet stayed stationary.

David clapped me on the back, grinning. "Look at this, Raf. An entire camp full of joyful Jews!"

Levi raised his arms skyward. "We've found our PEOPLE!"

As we departed from the terminal, we joined a band of survivors heading toward the settlement. The path wound through open fields, and after ten minutes, we came upon the registration building. As I waited in the check-in line, I whispered to my friends, "Look! Everyone is wearing pajamas!"

The young woman behind the desk chuckled, making it obvious she heard me. "Yes, this used to be a camp for Hitler Youth. After they fled, we liberated the pajamas from an enormous warehouse. Every resident gets a pair as a welcome gift."

David broke into a laughing fit, slapping his knees in his hysteria. The clerk's eyebrows quirked, and we all stepped back to keep from getting struck by David's appendages.

Levi quipped, "He's just excited. We've never had a greeting quite like this before."

The clerk smiled as she finished up our paperwork. I wondered if she might be interested in David, or else, just thought he was totally nuts.

The camp's lodgings consisted of prefabricated wooden buildings crammed with beds. They assigned us to one near the center of the camp, close to the kitchen and administration buildings. But the sweetest surprise came when we discovered our dorm sat right next to the women's bunkhouse. The chance to meet Jewish girls our age—girls who had also survived the horrors of the concentration camps—filled us with a rush of added vigor we hadn't felt in years.

David nudged me, a mischievous glint in his eye. "Looks like you'll be making some new friends, Raf!"

I smirked. "You're not jealous, are you?"

David rolled his eyes. "Jealous? No. Just thrilled you'll finally get to flirt with someone other than me!"

The first night, I couldn't sleep, even with my head resting on a fluffy pillow. Feldafing hummed with activity, and the excitement made me restless. The next morning, we attended a camp orientation for newcomers in the central hall. After taking our seats, an older Jewish man with a graying beard, dressed in civilian clothes, stepped up to address us.

"Welcome to Feldafing. This place is ours—a community built by us and for us. We have schools, religious centers, a hospital, and social gatherings. We even have a theater and a newspaper!"

Levi grinned. "It's like a mini city."

"Tonight," the man continued, "there will be a gathering in the mess hall for all the young men and women. Don't be shy! Make new friends and share your stories."

Levi and David nudged me. It was all I could do not to laugh.

I struggled to think about my looks objectively. My hair had grown back, my cheeks had filled out, and an American dentist had taken care of my worst dental issues. But for the longest time, I hadn't thought about my appearance at all. Now, with girls around, I found myself at a loss. Curious, I asked Levi to rate me on a scale from one to ten. He barely hesitated before saying, "Solid five, maybe six if you were a little taller."

By the time the three of us entered the mess hall, it was already in full swing. I noticed young women clustered in groups, some even glancing our way with curiosity.

"Hello there," a girl with dark chocolate hair, hazel eyes, and a sweet smile greeted me. She thrust out her hand. "I'm Lidka."

My face got hot. In fact, all of me did.

"Rafal. That's my name. But I go by Raf." *Oy, why am I so nervous?*

"Nice pajama top!" She pointed at my shirt. "Do you always get so dressed up for mixed socials?" We both chuckled, the tension dissolving.

I grinned. "It's the fanciest shirt I've worn in years."

Lidka turned serious. "It's strange, isn't it? To find moments of happiness here? It's like a miracle."

"Yes, it is." I scratched at the stubble on my chin, wishing I'd thought to shave.

As the night wore on, I spoke with so many young people my age. It was so invigorating to be among fellow survivors, swapping stories and debating difficult topics. Whenever conversations became too difficult, we would look at the pajamas half of us wore and bust up with laughter.

$\triangledown \quad \triangledown \quad \triangledown$

A MONTH AT FELDAFING FLEW BY in a whirl of gatherings, meals, and new friendships. It was great to be around others my age who understood my situation and welcomed me. But while I relished every moment, a growing part of me craved independence.

Sitting with Levi and David by the fire in the mess hall, I broached the idea of leaving. "Come with me to Munich. We could find work, maybe learn a trade. That way, when we leave Germany, we'll be able to support ourselves." *And possibly a family one day*, I thought but didn't say out loud.

David chuckled, leaning back. "Feldafing is just fine for now. Besides, the girls are finally coming around."

Levi nodded in agreement. "I'm not in a rush either. I feel at peace here, and I'm not ready to lose that."

I sighed. "I get that, I do. Germany is licking its wounds right now, bending over backward for us, and it's nice to take advantage of their hospitality. But at some point, the government will realize they can't afford to support us anymore. When that happens, I want to be prepared."

David ruffled my hair. "Do what feels right for you, Raf. But before you leave Germany, you better come back here and tell us first."

I shook hands with them both. "It's a deal."

THE FOLLOWING DAY, I took the train to Munich, a half-hour ride passing through the famous ski resort, Garmisch-Partenkirchen.

The Munich train station was in ruins, its condition much like the Frankfurt station. The ceiling was gone, but passenger trains still ran regularly within its bombed-out shell. I had chatted with some other young survivors on the train, and they recommended the Deutsches Museum as a meeting place and information center for surviving European Jews. I was eager to discover if any friends or extended family members had survived the Holocaust.

A streetcar dropped me off at the museum, and I found the venue packed with young Jewish men and women seeking information about their loved ones. Although I knew my immediate family's fate, I checked the lists of known survivors for any relatives or school friends. My search yielded no results, a disappointment but not a surprise.

At the end of one list, I printed my name, Rafal Kantor, for the first time since I lost my entire family. The full weight of being the sole surviving Kantor hit me anew, and all my suppressed emotions poured out on the tile floor of the Deutsches Museum. I felt as though Adolf Hitler, the most despicable, most evil mass murderer the world had ever known, was still torturing me. "Rot in Hell for all eternity, you bastard," I cried, and I was far from the only one so affected.

I spent hours drifting through the crowd, hoping to find someone, anyone, I might have known in my pre-war life. Or perhaps a survivor from Buchenwald or the Rakow plant who, like me, would be searching for a connection. Alas, my efforts yielded no results. I failed to find a single person I recognized.

Dejected, I collapsed onto a seat at a cafe outside the museum and ordered a coffee. The host brought me a cup brimming with the velvety black liquid, steaming hot. It was such a change from the watered-down pigswill the Nazis passed as coffee. I kept sniffing it like a crazy person.

"I recommend you drink that while it's hot," an older Jewish man said. "I hope you don't mind if I join you. I'm Moshe Rubenstein. And you are?"

I shook his hand. "Pleased to meet you, Mr. Rubenstein. My name is Raf Kantor."

He chuckled. "Mr. Rubenstein is my father. Call me Moshe."

Moshe was in his 40s and came to the museum daily to check the lists. He had also survived a concentration camp and spoke German and English, but not Polish. Since the end of the war, he had built a small business exchanging valuables from civilian Germans for food and money from American soldiers stationed at a nearby base.

When I told him I also spoke English, his eyes lit up. "I'll bet you could land a job with Kaserne-Freimann, the American Military base in Munich. You're welcome to stay in my flat, as I would enjoy the company." Beyond grateful, I accepted his offer.

The sun was low in the sky when we arrived at his apartment, and Moshe cooked us an excellent meal. The following morning, I hiked to the entrance gate of the American base and engaged the guard in a conversation about my background and qualifications. I made sure to mention that I was conversant in three languages.

Black companies of the Quartermaster and white companies of the Ordinance occupied the base. The guard I talked to at the gate was with the black company, and he summoned another soldier from the guardhouse to escort me to the office to meet the sergeant of the guard.

The sergeant, a young black man in his mid-twenties, oversaw the guardhouse and operated a small jail in the basement for soldiers who committed minor infractions. He didn't need help in those areas, but impressed by my language skills, asked if I wanted to be his assistant and interpreter. Excited about scoring my first paid job, I not only agreed but started working on the spot.

The sergeant outfitted me with an American uniform and took me to lunch in the mess hall, where I received a military mess kit and a canteen. This was my first G.I. lunch, served cafeteria style. My eyes jumped out of their sockets when I saw the selection of meats, fruits, vegetables, and cookies—a literal feast.

I spent the day with the sergeant, exploring the base and meeting American soldiers. He printed an identity card for me, which allowed me to enter and exit the base without a guard. I almost asked how he could trust me, a virtual unknown. But I wisely kept my mouth shut.

In the evening, following a dinner at the base, I returned to Moshe's flat. I carried my civilian clothes under one arm and a box of food under the other. When I appeared before him in the American military uniform, he clapped his hands and pounded me on the back.

"I knew you would succeed! Well done, my friend!" Although I had just met Moshe, he treated me like family. Without his advice, I would have never found the job. And I still couldn't believe he had welcomed me into his apartment without charging me a thing.

My new assignment consisted of translating administrative documents from English to German. I also worked with a corporal in charge of the Post Office, distributing letters and packages among the American soldiers here on base.

Despite my duties, I had plenty of spare time to do as I pleased. It gave me the opportunity to befriend most of the enlisted men and officers in the company. In the evenings after dinner, I joined my co-workers on trips to places of entertainment reserved for American troops. A fun place was the American Red Cross in downtown Munich for dancing and snacks.

My language skills improved each day, and I became familiar with every corner of Munich. In the suburb of Freimann, where I lived, I became known as the American Pole who spoke German.

Chapter 53

Changes

American Base, Munich — September 1945

At the end of my second week in Munich, I traveled back to Feldafing straight from work. Levi and David found the sight unbelievable and shared with everyone that I'd got a role in the American military. "Women sure love a man in uniform," Levi ribbed.

Most weekends, I found myself on the road back to Feldafing, eager to see my friends and to give Moshe his privacy. Whenever I showed up, Levi and David wrapped their arms around me as if I'd been gone a year instead of seven days.

One weekend, I met a young man named Czeshik whom the Nazis deported to Dachau. He, too, was the lone survivor of his family. He told me he'd been a tailor's apprentice and still dreamed of owning a store one day. Czeshik was a sharp dresser, but it was his wit and charisma that pulled me into his orbit.

When he observed my uniform, he commented, "The fabric's not bad, but it needs a bit more flair. Lucky for you, I can help with that."

I chuckled. "You might find work at the American military base where I'm assigned. You should come to Munich with me. I share a flat with another guy, but I'm sure he wouldn't mind if you join us."

He didn't hesitate. "I can't turn down an offer like that. Count me in."

As I'd hoped, Moshe welcomed him warmly. Within days, Czeshik secured a job at the base, reconditioning uniforms for the soldiers. His smooth transition into his new role made me smile—we were two Jewish survivors making money in Germany, of all places.

A few weeks later, my supervisor pulled me aside with a new assignment. They needed an interpreter at a nearby German POW camp to oversee communication and enforce policies among the prisoners. I found myself completely torn and asked for a day to think it over.

That evening, Czeshik cornered me. "What's got you all wound up?"

I wrung my hands together as I told him about the offer. "Part of me wants to make the Germans squirm, make them experience a fraction of what they put us through. The other part of me thinks I shouldn't go anywhere near them, that my anger will consume me."

Czeshik rubbed his chin, weighing my words carefully. "Only you know what you can handle. But remember, revenge is a double-edged sword."

I debated the decision all night long. Ultimately, I decided to go through with it. After taking an entrance exam, I met with a hardened American captain who told me he lacked experience handling prisoners. When I shared highlights of my story, I didn't spare him the ugliness. He listened without interrupting, and when I finished, he told me I was perfect for the job.

At first, I handled curfews, roll calls, and maintaining order. But what bothered me most was the food. The German prisoners received meat, whole pieces of bread, and unlimited access to real coffee. All of it felt like a slap in the face, especially the coffee.

I enacted my first change. One cup at breakfast. One cup at dinner. Period.

You'd have thought I declared war from the way they reacted. I stared at them in disbelief. Did they know how lucky they were?

I made sure they did.

I told them how the Nazis starved us, tortured us, worked us to death. How the Nazis degraded my family members before murdering them. I didn't know if these prisoners followed Hitler willingly or were too afraid to resist. But as they listened to me, I observed their faces. Some looked down, unable to meet my steely gaze, while others shook their heads in disbelief. Regardless, they stopped grousing about the coffee limitation.

Over the months I worked there, my perspective slowly changed. Observing the POWs carefully, I couldn't help but witness their exhaustion, homesickness, and unguarded moments of regret. Gradually, I began to view them as fellow humans deserving of some respect and understanding.

My greatest hope was that when they looked at me, they viewed me the same way.

CHAPTER 54

Retribution

Munich, Germany — October 1945

I ACCEPTED A TEMPORARY ASSIGNMENT, helping to requisition a mansion owned by a high-ranking Nazi official, a former judge. This was a high-level party member who helped enforce the Nazi decrees, a far cry from the rank and file at the POW camp. While I was able to forgive them, I would never be able to forgive the monsters who engineered and enforced the Holocaust.

The American captain wanted this mansion for his new quarters, and I couldn't wait to deliver the evacuation notice myself. Two American G.I.s accompanied me, and we were wowed by the mansion as our jeep rumbled up the winding driveway. It stood untouched—its lush rose gardens and manicured hedges were a surreal contrast to the devastation throughout Munich.

We parked on the cobblestone driveway, and the soldiers flanked me as I rang the doorbell. After a moment, a middle-aged woman, clearly a servant, opened the door and eyed us with obvious unease. I switched to German and asked to speak with the owner. She left us standing in the foyer, the ticking of an antique grandfather clock filling the silence as we waited.

A tall, blond man in his 30s strode into the room, his blue eyes and square jaw giving him the look of an Aryan poster boy for Nazi recruitment. His crisply pressed shirt showed a discolored patch where someone had removed an SS insignia. He regarded us with open disdain, and I couldn't wait to wipe the smirk from his face.

Moments later, an older woman swept in, contempt shown in her tightly pursed lips and lifted chin. Her blond hair was streaked with gray and wound into a severe bun, and she wore a forest green dress cinched tightly at the waist. There was no doubt she was the young man's mother.

"Why are you here?" she snapped. "Leave us alone!"

Ignoring her outburst, I held her gaze and asked to speak with her husband.

"He is unavailable," she replied haughtily. But from her sudden twitch, I sensed he was hiding or on the run.

I squared my shoulders and pulled out the papers, switching to flawless German. "You're ordered to vacate the house by 10 a.m. tomorrow. Noncompliance will cause forced removal."

She frowned and pointed her index finger at me. "You can't just throw us out on the street like vermin!"

I kept my tone even. "It doesn't feel good to be ripped from your home, does it? At least you have a warning. When the SS seized our homes, they cast us into the streets and murdered innocent people without mercy."

The woman's face blanched, and then she muttered, "Juden." Her hand flew to her mouth as though she'd let out a swear word.

"Yes. And unlike us, you won't be rounded up, stripped of your dignity, and packed into freight cars. Your home will still stand when Germany is no longer occupied—while ours were burned to the ground."

She opened her mouth, but no words spilled out. Sharp daggers flew from her son's eyes, but he remained silent. In a passing moment of insanity, I wanted to throw a mocking Hitler salute to them. But I heard my mother's voice reminding me to respect everyone, even those who didn't deserve it.

"Pack only your *personal* belongings. All other items must remain in the house."

I didn't wait for her response before turning away from the door. As we strode back to the jeep, one of the American G.I.s clapped me on the shoulder. "Raf, you really put her in her place. For that, we'll let you have the master bedroom!"

I chuckled along, imagining the frau's face if she ever discovered a Jew had slept in her bed. It was just a joke, but I savored it all the way to the military base.

▽ ▽ ▽

WHEN WE ARRIVED BACK at the mansion the following day, servants were bustling around, packing up the last of their belongings. I suspected they were taking more than allowed, but I ignored them, instead choosing to inspect the house quietly.

During my pass through, clanking sounds from the dining room caught my attention. I entered to find the son stacking plates and dishes into an open box. The sneaky bastard was trying to smuggle out the family's fine china.

"The fine china stays," I said in my most authoritative voice.

I shocked him so much, he dropped a plate on the hardwood floor. Viewing the shards, he shot me a sharp glare, the kind I knew all too well—disgusted, incredulous, full of arrogance.

I held my ground, crossing the room to face him. "You consider this china to be a personal effect?"

"They are family heirlooms," he snarled, no doubt assuming I would back off.

On the table, I noticed a folded set of cloth napkins, each one emblazoned with a crisp black and red swastika emblem. My anger built as I recalled a similar looking cloth used to clean Jewish blood from Nazi jackboots.

I gestured at the napkins. "You plan to take these, too?"

His cheeks flushed with defiance. "It's why I put them there."

I traced the swastika with my fingernail. "Where did you get these beautiful napkins? From Hitler himself?"

The Nazi bristled, his left eye throbbing. "Nein, nein—they were a gift from a friend."

"Ah, so I take it your friend was a loyal Nazi party member?" I refused to let him weasel out of this.

He stamped his foot on the floor, the equivalent of a toddler throwing a tantrum. "Nein!"

"Glad to hear it. Since you won't be hosting any more dinner parties for your Nazi friends, you won't need these nice dishes."

I hefted the box of china and hurled it out the open window. Dishes spun through the air, shattering on the ground below in an explosion of porcelain. To me, the crash sounded like justice served. He let out a howl of outrage, whipping around to face me, his features twisted in fury.

"You... you... filthy, worthless Jew!" he screeched, loud enough to bring the G.I.s rushing into the dining room, rifles raised. With muzzles aimed at his face, he stumbled back into the cabinet, cowering.

"Stand down," I signaled. "Everything is under control."

While he was still cowering, my gaze shifted to the offensive napkins. They reminded me of the SS officer cleaning his hands after beating Tatte, and of Becker wiping Albert's lifeblood from his steel-toed boots.

"Got a light?" I asked one of the American soldiers.

He nodded and handed me his lighter. Holding them in my fingertips, I lit the napkins on fire, delighting as the flames devoured each swastika, one by one. Before dropping them into the fireplace, I shoved the flaming napkins into the Nazi's face. The flames reduced the symbol of his beliefs to ash, rendering him speechless.

"Leave," I ordered, pointing to the door. He stormed out of the dining room and straight outside, his face crimson. Through the window, I caught sight of his mother berating him, and the joy of retribution filled me with a delicious sense of power. *How dare they retain their superior attitudes, act like nothing has changed.*

But the rush didn't last. It burned out quickly. My feelings of triumph quickly turned to frustration and unease. Was this all there was? Would I spend the rest of my life trapped in this cycle of hatred and revenge?

I loathed the way they could move on with their life. How surrender had saved them while the rest of us had to claw our way out of the grave they'd dug for us.

And who was I supposed to take revenge on anyway? The Nazi party member in front of me? The German soldiers who might have pulled the trigger, or the civilians who had simply stood by? What suffering could they endure now that would make up for what they had done?

My family was never coming back, no matter how many deserving Nazis I punished. The scale of human suffering would forever be unbalanced, no matter how much I wished otherwise.

It's time to look forward, Raf, I chastised myself.

CHAPTER 55

New Apartment

Munich, Germany — October 1945

CZESHIK FOUND HIS STRIDE mending uniforms for American soldiers, and after making enough to buy new clothes and other essentials, he could almost pass as a regular German businessman. His dapper style added to his confidence, which made him a perfect partner for our ventures—both in business and in life. Czeshik had become my confidant, and around him, I felt safe enough to let my true self show—rough edges and all.

Soon, we both felt we were taking up too much space in Moshe's small flat, and Czeshik was tired of sleeping on the couch. While Moshe never once complained, we couldn't keep imposing. Since we had both saved a decent amount, we decided it was time to get our own apartment.

After reviewing a few cramped apartments, we found a place close to the military base. It was a small, two-bedroom flat, which we ended up sharing with two Russian women. Our landlord informed us that their husbands were POWs, and they hadn't heard from them in two years. It was a stark reminder that the war left wounds in all directions.

Settling in was easier than I'd thought. We split the rent and utilities with the women, which lightened the financial load. Once we had things sorted, we invited Moshe for dinner. When he entered, I gifted him a bottle of wine I'd "liberated" from the judge's mansion. His eyes lit up as he read the label.

"A fine vintage," he said, grinning. "From the best collection in Munich, no doubt?"

I winked. "Only the best for you, Moshe Rubenstein! What better way to show my gratitude for your generosity?"

A month later, my American soldier friends invited me to celebrate Thanksgiving with them. They loaded the table with food I'd only heard about—turkey, stuffing, cranberry sauce, and my favorite, apple pie!

As they carved up the feast, I joined them in their blessings, realizing I had much to be thankful for, too. Although I yearned to move to Palestine, for now I lived and felt like an American.

I stayed in Munich and celebrated Christmas 1945 with them, too—my first and last—and reveled in the beauty of the lights and the spirit of giving. When we rang in the New Year, I reflected on how these Americans had welcomed me so freely—a Jewish survivor from Poland, with no family and no home. Yet here I was, surrounded by new friends, toasting to 1946 with a full glass in my hand and hope in my heart for better days ahead.

CHAPTER 56

Dreams of Equality

Munich, Germany — October 1946

I CHANGED ROLES ONCE AGAIN and now had the responsibility of supervising Polish para-military units. These Polish laborers, forced to work in Germany against their will, had refused to return to Poland—a conviction I understood well. The U.S. Army hired them as guards for military and civilian installations.

They assigned me to be a liaison between the Americans and Polish guard units. The responsibilities included interpreting, creating morning reports for the American company, and reviewing reports from the Polish units. I sat in on meetings with the American captain and the Polish officers and accompanied the captain on inspections and other duties.

In pre-war Poland, where antisemitism was prevalent, people would have resisted and shown intolerance toward a Jewish man's authority. I wondered, therefore, how the Polish officers and their men would take to me being in a leadership role.

At first, we treated each other with cool courtesy. Right off the bat, I made it unmistakably clear to them I was Jewish and proud of it. But their commanding officer spoke very little English and depended on me to translate his frequent requests to my American captain. Under these circumstances, he soon became friendly, even inviting me to his home outside the camp, where he and his wife served me a lovely meal of beef, scalloped potatoes, and a melange of vegetables. When she brought out a beautifully decorated homemade chocolate cake, I nearly cried.

After the delicious meal, we sat together in his office, and our talk turned to Polish life. I couldn't help but reminisce about our "good old days," reminding him of my status as a second-class citizen, of being restricted from attending higher school, running for political office, or advancing in the military. He seemed receptive, so I kept going.

"If the Poles hadn't cooperated with the Nazis, how many more Jewish lives could have been saved? You all knew what was happening in the ghettos, and how men, women, and children were sent to labor and concentration camps. How were you able to sit back and do nothing?"

I had waited so long to unburden my soul about my mistreatment within the country of my birth. But as he listened respectfully and didn't rise to his own defense, I apologized for making it a personal indictment.

"Rafal, I understand why you feel this way, and I don't blame you one bit." He stood up, poured himself a glass of brandy from the decanter on his credenza, and offered me one. When I declined, he took a deep sip and continued.

"Poland has a complicated history. My parents and grandparents taught me to mistrust Jews, to hold them in contempt. I won't deny it made me happy that Jewish families lived in their own quarter, separate from the Christian majority. But after all I've witnessed, I can't find the proper words to express how much I regret my years spent mired in prejudice against the Jewish Poles, not taking a stand, not being brave enough to reach beyond my upbringing and form my own opinions."

He swirled the brandy in the glass and took another sip. "The Nazis, Raf, they steamrolled us, and our country was too weak to fight back. I had to serve their despicable agenda, even though it literally made me sick. I saw things I can never unsee. Horrors I'd never imagined. Once they took over, they killed anyone who objected, their families, too." He put his hand on the back of a chair to steady himself.

"You may think me weak, but I had my wife to protect. The Nazis considered themselves superior, treating all Poles like ants they could easily crush. But the evil they dealt to the Jewish people will damn them to hell for all eternity." He pulled out the chair and sat down heavily. I almost told him to stop, but I could tell he needed to unburden his soul as much as I needed to hear his confession.

"My wife and I are desperate to find somewhere new, somewhere free of this endless hate and prejudice. I have no desire to go back to Poland, not after everything I've seen and done. We want to live where people judge others by their actions, not by their religious beliefs."

I nodded, agreeing wholeheartedly with his sentiment. But then he leaned toward me, his gaze piercing.

"Rafal, I must ask you something, and I ask it not in judgment, but because I think you'll understand. When you lived in the ghettos, or in those wretched camps, did you ever put your own needs before the needs of others? Did you ever make choices that saved you, perhaps at someone else's expense?"

His question hit like a punch to my gut. I cast my eyes downward as I recalled the countless impossible choices I was forced to make. Memories that I'd buried for self-preservation.

"Yes," I admitted, staring at my shoes. "I, too, never spoke or acted against the Nazis. I let them take my friends and family away without a fight. It doesn't feel fair that I survived, and they didn't, when each of them was a better person than I am."

The lines on his face softened. "Don't discount your own worth, Rafal. I struggle with that feeling, too. We both found ourselves trapped, forced into ungodly positions we never wanted and never deserved. Maybe it took a war of this magnitude for people to realize that we're all human beings. That hatred is a poison that spreads beyond those it touches."

The depth of his regrets and dreams for the future blew me away. I saw him not as the man who once looked down on my suffering, but as someone who suffered his own torment. My conversation with him was immensely healing, for the both of us, I think. The faint stirrings of forgiveness began to melt my icy heart—something I hadn't considered possible.

CHAPTER 57

Surprise Visitors

Munich, Germany — January 1946

ONE LATE JANUARY EVENING, I returned from work, worn out and ready for a quiet night. But the moment I stepped into the apartment, I knew that wasn't going to happen. Czeshik was pacing like there was a fire lit under him. The second he saw me, he shouted, "It's about time you got home!" and shoved me toward my room.

"Go change. We're having company tonight!" Czeshik had fussed over his appearance more than usual, slicking back his unruly hair, wearing his best shirt, and pressing a perfect crease into his dress pants. My roommate was primping, and I couldn't wait to find out why.

"Raf, you won't believe what happened today," he began, bouncing on his heels as I unbuttoned the smelly shirt I'd worn all day. "Are you aware of my daily checks of the Deutsches Museum survivor lists?"

I nodded, as he'd mentioned his daily ritual more than once. When I chose a fresh shirt from my closet, he pulled me back to my bed, pointing to the outfit he'd already laid out for me. I didn't blame him for not letting me choose, as he was by far the better dresser.

"Well, I saw a familiar face—a girl from Sosnowiec! We went to school together, Raf! I couldn't believe it. We hugged, held hands, and cried our eyes out." He reached over to button my shirt, as he thought I was moving too slowly.

"Her name's Lidka. I knew her entire family." His eyes fluttered as he remembered, but he rallied, his enthusiasm uncontainable. "She told me there's another survivor from Sosnowiec, who I might know *very* well. But she wouldn't tell me who it was right away! No, she batted her lashes at me, letting me squirm." He plopped onto my bed, then, like a yo-yo, bounced back up and paced around the room.

"Her name is Sala. She's the girl I dated off and on in high school! I've dreamt about her every night, imagining she was gone like everyone else. But no! She's alive, and living in Feldafing, rooming with Lidka!" Czeshik panted like he'd just ran a marathon.

"Wait a minute," I said as I looped a belt around my pants. "If they're in Feldafing, why are we getting so dolled up?"

Czeshik grinned like the Cheshire cat. "Oh! I forgot to tell you! They're coming over tonight. In fact, they should be here any minute. Hurry and finish getting ready!"

As I sputtered, Czeshik bolted out of the apartment to wait for the women downstairs.

I shaved, realizing I should have done that before I got dressed. Wiping off my chin and blotting the spatters on my shirt, I reflected on how crazy life had gotten. Making new friends, making money, and now, about to meet two girls. At one time in my life, I supposed those things would have seemed normal. Now, they felt miraculous.

I entered the living room and saw that Czeshik had laid out a spread of cheese, sausages, crackers, and even brought out some wine—a rare treat for us. When the girls arrived a mere two minutes later, he poured a full glass for each of us. No sooner did they sit down when Czeshik took center stage, recounting the day's events in vivid detail, punctuating his performance with dramatic gestures. It certainly broke the ice as we all convulsed in stitches. Lidka let out a snort, and Sala was so overcome with laughter, happy tears sprung from her eyes.

As we noshed, sipped, and talked, I found myself drawn to Lidka, convinced we'd met before but not able to remember the time or place. She must have noticed my less than subtle attention and quipped, "Do pajamas ring any bell?"

I laughed nervously. "Of course. You were the first friendly girl I spoke with at Feldafing."

Czeshik nudged me. "Smooth one, Raf!"

I hit my forehead with the palm of my hand. "That didn't come out quite right. I meant…"

"Quit while you're behind," Lidka said. Luckily, before I could stick my foot in my mouth further, Sala began ribbing Czeshik about his caddish behavior in high school, and Lidka chimed in.

Feeling embarrassed and more than a little tired, I slipped into the kitchen for a quick cup of tea. I pushed open the door and startled our Russian roommates, who'd been eavesdropping on our conversation. The women tried to appear busy, but their smiles gave them away. They shooed me back to the living room, promising to bring tea out for everyone.

When I rejoined the group, I caught Czeshik saying with a remarkably straight face, "I can't help it if all the girls wanted me. I was quite the catch!"

"You were a good-for-nothing catch," Sala retorted with a grin, "and it doesn't seem like you've changed at all."

Czeshik preened like a peacock, loving every second of the attention. By the time the teacups were drained, so were all of us.

"Thank you for the invitation," Sala said, rising to her feet.

"Yes, it was a lovely evening," Lidka added, her gaze pointed at me.

"We'll walk you to the train station," Czeshik offered brightly.

At that precise moment, a yawn slipped out of me. Seeing that, Lidka said, her lips pressing thin," It's just around the corner. We don't need an escort." Before I could apologize, they were gone.

Czeshik cleaned up the cups and plates, but I was dead on my feet. I barely had enough energy to change into my nightclothes and climb into bed when Czeshik burst into my room. "So, what did you think of my girlfriend?"

"Which one?" I teased, pulling up the blanket.

"Sala, you dolt!" he replied, and then turned serious. "I'm going to propose."

My mouth dropped open. "After one night?"

A dreamy expression passed over his face. "No. But I will, mark my words, and I guarantee she'll say yes."

I chuckled. "I admire your confidence. Now, would you let me get some sleep?" I reached over and switched off the bedside lamp.

Czeshik hung in my doorway. "You should go for Lidka. I saw the way she gazed at you."

Lidka was cute as a button, and clever, too. But I might have blown my chance at the end. "Would you let me sleep? I have another busy day tomorrow."

The door clicked shut, and I rolled over with a sigh. Tired as I was, I couldn't shake thoughts of Lidka from my head. As I tossed and turned, I wanted to throttle Czeshik for planting the seed of possibility in my brain.

▽ ▽ ▽

THE NEXT WEEKEND, Czeshik and I made the trip to Feldafing. Predictably, the moment we arrived, he took off with Sala, leaving me in the dust.

I was on my own, and the only person I wanted to see was Lidka. I figured I could invite her for some coffee, maybe take in some music. If I was lucky, she'd agree to a dance or two. But when I found her and offered my invitation, her response made me blanch.

"No, thanks. I have plans tonight."

That was it. I stood there feeling like an idiot.

I tried to find Levi and David but discovered they'd gone away for the weekend. Feeling rejected, I sat in the cafeteria alone, trying to shake the sting of Lidka's brush-off. I kept replaying it in my head, realizing with growing embarrassment just how little I understood about dating. The evening at our house had gone well, better than I could have imagined. Except for the end, of course. Couldn't she forgive me?

Later that evening, I tracked down Czeshik and told him how Lidka rejected my advance. He listened, snickering the entire time.

He knocked me on the shoulder with surprising strength, practically pushing me off my feet. "Rafal, you fell for the oldest trick in the book. She's playing hard-to-get, trying to reel you in hook, line, and sinker."

I smacked my forehead. *Czeshik might be right! And it's working, too.*

I couldn't stop thinking about Lidka and how to win her over. The next weekend, as soon as we got back to Feldafing, I made a beeline for her apartment. Steeling myself, I took a deep breath and knocked. The door swung open, and her sister Alma answered, eyeing me before calling out, "Lidka! Some guy is here for you."

Did I misread her signal after all? Was she trying to tell me to get lost? But then she appeared in the doorway, and despite her unreadable expression, I knew this was my last chance to redeem myself. "I'm sorry if I offended you last week. Will you let me make it up to you?"

Her expression softened for the briefest moment, so fleeting, I wondered if I imagined it. "I traveled to Munich and back to see you. What kind of effort did you make? You kept yawning, acting like our conversation was boring you."

I thought I had engaged in the conversation and wasn't even aware that I'd yawned more than once. "I… I was tired." The excuse sounded weak, even to my ears.

She arched an eyebrow, unimpressed. "You had plenty of energy for your Russian roommates. Is one of them your girlfriend? That would be… convenient."

My eyes widened in shock. "Absolutely not! They're both married and waiting for news about their husbands. We split the rent, that's all. I swear!"

"You claimed you remembered our first meeting. Do you remember what I was wearing?" She folded her arms again and tapped her shoe on the floor, expecting I would fail her test.

But she didn't know she was the most attractive girl I'd spoken to in over six years. I recalled every detail of our meeting. "You were wearing a royal blue skirt and matching top, and you looked so sophisticated. Every man in the room was staring at you, and I was afraid one of them would beat me up if I commandeered too much of your attention."

The corners of her lips quirked upward. "I suppose one date won't kill me. I've lived through worse."

CHAPTER 58

Lidka

Feldafing D.P. Camp, Germany — Early 1946

ONE DATE BECAME TWO, then three, and soon, I was spending every free moment with Lidka. The more I learned about her, the more I admired her strength, beauty, and spirit. She told me about her family life back in Sosnowiec, and with every story, I could feel the love and devotion she carried in her heart.

"My father was a master harness maker," she told me one evening during our post-dinner stroll around the grounds. "People respected and admired him. He perished in Auschwitz, the same evil place that claimed my dear mother, as well as my brother's cherished wife and their darling baby." She stopped walking and took a moment to wipe her eyes. "My faithful brother perished in a Nazi labor camp, and not a day goes by that I don't think of him."

I removed a clean handkerchief from my pocket and offered it to her. She accepted it and wiped her tear-stained cheeks. I asked if she wanted to stop, but Lidka insisted on continuing.

"Somehow, my two sisters and I survived the selection process. Alma, my younger sister, was so fragile, pale as a ghost. She was continually sick, getting weaker and weaker every day. You know what the Nazis did with those who appeared weak…"

I took her hand and led her to a nearby bench. I held on while she collected herself, trying to convey my understanding and support. As much as it hurt to see her so distressed, I knew how important it was for her to tell the whole story. I was incredibly honored she trusted me enough to share it with me.

Lidka took a deep breath. "Sarah, my older sister, removed a safety pin from her skirt, pricked her fingers, and passed it to me so I could do the same. We dabbed Alma's cheeks with our blood, rubbing in the color until she looked healthy. Sarah and I sent her through selection first, with an unspoken agreement that we would stay together, no matter what the Nazis decreed." Lidka shot to her feet and began pacing. Oddly, in that instant, a waking nightmare gripped me.

A brutal voice. The sharp crack of a riding crop. Rivka reaching for me, her wide, terrified eyes locking onto mine. Her desperation crashes over me— my heart aches to be her salvation, her shining knight. But fear roots me in place. I do nothing. She dissolves into ash, slipping through my fingers like dust, and I am powerless to stop it.

A sharp snap of fingers jolted me back. Lidka was standing in front of me, concern etched across her face. "Are you okay? Your eyes glazed over—I couldn't get your attention."

"Forgive me," I pleaded, shaking my head to banish the horrific images. "Please keep going."

She remained standing. "We were sent to a labor camp in Sudetengau, Czechoslovakia, with twelve-hour shifts in a loom factory. It was grueling work. The rations were pathetic, and I worried that none of us would survive. But somehow, we hung on by the skin of our teeth until the Russians liberated us." She took a deep breath. "We returned to Sosnowiec afterward, searching for any trace of our family."

My heart leaped toward hers. "What did you find out?"

Lidka shook her head. "The town was soaked with Jewish blood, and it was there that we learned the fate of my parents, my brother, and his family. Despite asking everyone we met, Eva's fate was still unknown." A soft smile lit her face. "Then I found my friend Sala. She told us Eva was sent to Auschwitz but might still be alive."

I'd met Eva in the D.P. camp, but I nodded for her to keep going. Lidka clutched my arm. "Oh my God, Rafal, it was a miracle! After a few weeks at Auschwitz, the Nazis sent Eva to work in an ammunitions factory. I don't know how she survived, but she did. I'll never forget our reunion as long as I live."

"How incredible," I gushed, giving her a warm hug. "I'm truly happy for you."

"Now, Eva and Sarah are married, and Alma is engaged to a wonderful man. Somehow, despite all the sadness, we've found family, old and new." She dabbed her eyes again, but these were tears of happiness.

As we spent more time together, our conversations gradually shifted. We spoke less of the past and more about our dreams for the future. I became increasingly certain that Lidka and I could build a wonderful life together. I was extremely hopeful she felt the same way.

▽ ▽ ▽

OUR STROLLS AROUND FELDAFING became a ritual, a pocket of time when we were in our own world. One Saturday, as we wandered along a tree-lined path, I gathered the courage to ask Lidka the big question. I tried to keep my tone casual, to keep calm and cool, but no doubt failed.

Lidka stared at me in surprise. After a tense moment, her expression softened. "I need to think about it."

I was relieved she didn't shut me down outright, but this was far from the enthusiastic response I'd hoped for. I waited a solid week, but with each passing day, I worried more and more that she only saw me as a friend. Soon after arriving the following Saturday, I received word to meet her in the Feldafing cafeteria. I made a beeline there, desperate to hear her verdict for better or worse. But as I entered the building, she ran up to me with a big, beautiful smile and declared, "Yes, Rafal—I'd love to marry you!"

I was absolutely stunned as she stood on her toes and kissed my lips in front of everyone there. A cheer rang out, and I thought my heart might burst with happiness. We spent the rest of the weekend dreaming about our future and planning the right time to tie the knot.

When we shared our news with Czeshik and Sala, their joy was boundless. With their own engagement fresh, we decided on a shared celebration. Our joint wedding was held on April 11, 1946—a day that marked the one-year anniversary of my liberation from Buchenwald.

The morning of our weddings, Czeshik and I woke early, grateful to see the sun making its ascent. As I adjusted my tie in the mirror of our Munich apartment, I ached to share this day with my family. How I wished Tatte were here to give me one of his warm blessings. I could picture Mama and Rivka in the audience, beaming with joy, and Shlomo at my side, cracking jokes to steady my nerves. Overall, I felt a strange mix of emotions—excitement, sorrow, gratitude, and hope.

Czechik and I were both quiet on the train ride to Feldafing, each mired in our personal thoughts and memories. When we arrived, we headed straight for Villa Kaiser, where Lidka's sisters had been preparing for the event. The house was bustling with activity, and friends soon began arriving. I welcomed David and Levi warmly, so thankful they'd come to witness the signing of the

Ketubahs (*wedding contracts*) for me and Czeshik. Though our lives had split in different directions, our connection remained strong.

When the rabbi arrived, himself a Lithuanian survivor, the room hushed. Upstairs, in the quietest corner of the house, Czeshik and I each signed the Ketubahs, our pledges to provide financial support for our wives, in marriage and after death. After sharing a toast with the rabbi, David, and Levi, we descended into the living room to begin the ceremony. Czeshik and Sala went first, and then it was my turn.

Lidka glided toward me, her hazel eyes glittering, and I almost forgot to breathe. She wore a simple dress, but to me, she was the most beautiful woman in the world.

The rabbi led us through the vows, and as I recited the words of betrothal, my voice grew stronger. Next came the ceremonial sip of wine, the breaking of the glass wrapped in cloth, and the kiss that sealed our promise to be faithful through good times and bad. Musicians added a splendid touch, the perfect finale to the best day of my life.

The celebration stretched late into the night, with music, dancing, and freely flowing drinks. When the night wound down, I found myself on a bed next to Lidka, but we weren't alone—our friends and family were sprawled across every available surface. It was far from what I'd dreamed a wedding night would be like, but with so much love surrounding us, I couldn't complain a bit.

The following morning, Czeshik and I accompanied our new brides to the train station, our hands linked as we stepped toward our new lives.

CHAPTER 59

Big News

Feldafing DP Camp, Germany — September 1946

LIDKA TOOK MY HAND as we sat on the edge of our worn-out couch. "Rafal, I think… I think we might have a baby on the way."

My initial reaction was outright panic. *A baby, here in the rubble of Germany? In the country that sought to destroy us and nearly succeeded?* But seeing the wonder in her eyes, I swallowed my doubts and plastered a smile on my face. "That's incredible news," I said as brightly as I could manage. When the Feldafing camp doctor confirmed Lidka's belief, my excitement was genuine.

"Me, a Tatte!" I kept repeating, completely stunned. I could still hear the doctor pronouncing, "Congratulations, Kantor family. You're having a baby!"

But when we boarded the train for Munich, Lidka became distant and silent. For the first fifteen minutes, she gazed out the cabin window, lost in her own thoughts.

Worried, I nudged her shoulder. "Lidka, is everything all right?"

Her hazel eyes pierced my soul. "Raf, are we ready for this? Are we sure we want to bring a baby into this broken world?"

I put my arm around her shoulders and rubbed her back. "I understand your concerns, but a baby is a *berakah*, a blessing, a way to repair the world."

Lidka sighed. "Everything's still a mess. How can we promise our child a better life without a real home?"

I closed my eyes, remembering when Mama brought Rivka home from the hospital, just a tiny pink bundle. I'd stood over her crib, watching her face scrunch up in sleep, her tiny hands curled into fists. I remembered her funny way of chewing her thumb, and how it wasn't long before she begged me to play with her and started calling me Rafal. Rivka's presence had brightened our entire home, even during the most difficult times.

"I know the world's a mess, but I promise it will get better." I stroked her hair. "A baby's innocent. A clean slate. We'll fill this world with our love."

Her eyes softened. "We will."

WINTER CAME, and as Lidka's belly grew, our need for a larger home became urgent. We hunted every corner of Munich for a quiet, comfortable apartment close to the streetcar, so Lidka wouldn't have to walk far in the cold. After weeks of searching, she found a place on Hohenzollern Strasse in Schwabing. Moving into that apartment, with its creaky floors and old-fashioned furniture, felt like a step toward normalcy—even if it was still in Germany.

Finally, we had privacy—and a proper place to plan our future. I took on more work, and Lidka became a fixture downtown, finding everything our apartment needed to make it a home.

My work as a liaison with the Polish guards ended, and I needed a new job to support my growing family. When I learned that the Hebrew Immigration Aid Society (HIAS) wanted someone to help Jewish orphans, I jumped at the opportunity.

In this role, which was personal to my heart, I helped individuals find family members across the U.S., South America, and other countries. Whenever I made a connection, it gave me great pride and joy.

Before long, I earned a promotion to work with U.S. immigration—a great privilege. For so long, I had focused on my own survival, wallowed in the pain of loss. But helping others rebuild their lives after immense losses ignited a renewed sense of purpose in me. I stepped into the role of department head at a pivotal time in history, when President Truman was working to raise U.S. immigration quotas.

But in early 1947, I began experiencing abdominal pains, sharp and persistent. At first, I brushed them off as stress related. But soon, the pain became so intense that it was debilitating. A German doctor suspected an ulcer and put me on a strict diet of baby food and milk. I couldn't let this slow me down, not with Lidka and so many families depending on me.

Lidka's pregnancy progressed normally, and our plan was for her to deliver in Feldafing, under the care of a Jewish doctor. I hoped our firstborn would be a boy, especially because my two brothers-in-law boasted about their newborn boys. On the last weekend in May, we journeyed to Feldafing with a plan to stay there until the baby arrived. On the morning of June 1st, as Lidka was making breakfast, she dropped the spatula.

"Rafal, the baby's coming!"

I ran around the apartment, gathering Lidka's clothes and sundries as if she was going away for a month instead of days.

After spending most of the day pacing at the Feldafing hospital, the midwife on duty told us the baby might not arrive for some hours. With dusk approaching, both Lidka and the midwife persuaded me to head back to our temporary lodging to get some sleep.

They assured me the baby wouldn't appear until the next morning.

I was reluctant but kissed Lidka's brow and went home to rest. Early the next morning, I rushed to the hospital, eager to see her and to be present for the delivery. But as I bolted through the entry door, my sisters-in-law greeted me with beaming faces.

Sarah grinned. "It's a girl! Just kidding! You have a healthy baby boy!"

"A boy?" I repeated, incredulous. I hurried to Lidka's room, and along the way, I was peppered with congratulations from friends and nurses. When I stepped through the door, I gasped.

"Rafal, meet Abraham," Lidka said proudly. As I took our healthy, beautiful son into my arms, she declared, "We can call him Abri." I was too overwhelmed to respond.

Eight days later, we held a small celebration for Abri's bris, filling the day with love and well wishes. Afterward, Lidka and Abri stayed at the Feldafing villa with her sisters, where she had extra support, while I commuted back and forth from Munich daily.

One night, Lidka dropped onto the couch beside me as I pored over reports. She let out a sigh, then nudged me. "Maybe we should stay in Feldafing. Abri will grow up surrounded by family, in a Jewish community. Unlike in Munich, where there are still pockets of antisemitism."

Nights alone in Munich had been tough for me, and as much as I enjoyed city life, I knew it wasn't the ideal place to raise our precious son. No one had prepared me for how much a baby changes everything. But as I held Abri in my arms, I knew our choice to remain here in Feldafing was the right move.

Chapter 60

Israel

Feldafing DP Camp, Germany — 1947–1948

WITH SO MUCH EXCITEMENT IN MY LIFE, I didn't pay enough attention to my health. Only when the pain reached the stage where it kept me up all night, moaning in agony, did I consent to visit Dr. Weiss in Freimann again. I had been taking his "secret formula" for weeks now, a blend he assured me would settle my digestive system.

It didn't work. When I entered his office, clutching my stomach, he sighed.

"Rafal, your condition is worse than I thought. You need to go to the hospital for proper observation. I'll arrange your admission in Schwabing."

I nodded, half-dazed. The entire trek home, I thought about Lidka and Abri, what they would do without me if this turned life threatening. But Lidka only squeezed my hand when I expressed my concerns.

"You'll be home soon, Rafal," she said, giving me a reassuring smile. "We'll get through this together."

Unfortunately, after a ten-day stay in Schwabing, there had been no improvement. All tests proved negative, baffling the doctors and me. Upon their advice, I consulted a German professor at his private clinic in Tutzing.

"Two weeks should be all we need," he assured me, jotting down notes on my chart. He admitted me to the hospital, ordered a whole new battery of tests, and prescribed a new diet. I spent endless hours staring at the ceiling, bored out of my mind.

I never did well when I wasn't active. With nothing to occupy my time, my thoughts drifted back to Buchenwald. To the nights of agony when I was afraid my body was failing me. Once again, I worried I might never recover.

When Lidka visited, she tried to hide her concern, but as I lay there, gaunt and weak, she finally spoke her mind. "I don't trust these doctors," she whispered, her hand on mine. "You need to come home. With my constant care, I know you'll get better."

I was too weary to argue, so I agreed. Once we returned to Feldafing, she put me on a diet recommended by Jewish nutritionists. She prepared each meal and ensured I got the proper rest. Seeing her belief and determination gave me the drive I needed to keep fighting for my life.

Her ministrations worked, and gradually, my strength returned. One night, I got choked up and said, "You're saving my life." And it was true.

When I returned to work, I wasted no time registering our family for resettlement in the newly named State of Israel. We wanted to be part of Israel's development, to build a life without the past hanging over us. Sarah and her husband had already left for Israel, and we couldn't wait to join them.

Lidka and I threw ourselves into preparing for the move. We packed a little every day, chuckling over this item and that, each one a piece of the new life we would soon build in Israel.

We wrote to Sarah and her husband, detailing our plans. But once again, my body betrayed me. Some days, I felt strong—raring to leave. Other days, I was weak, exhausted, and barely able to move. Frustration mounted as I impatiently waited for my strength to return for good.

In the meantime, I kept working at the HIAS, running the American desk, but my heart was already in Israel. I scoured every available opportunity to work in administration there, eager to be part of Israel's early growth.

One morning, Lidka wordlessly handed me a letter from Sarah. Her fingers trembled as she passed it to me.

When I finished, I set the letter down, staring blankly ahead. Sarah and her family were living in tents, unable to secure jobs. They advised that we go to America, where I'd get better healthcare and have a better chance of finding employment.

"Rafal?" Lidka's voice shook with distress and disappointment. "What should we do now?"

Swallowing hard, I tried to process the news we'd both just learned. "Life in Israel is so much harder than I imagined. With everything I've heard at HIAS, I should have expected it." A heavy sigh escaped. "Lidka, I'm so sorry. I don't want to disappoint you, but maybe Sarah is right."

She shook her head vehemently. "You haven't disappointed me. If we're together, it doesn't matter where we live. If America will take us, I think we should go there."

For my health. For Abri's future. For our financial security. I reached for her hand. "America is it. If they will take us."

▽ ▽ ▽

THE UNITED STATES passed the Displaced Persons Act, allowing thousands of new refugees into the country. Our immigration paperwork took months, with countless interviews and a thousand questions, all of which gave me full appreciation for the frustrated people I'd encountered daily at HIAS. I trained my replacement, eager to leave Germany once and for all.

In March 1949, we received our instructions to report to a camp in Munich for our final processing. After a tear-filled fare-well to all our friends and neighbors in Feldafing, we boarded a train to Munich the following day.

On the brief journey, I stared out the window, watching the world whizz past. Lidka noticed my silence and leaned close to whisper, "Are you worried?"

"What if things aren't so different in the States? I once met an American soldier in a bar—drunk and cursing the Jews. I want to raise Abri in a world free from discrimination and blind hatred." I paused, searching her eyes. "I want to believe it's different there—for you, for me, and for our son."

She rested her head on my shoulder. "Then let's believe it."

CHAPTER 61

U.S. Immigration Center

Bremen, Germany — April 1949

WE STAYED OVERNIGHT in the Munich camp, and the next day, army trucks drove us to the Munich train station. As night came, we boarded an overnight train to Bremen. When we arrived, United Nations trucks drove us to the U.S. Immigration Center, where they placed us in temporary housing.

After three days, we met with a U.S. immigration officer. The man examined our papers, flipping through every document. Lidka squeezed my hand throughout his careful review.

At last, he laid the papers on his desk. "Mr. and Mrs. Kantor, everything is in order. I'm happy to inform you that you're approved for entry to the United States. You'll depart on the fifteenth. Congratulations—and best of luck in your new life."

Lidka wore an expression I'd never seen before—a mix of relief, awe, and joy. As we stepped out of the office, she let out a whoop. "America, here we come!" She gave Abri a tight squeeze and kissed his cheek, making him gurgle with delight.

A few days before our departure, an officer from the American Consul pulled me aside. "Mr. Kantor, we'd like to ask you to be the ship leader for the immigrants on board. Your English skills are solid, and you've handled yourself here with great patience and good humor. What do you say?"

Lidka gave me a nod of encouragement. I took the clipboard from his outstretched hand and said, "I'd be honored."

This position enabled us to board the ship a day early, giving us a chance to settle in. I wrapped an arm around Lidka as we made our way to the harbor, the three of us bundled up against the wind.

The sight of massive American Navy vessels preparing to carry troops back to the United States overwhelmed us. Ours, the *General Langfitt*, an imposing army transport vessel, stood among them.

Lidka's eyes widened as she craned her neck to take in the full height of our ship. "Can you believe we're getting on that thing?"

"First time in a harbor and first time on a ship. The first of many exciting experiences to come!" I shifted Abri's small suitcase in my grip as we climbed the metal gangway.

On board, we discovered bunk beds stacked five high and rows of communal bathrooms. The officer explained that men and women would sleep in separate quarters, but mothers with children would get small cabins. Lidka smiled, relieved, and I knew Abri would sleep better in a quieter space.

After helping them settle in, I headed up to the top deck for my orientation meeting. I greeted a group of other men who would lead their sections. The officer in charge handed me a sheet with my official title, "Head of Liaison and Coordination."

The first day, I was running in circles, coordinating everything from meals to medical requests. But after leaving port, everyone settled into ship life. Lidka would often join me on deck, Abri bouncing in her arms as she took in the vast expanse of ocean.

Over the next ten days, all the passengers became one close-knit family—people from all walks of life, speaking different languages, practicing different faiths, all looking forward to bright new futures in America. Despite the cramped quarters and endless lines, no one complained.

On our last night at sea, I strolled along the deck, letting the cool, salty spray kiss my skin. Beside me, a young boy sporting a crew cut gripped the railing. He pointed to a faint shape on the horizon. "Look. America!" he yelped, his voice filled with wonder.

CHAPTER 62

New York Harbor

United States — April 26th, 1949

THOUGH IT WAS DARK, the ship hummed with excitement as hundreds jammed on deck to see the lights of America come into view. The date was April 26th, and after a journey across a vast ocean, Lidka and I viewed the distant glow from New York City in disbelief.

The mighty ship cut its speed as we approached the harbor. The skyline rose before us, every skyscraper gleaming against the night. Neither of us had ever seen such awe-inspiring majesty. I gazed at Abri, asleep in Lidka's arms, his little face peaceful, unaware of the momentous event unfolding around him. I brushed a hand over his head, whispering, "One day, you'll learn about how you arrived in the land of the free."

Lidka rested her head on my shoulder, her eyes shimmering as she stared at the view. "Rafal, what would our parents think?"

I placed a protective arm around Lidka and Abri. "They would be proud. We will carry them always, in every step we take."

We retired to Lidka's small room for a few hours of rest, mostly for Abri's sake, as we didn't sleep a wink. When we rushed back to the deck in the morning, the ship had already docked at the pier. Before us stood a sea of people, cheering and waving flags, as if they'd been waiting for every single one of us. The welcome stole our breath away, and I knew we would carry it in our hearts for the rest of our lives.

"Rafal, we made it!" Lidka's face lit up as she waved to the cheering crowd.

I jiggled Abri in my arms. "We'll build a good life here. I promise."

Abandoning my usual restraint. I let out a triumphant shout, letting the weight of the past slip away. Afterward, we bowed our heads for a moment of silence to honor the family and friends lost to us. This was their victory as much as ours.

As we took our first steps on American soil, our family's future stretched ahead of us. Brimming with hope and love.

The End.

Rafal Kantor, Holocaust survivor (top left).

Epilogue

IN 1949, RAFAL KANTOR leveraged his role with the Hebrew Immigrant Aid Society (HIAS) to immigrate to the United States with Lidka and Abri. Upon arrival, they adopted the Americanized versions of their names, becoming "Ray" and "Lydia."

They settled in Cincinnati, Ohio, where Ray managed a furniture store. Over 40 years of marriage, they raised three children and became grandparents to two grandchildren.

In their new homeland, Ray and Lydia integrated into the Jewish-American community, taking part in various Jewish organizations and attending communal events and celebrations. Sundays became a cherished tradition as they joined other Jewish families for gatherings at Meadow Brook Park in Ross, Ohio, enjoying picnics, songs, and games. Most of these get-togethers were with fellow Holocaust survivors, united by their shared losses and resilience. These survivors not only celebrated life but also reaffirmed the importance of community and remembrance.

In 1979, Ray drafted personal memoirs of his survival experiences from 1939 to 1949. Later, he videotaped his story for the USC Shoah Foundation, whose mission it is to record, preserve, and share the testimonies of Holocaust survivors.

Throughout his life, Ray took on many leadership roles in several Jewish organizations. He served as President of the Greater Cincinnati Jewish Society and The Jewish Survivors of Nazism, the forerunner of the Nancy and David Wolf Holocaust and Humanity Center.

In 1998, Ray fulfilled a long-held desire to revisit his Jewish roots in Czestochowa, Poland, accompanied by some of his family members. There, surrounded by the echoes of his childhood home, Ray recounted stories from his youth. They also visited the solemn sites where the Nazis had committed atrocities against the citizens of Czestochowa—a stark reminder of the horrors he survived, and of so many precious lives lost.

One of Ray's greatest sources of pride was his remarkable talent as a cantorial singer, a passion rooted in singing while attending synagogue in Czestochowa and performing in school theater programs. As an adult, Ray's resonant voice later guided congregations in heartfelt prayer, first at a synagogue in Newport, Kentucky, and later at Adath Israel and Etz Chaim (B'nai Tzedek) congregations in Cincinnati. Known for its power and deep emotion, Ray's singing left a profound and lasting impression on all who had the privilege of hearing him.

In conclusion, the Holocaust shaped Ray's life. Driven by a deep sense of duty to honor the memory of the six million Jews who perished, he recounted his family's suffering under Nazi rule. By invitation, Ray spoke to high school students, lectured at universities, and addressed church groups and other organizations, reliving the horrors so that future generations would not repeat the evils of the past.

Ray and Lydia Kantor now rest at the Jewish Cemetery of Greater Cincinnati (JCGC), their graves marked by a special medallion honoring victims and survivors of Nazi persecution. Their legacy endures through their family and the community they enriched with their faith and commitment to remembrance.

PHOTOGRAPHS AND DOCUMENTS

Lidka Kantor (17) wearing the star of David armband. Circa 1940.
Photo courtesy of the Kantor family.

Rafal Kantor. Buchenwald Concentration Camp.
After liberation. April 1945.
Photo Credit: United States Holocaust Memorial Museum
(USHMM), courtesy Judith Saul Stix.

Rafal (left) with a friend after liberation. Circa 1945–1946.
Photo courtesy of the Kantor family.

Left, Rafal, Lidka, and friends. Most likely
at the Feldafing DP camp. Circa 1945–46.
Photo courtesy of the Kantor family.

Rafal and Lidka.
Most likely at the Feldafing DP camp. Circa 1945–46.
Photo courtesy of the Kantor family.

Rafal and Lidka with Abraham. Feldafing Camp. Circa 1947.
Photo courtesy of the Kantor family.

Rafal and Lidka.
Photo courtesy of the Kantor family.

Ray Kantor

Kantor to sing at B'nai Tzedek

For the second year, Cantor Ray Kantor will lead High Holiday services at Congregation B'nai Tzedek along with Rabbi Ed Boraz. Congregation B'nai Tzedek invites the community to join in their services which are held at the Jewish Community Center.

Rafal was a European-trained chazzan who learned to lead services in a Chassidic congregation before the war. The above article states: "We're delighted Kantor is returning to lead our services. His high-quality voice and wonderful style offer a phenomenal religious experience. Congregants said our High Holiday services were the most moving they had ever encountered."

Ray (Rafal) and Lydia (Lidka) Kantor. Holocaust survivors.
Jewish Cemetery of Greater Cincinnati.
Photo courtesy of the Kantor family.

German soldiers entering Czestochowa. Circa 1939.
Photo Credit: Bundesarchiv, Bild 101I–380–0086–27 /
Greiner / CC–BY–SA 3.0

Germans on the streets of Czestochowa, Poland,
shortly after the occupation. Circa 1939.
Photo Credit: The Chris Webb Private Archive.

A German soldier appears to be mocking a Jewish man in
Czestochowa, Poland. Circa 1939.
Photo credit: United States Holocaust Memorial Museum (USHMM)

German soldiers round up a group of Jewish men on Strazacka
Street in Czestochowa. Circa 1939.
Photo Credit: The World Society of Czestochowa Jews
and Their Descendants.

Jews are arrested in Czestochowa. Circa 1939–40.
Photo Credit: The World Society of Czestochowa Jews
and Their Descendants.

Round up of Jews in Czestochowa, circa 1939.
Photo Credit: USHMM

The German army seized Czestochowa on Sunday, 3 September 1939, in the early morning. By noon the next day, they had brutally brought the city into submission. Several hundred people were killed (some sources report as many as one thousand), including many Jews. Photo Credit: The World Society of Czestochowa Jews and Their Descendants.

A group of Jewish men, rounded up by German soldiers, await execution on a street in Czestochowa. In front of them lie the corpses of those who were shot earlier. 3–8 September 1939. Photo Credit: The World Society of Czestochowa Jews and Their Descendants.

The deportations of Czestochowa ghetto residents to the Treblinka death camp began early in the morning on 22 September 1942. The Germans, with perfidy and cynicism, chose the most important day on the Jewish calendar—Yom Kippur (the Day of Atonement)—to liquidate the Czestochowa ghetto. Around 40,000 women, children, and men, in five transports, were deported to the gas chambers of Treblinka. Photo Credit: The World Society of Czestochowa Jews and Their Descendants.

Pelcery Plant Czestochowa.
Rafal's place of forced labor.
Circa 1942.

Photo Credit: The World Society of
Czestochowa Jews and their Decedents.

In the spring of 1942, Capt. Paul Degenhardt assumed command of the Schutzpolizei—the uniformed German police—in Czestochowa, Poland. Under his watch, more than 40,000 Jews were deported to their deaths at Treblinka. During selections for "resettlement," riding crop in hand, Degenhardt directed prisoners left or right—left meant death, right meant forced labor and a temporary reprieve.

He also committed or ordered numerous individual murders. Tried in the Lüneburg District Court, he was convicted on May 25, 1966, of twenty-eight counts of murder involving seventy-one victims, and sentenced to life in prison. He served only seven years before his release and died shortly after. Photo credit: The World Society of Czestochowa Jews and Their Descendants.

Jews boarding a deportation train to an extermination camp.
Photo courtesy of Yad Vashem.

-5-

116211 Gorgiel, Beniamin
12 Gelbart, Pinkus
13 Wolfman, Mojzesz
14 Wolfman, Chaim
15 Kac, Ajzyk
16 Grynewajg, Fajwel
17 Boms, Hiler
18 Szczerczowski, Zygmunt
19 Rozencwajg, Izrael
20 Gliksman, Wolf
21 Goldberg, Jozef
22 Osja, Eljasz
23 Joelewicz, Mojsze
24 Besser, Herszlik
25 Goldberg, Benek
26 Besser, Mortka
27 Besser, Szaja
28 Gelassen, Mojzesz
29 Szmulewicz, Szmul
30 Kamionka, Motek
31 Sultanik, Abram
32 Gallster, Abram
33 Scharfstein, Marcel
34 Kohn, Abram
35 Glikson, Jakub
36 Tapor, Majer
37 Sandler, Lajma
38 Markowicz, Wolf
39 Feiner, Kiwa
40 B Szpiro, Josef
41 Szpringfeld, Jozef
42 Szpringfeld, Majer
43 Szymanowski, Uszer
44 Peter, Michal
45 Neumark, Bachmil
46 Krzepicki, Josek
47 Kac, Izlama
48 Bajgelman, Jonas
49 I Fajtek, Jakub
50 Grynberg, Abysz
51 Sendrowicz, Gustaw
52 Szaja, Herman
53 Krause, Polek
54 Jarzabek, Isk Jacob
55 MAX Sulkowski, Wolf
56 Dawidowicz, Henoch
57 Gruszka, Zajnwel
58 Ehrlich, Symcha
59 Berger, Marjan
60 Hartka, Jozef
61 Glatter, Leon
62 Emzel, Szaja
63 Platkiewicz, Eliasz
64 Klasner, Moszek
65 Fefer, Salek
66 Zyngier, Berek
67 Wajchman, Burech
68 Gurfinkel, Zymcha
69 Kornfeld, Karol
70 Fajfer, Moszko

116271 Dafner, Rubin 53
72 Schpringer, Dawid
73 Silberberg, Chil
74 Smiga, Nuchym
75 Eis, Henryk
76 Bienstock, Hermann
77 Nirenberg, Icek
78 Smiga, Hersz
79 Dlugonoga, Jozef
80 Nowak, Markus
81 Frank, Moszek
82 Laib, Symcha
83 Edelman, Izrael
84 Karmiol, Jakub
85 Blum, Chil
86 Libson, Kuba
87 Seistowski, Szmul
88 Borkowski, Szymon
89 Scislowski, Jankiel
90 Brauner, Chil
91 Buzyn, Gerszon
92 Tag, Samuel
93 Filip, Lajb
94 Kenig, Chaim
95 Heler, Abram
96 Waksberg, Icek
97 Kantor, Rafal
98 Fischel, Lewi
99 Lokiec, Moszek
300 Stelzer, Peisack
1 Tag, Mechel
2 Sztelcer, Hilel
3 Magiet, Chaskiel
4 Prajs, Zelik
5 Gomolinski, Majer
6 Sztrauch, Hersz
7 Racker, Baruch
8 Kirsz, Hersz
9 Krzepicki, Wolf
10 Horowicz, Hirsz
11 Bajgelman, Haskiel
12 Kaluszynski, Daniel
13 Helfgot, Abram
14 K Jakubowicz, Icek
15 Kaluszynski, Szlama
16 Lipiec, Szaja
17 Bergman, Icek
18 Bergmann, Abram
19 Fajersztajn, Moszek
20 Fajersztajn, Kopel
21 Meloch, Aron
22 Rosenzweig, Grischa
23 Laznowski, Fiszel
24 Rozenwald, Josek
25 Hansla, Aba
26 Klug, Zyskind
27 Zajdman, Aleksander
28 ZZ Kujawski, Henryk
29 Ungier, Chaim
30 Unger, Markus

All Buchenwald prisoners were assigned identification numbers. Likely, this is the list of the men who arrived in Buchenwald with Rafal. Document courtesy of Yad Vashem.

KL. BUCHENWALD   (Männer)   T/D Nr.   1 7 5 5 6 8

KANTOR,   Rafael
NAME   Vorname

4. 7. 1923   Czestochowa   116 297
Geb.-Datum   Geb.-Ort   Häftl.-Nr.

Häftl. Pers. Karte . . . . [1]	Mil. Gov. Quest. . . . . [ ]	Dokumente: 7
Effektenkarte . . . . . . [1]	Order f. Disp. . . . . . [ ]	
Effektenverzeichnis . . . [ ]	Todesmeldung . . . . [ ]	Inf. Karten:
Postkontr.-Karte . . . . [1]	Soz. Vers. Unterlagen . . [ ]	
Schreibst.-Karte . . . . [ ]	Zahnbehandlungskarte . [ ]	Bemerkungen:
Häftl. Pers. Bogen . . . [1]	Korrescondenz . . . . . [ ]	
Revierkarte . . . . . . [1]	[ ]	
Krankenblätter . . . . . [ ]	[ ]	
Arbeitskarte . . . . . . [1]	[ ]	Umschlag-Nr.:
Geldverw.-Karte . . . . [ ]	[ ]	
Nummernkarte . . . . . [1]	[ ]	

All Buchenwald prisoners were required to fill out registration
paperwork upon arrival. The document above is Rafal's actual paperwork, summarizing the forms kept in his personnel file. Rafal's
file included seven documents: the Buchenwald Personal Detention
Card, Effects Card, Postal Contacts, Liable Sheet, Territory Map,
Work Card, and Number Card. Rafal entered the camp on January
10, 1945, and his paperwork was completed on January 20, 1945.
Documents courtesy of Yad Vashem.

Pole Häftl. Nr. 116297 **Kantor** Rafal
Jude
Name   Vorname
geb. 4.7.23 in Czenstochowa

Walzwerkarbeiter Posteingang

Januar	Februar	März	April	Mai	Juni	Juli	August	Septemb.	Oktober	Novemb.	Dezemb.

RSHA **Postausgang**

Januar	Februar	März	April	Mai	Juni	Juli	August	Septemb.	Oktober	Novemb.	Dezemb.

Postsperre:

vom .... bis ....

" .... " ....

" .... " ....

Bemerkungen :

Rafal's Work Card: The German word "Walzerkarbeiter," trans-
lated into English, means "Rolling Mill worker," likely describing
one of Rafal's jobs at the Pelcery plant in Czestochowa, Poland.
The card was dated January 20, 1945. Documents courtesy of
Yad Vashem.

KL.:   Weimar-Buchenwald   Jude

Häftl.-Nr.:
116.297   P

Häftlings-Personal-Karte

Fam.-Name: Kantor
Vorname: Rafal
Geb. am: 4.7.23 in. Tschenstochau
Stand: led.   Kinder:
Wohnort: w.o.
Strasse: ul. Warszawska 20
Religion: mos. Staatsang. Pole
Wohnort d. Angehörigen: Mutter:
Chawa K.,w.o.

Eingewiesen am: 20.1.1945
durch: RSHA
in KL.: Buchenwald
Grund: Polit.Pole-Jude
Vorstrafen:

Überstellt
am: an KL
am: an KL
am: an KL.
am: an KL
am: an KL.
am: an KL

Entlassung:
am: durch KL :

mit Verfügung v.:

Strafen im Lager:
Grund: Art: Bemerkung:

Personen-Beschreibung:
Grösse: cm
Gestalt:
Gesicht:
Augen:
Nase:
Mund:
Ohren:
Zähne:
Haare:
Sprache:

Bes. Kennzeichen:

Charakt.-Eigenschaften:

Sicherheit b. Einsatz:
I.T.S. FOTO Nr. 697

Körperliche Verfassung:

KL.5/114.4. 500.000   40886

Rafal's Buchenwald Personal Information File. The upper left (KL) indicates that the concentration camp was Buchenwald, located in Weimar, Germany. The upper right indicates Rafal's prisoner number: 116297. The German word "Grund" means "reason," and in Rafal's case, it appears the reason for his incarceration was that he was a political prisoner—from Poland—and a Jew.

P. Jude
Vor- und Zuname: _____ Rafal Kantor _________________ ⁴¹⁷³ Haft-Nr. 116247

Beruf: _Arbeiter_________ geboren am: _4. 7. 23_____ in: _Czestochowa____

Anschrifts-Ort: ____ Straße Nr. ________

Eingel. am: _20.1.45___ Uhr von _RSHA.________ Entl. am _______/_____ Uhr nach ________

Bei Einlieferung abgegeben: Koffer ____ Aktentasche ____ Paket

Hut/Mütze	Paar Schuhe/Stiefel	Kragenknöpfe	Feuerzeug	Wehrpaß
Mantel	Paar Strümpfe	Halstuch	Tabak _ Pfeife	Fremdenpaß
Rock _ Jacke	Paar Gamaschen Tuch/Leder	Taschentuch	Zigarren/Zigaretten	Arbeitsbuch
Weste/Kletterweste	Kragen	Paar Handschuhe Tuch/Leder	Zig.-Blättchen	Invalidenkarte
Hose	Vorhemd	Brieftasche mit	Ziertuch	
Pullover	Binder/Fliege	Papiere	Messer _ Schere	
Oberhemden	Paar Armelhalter	Sporthemd/Hosen	Bleistift/Drehblei	
Unterhemden	Paar Sockenhalter	Abzeichen	Geldbörse	
Unterhosen	Paar Mansch.-Knöpfe	Schlüssel a. Ring	Kamm	Wertsachen: ja — nein

Abgabe bestätigt: Effektenverwalter:

Rafal’s signature appears in the lower left corner. Dated January 20, 1945. Documents courtesy of Yad Vashem.

Buchenwald prisoners standing during a roll call. Each wears a striped hat and uniform bearing colored, triangular badges and identification numbers. Circa 1938–41. Public domain.

Prisoners inside the hospital crib at the Buchenwald camp. An officer from the U.S. Army Chief Surgeon's office took the photograph when he arrived at the camp three days after Weimar was captured by the U.S. Third Army. Photo credit: U.S. Army Signal Corps. Dated April 14, 1945.

American troops and liberated prisoners at the front gate of
Buchenwald Concentration Camp. Germany, May 1945.
Courtesy of USHMM

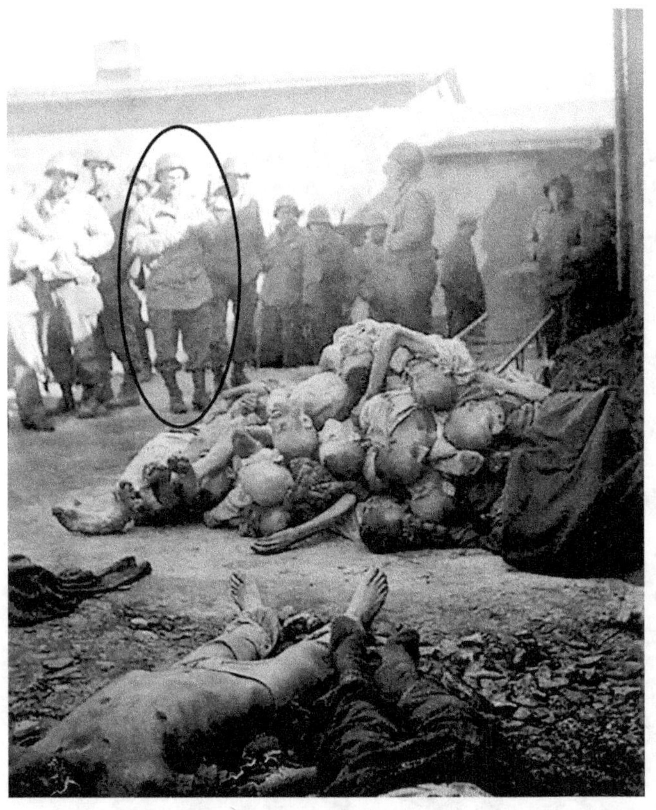

The author's father, U.S. Army combat medic Staff Sergeant Edmund D. Kruszynski (circled) observing a pile of dead bodies outside a barracks in the Buchenwald concentration camp. The photograph was taken by Sgt. John Poulos, MP, of the 512th MP Battalion. Sgt. Poulos was an early liberator of the camp. Courtesy of the Jewish Virtual Library. Dated April 17, 1945.

Rafal after liberation. Circa Summer 1945.
Photo courtesy of the Kantor family.

Rafal (left) worked as a tour guide at the Buchenwald concentration camp, helping Allied soldiers and others understand the atrocities and horrific conditions that prisoners endured at the hands of the Nazis. Circa June–July 1945. Photo courtesy of the Kantor family.

"I owe my life to the United States Army. I survived the Holocaust because of the courageous American soldiers who risked everything to fight their way into the camp and free us from unthinkable persecution." –Rafal Kantor (back row far right) with his American military friends. Circa 1945–1946. Photo courtesy of the Kantor family.

Rafal working with the American Military. Munich, Germany.
Circa 1946–1947. Courtesy of the Kantor family.

Rafal (center) with two friends. Circa 1946–1947.
Photo courtesy of the Kantor family.

Rafal (right) with a friend. Circa 1946–1947.
Photo courtesy of the Kantor family.

Rafal's visa/passport photograph for his immigration
application to enter Palestine. Circa 1947.

HIAS immigrants traveling to America in 1949.
Photo courtesy of the HIAS.

The Many Faces Of Horror

... survivors of Buchenwald can barely raise their heads from the wooden racks where they slept

The Holocaust

Local Survivors Recall Savage Slaughter Of Jews

By PAUL H. HARASIM
Enquirer Reporter

Day after day, villagers were marched up a hill outside Kaunas, Lithuania, and ordered to stand by the freshly dug graves.

Then the machine guns opened up.

The year was 1942 and 12-year-old David Levine and his mother, huddled with others in a ghetto ringed by armed Nazis, listened as the guns roared day and night.

For two days Mrs. Levine stared straight ahead and talked to no one. When she spoke, she tried to reassure herself and others.

"No, they couldn't have killed them all. They're just firing over their heads to scare us."

HER MIND couldn't conceive of that happening," said David, now 47 and in the dry cleaning business in Cincinnati.

"Normal people can never conceive of what happened in that time," said Barry Powers, like Levine a survivor of what has come to be known as The Holocaust — the Third Reich's savage slaughter of six million human beings who happened to be Jewish.

Sitting Thursday in the Roselawn home of Powers were Levine, Ray Kantor and Louis Weisser — all members of the Cincinnati chapter of Jewish Survivors From Nazism.

FOR FIVE hours the foursome remembered what they and their families had been through from 1933 to 1945 — the period when Hitler tried to carry out the extermination of Jews.

Each of the four men lost more than 50 members of their families. And the memories of what happened — the beatings, shootings, burnings, debasement and humiliation — still haunt them.

"I know I won't be able to sleep tonight without a sleeping pill," Levine said as he finished his recollection. "It seems as I get older the closer it all comes."

Except for Weisser, each of the men served time in German labor camps, where the Nazis' need for their labor saved them from the fate of the six million. They later were liberated by Allied forces and immigrated to the United States.

For some time now, the survivors in Cincinnati and other cities have worked hard to make sure that The Holocaust will not be forgotten. By invitation they have spoken to high school students, lectured to university students, church groups and other organizations.

"WE HOPE that by doing this The Holocaust will never be repeated," said Kantor, president of the Cincinnati survivors group.

Today is Yom HaShoa, the observance of The Holocaust. It commemorates the 27th day of the Hebrew month of Nisan — the day recognized as the first real sign of Jewish resistance to the Nazis.

It was on April 19, 1943, the 27th day of Nisan, that Germans attempted to enter the Warsaw ghetto. For a month, the Jewish resistance battled the Nazi troops.

The 32nd anniversary of the liberation of Nazi concentration camps will be observed in Cincinnati on Sunday at Ohav Shalom Synagogue, 1834 Section Rd., Roselawn.

HOW THE killing of Jews went on in Europe so long without even more resistance was explained by Kantor. Noting that there were other battles against the Germans and their allies, Kantor said.

After the Romans destroyed the second Temple (about 70 A.D.), the Jews further dispersed to the farthest points of the Roman Empire. Jews became the victims of abuse by the Christian world, suffering forced conversion, torture and death for their refusal to convert.

But while Jews were equipped to suffer, said Kantor, they were not ready to accept total annihilation. They could not believe that a nation would set out to destroy all Jews. When it was realized, millions already were murdered.

SO AFFECTED by his experiences and his loss of family, Powers, owner of a poultry shop, now asks: "Where was God? Why did it all happen?"

Separated at 15 from his family in Poland by the Nazis, he was loaded in a cattle car and taken to labor camps in Blechhamer and Buudiug, Germany.

"We would travel for days with nothing to eat or drink," the 48-year-old Powers recalled. "It was so bad that persons would use their own urine to moisten their lips ... They reduced us to such primitive beings. That was their goal. We never had any idea where we were going."

POWERS WORKED in factories near the labor camps to produce airplanes and other military goods for the Germans. One day, because he was tired of eating only spinach soup garnished with sand, he tried to smuggle half a loaf of bread into the camp.

"That was a mistake," he said. "I was beaten with a leather whip with wires on it. By the fourth blow, I was unconscious."

Once, said Powers, a Nazi commandant ordered every member of the labor camp to watch as two German Shepherd dogs ate steak. On another occasion, they were forced at gunpoint to watch three fellow Jews hang.

KANTOR, 53, now the manager of a furniture store, worked in labor camps on the Russian border at 16. He can remember seeing children thrown in the air and shot.

His parents were killed in gas chambers at Treblinka and a brother was shot.

"If there is a hell that can be conceived by the devil, it cannot be more devilish than what we went through," Kantor said. "You became so hardened to death that you would use a dead person as a pillow."

Levine, who eventually ended up in Dachau, one of the most heinous concentration camps, remembered Nazis coming into his Lithuanian village in buses playing loud music.

"They would pick up all the children and drown out their screams with the music," Levine said. "The driver was separated from the children by a compartment and the exhaust was put into the back of the bus so the children would die from the fumes."

STARVING, LEVINE and other Jews were once taken to a Nazi kitchen. Shown soup so hot that hands would be burned by touching the bowl, the Nazis warned the Jews that if they began to drink the soup they must finish it in five minutes or be shot.

"We did not start to drink it because we knew we would be scalded," Levine said. "I hated the way they humiliated us. They were animals.

"I'll never forgive the degradation ... Some times they would urinate in bottles, put them on top of our heads and then try to shoot them off. If they missed, they killed us. If they didn't, the urine went all over us."

WEISSER, 53, a divisional merchandising manager at Shillito's, escaped six hours before the Nazis invaded Poland and fought with the Polish Army in Russia against the Germans.

"I am happy I had the opportunity to fight against the Germans," said Weisser, who was wounded three times in the leg. Although he was able to escape, the rest of his immediate family was slaughtered.

"Could such a holocaust ever take place again? Either in the United States or the world?

"It won't happen in the United States as long as we have the Bill of Rights and Constitution," said Levine.

"As long as men like President Carter stand up for human rights in the world, it won't happen," said Weisser. "That was the problem before. Nobody cared about what happened to people. And look what happened."

"If there is a hell that can be conceived by the devil, it cannot be more devilish than what we went through." Kantor said. "You became so hardened to death that you would use a dead person as a pillow." Source: *The Cincinnati Enquirer*. Circa 1977.

GLOSSARY

RAFAL KANTOR ENDURED brutal Nazi rule for almost six years. Throughout his ordeal, there were many times when he heartbreakingly thought, "How can people turn a blind eye?" or "Why hasn't the rest of the world stopped this madness?" or "The Jewish people are peaceful! Why is this happening to us?"

I'd like to take a few moments to reflect on the horrifying machinery of the Holocaust—the systematic and ruthless campaign that led to the genocide of six million Jews and millions of others who didn't match the Aryan ideal. It's helpful to understand how each organization within the Nazi campaign worked in concert, and critically, the integral role each group played during Raf's ordeal under Nazi oppression.

The **Einsatzgruppen**, mobile killing units formed in 1939, were responsible for the brutal task of rounding up Jews and other targeted groups, leading them to mass graves and executing them. They followed the advancing German forces, spreading terror and death across Eastern Europe. Led by high-ranking SS officers and supported by various auxiliary units, the **Einsatzgruppen** were the embodiment of the Nazi regime's genocidal intent.

Integral to the Holocaust's machinery was the **Gestapo** (Geheime Staatspolizei), the Secret State Police. Under the joint leadership of Heinrich Himmler and Reinhard Heydrich, the **Gestapo** played a pivotal role in the systematic persecution of Jews. They conducted investigations, gathered intelligence, and arrested individuals, spreading misinformation about their threats to the Nazi regime. Their relentless pursuit of Jews, political dissidents, and other "undesirables" coalesced into mass deportations to concentration camps and extermination centers. The **Gestapo**'s pervasive presence instilled alarm and mistrust, contributing to the terror and abuse that characterized the Holocaust.

The administration of concentration camps, like **Buchenwald**, was firmly in the hands of the SS—Totenkopfverbände (Death's Head Units), a division of the SS. These guards and administrators maintained the daily operations of the camps, enforcing the brutal policies set forth by their superiors. The SS, under Himmler, controlled every aspect of the camp system, from food to forced labor to the human extermination processes.

Outside Germany, there were also units like the **Ukrainian SS** and the **Ukrainian Police** who collaborated with the Nazis by implementing their genocidal policies. Their actions contributed to the suffering and death of countless innocents.

HASAG, or **Hugo Schneider Aktiengesellschaft**, was a German arms manufacturer that expanded into occupied territories to take advantage of cheap, forced labor. In Czestochowa, Poland, **HASAG** took over the Rakow foundry and the Pelcery plant, converting them into production sites for munitions and military supplies. Jewish workers were rounded up and forced into grueling shifts, with **HASAG** profiting immensely from their suffering.

The **Werkschutz**, or **HASAG** factory guards, were tasked with enforcing oppressive security measures within these plants. Acting as Nazi agents, the **Werkschutz** monitored every aspect of the workers' lives, forcing compliance through harsh discipline and brutality. Their presence served as a reminder that these factories were also prison-like camps where the slightest misstep could mean punishment or death. Under their watch, **HASAG** became a machine of profit and oppression, exploiting the enslaved Jewish workforce to feed the German war effort.

The Jewish **ghettos**, created by the Nazi regime, served as containment zones to isolate, control, and dehumanize Jewish populations, separating them from the rest of society and subjecting them to harsh living conditions. Within these cramped, walled-off areas, two types of police forces operated: the **German Police** and the **Polish Police**. The **German Police** enforced Nazi regulations with relentless brutality, ensuring absolute obedience. Meanwhile, the **Polish Police** often collaborated with the Nazis to carry out oppressive directives while maintaining order and overseeing daily life. Together, they kept the ghetto residents in a state of submission, near starvation, and fearing what horrors might come next, as whispers of the Germans' more sinister plans reached them.

An additional layer of complexity in the Holocaust system were the **Judenrat** (Jewish Councils) and **Jewish Police**, which operated within the ghettos. The fate of these organizations during the Holocaust was as tragic as it was complex. Initially appointed by the Nazis to manage the ghettos and enforce their ruthless policies, these Jewish leaders and officers found themselves in excruciatingly difficult positions. They implemented Nazi orders, which included organizing forced labor, distributing scarce resources, and facilitating deportations to the concentration and extermination camps. Despite their desperate efforts to protect their communities, duress often forced them to make agonizing decisions.

Tragically, as the Nazis continued their campaign of extermination, the roles of the **Judenrat** and **Jewish Police** were deemed expendable once they had served their purpose. As the Nazis moved to eliminate the remaining Jewish population, most members of the **Judenrat** and **Jewish Police** were murdered. The

Nazis saw them as witnesses to their atrocities who needed to be silenced, much as they viewed the last remaining Jews who survived the degradations of the concentration camps. Individuals who had been forced to participate in the Nazi machinery of oppression were executed in mass shootings, deported to concentration camps, or killed during resistance efforts. Their deaths, like those of millions of other victims, serve as a grim testimony to the Nazi web and the suffering and sacrifice of all who were caught in its deadly grip.

Rest easy Rafal & Lidka your story survives through these pages.
Ron Kantor (son) on the left and me on the right.

ACKNOWLEDGEMENTS

THERE WERE SO MANY PEOPLE who generously devoted their time and talents at various stages of this story's development. To every one of you, please accept my deepest gratitude for the support you provided along the way. Your feedback brought Rafal's story to life, and for that, I am truly grateful.

First and foremost, I'd like to thank Ron Kantor. If not for him, this story might have remained an untold footnote in history. From the very beginning, Ron was the driving force behind bringing his parents' remarkable story into the public eye. He generously shared 's original manuscript, family photographs, home videos, and personal archives. Ron met with me several times, patiently answered every question, filled in key gaps, and offered invaluable insights and anecdotes that helped shape this narrative. We began this journey as strangers, and through the process of telling this story, we became good friends.

Thank you to my wife, Tracy, who has been my greatest cheerleader, editor, sounding board, and occasional reality checker throughout this journey. She patiently reviewed countless drafts, weighed in on covers, titles, and blurbs, and never once complained when dinners ran late or when conversations were met with a blank stare—because she knew that even though I was nodding, my mind was off somewhere, facing a villain or lost in a plot twist. I couldn't have written a quality story without her love and encouragement!

I'm incredibly fortunate to have the best critique team a writer could ask for. These generous beta readers offered their time, invaluable feedback, fresh ideas, and thoughtful suggestions that helped shape and strengthen this story at every stage. Their honest input and sharp eyes pushed the manuscript to be better and better with each revision. I would have been in a world of hurt without their sound advice and insights. Heartfelt thanks to: Ron Kantor and his sister Gail, Valerie Ashton Rohde, Evan Ecklund, Dale Kay, Doreen Bochmann, Dick and Nadine Edwards, Julie Mervis, Steve Kiracofe, Tamra and John Bremmerman, Cherry Bochmann, Mary Faktor, Mike Wickiser, and Tracy Kruszynski.

My deepest gratitude to the extraordinary team at The Nancy & David Wolf Holocaust & Humanity Center—Jackie Congedo, Trinity Johnson, and Kara Driscoll—for your unwavering support of *Unbreakable*. Your belief in this story, your thoughtful endorsements, and your outreach efforts to connect me with the Kantor family have been instrumental in bringing this book to life. The programs and initiatives you lead continue to honor survivors and educate new generations, ensuring that stories like this one endure. It has been an honor to collaborate with you.

I also want to thank my fellow authors—Daniel Epstein, author of *Portraits in Faith*; Melissa Hunter, author of *All She Lost*; and Joyce Kamen, author of the *Upstander Series*. Your words of encouragement and your generous endorsements have meant more to me than you know. As writers who also explore memory, identity, and moral courage, your support affirms the importance of sharing these human stories of resilience and faith.

Each of you has played a meaningful role in helping *Unbreakable* find its voice—and its audience. I am deeply grateful.

Huge thanks to Robert Henry for being a steady hand throughout the entire publishing process. Your expertise, professionalism, and genuine care made all the difference in bringing *Unbreakable* to life. From formatting to final files, you handled every detail like the book was your own, and I'm deeply grateful.

This story has been greatly enriched by the extraordinary talents of Brigid Krane from Artists Eleven. A gifted graphic artist, Brigid specializes in restoring damaged photographs with meticulous care and unmatched expertise. Every image featured in this book has been lovingly restored to its original brilliance, thanks to her dedication and skill. Brigid also has a remarkable ability to distill a complex story into a single, captivating image—a striking book cover that draws readers in at first glance. Over the past six years, we've had the privilege of collaborating on two book covers, including this one, and her creative vision never fails to amaze me. As if her talent weren't enough, Brigid also happens to be my cousin, which makes every project we share even more meaningful and fulfilling.

And finally, I want to express my deepest gratitude to my editor, Laura Fineberg Cooper, for her invaluable contributions to this book. Laura's keen insight and thoughtful advice on character development, pacing, and resolving plot intricacies were instrumental to shaping this story. Her true gift, however, lies in her unwavering dedication to the craft of writing. With incredible patience and care, she helps writers like me refine our skills and bring our stories to life. As if that weren't enough, Laura even taught me a few Yiddish words, which we sprinkled throughout the story.

Laura's editorial brilliance can also be seen in my first book, *The Medic's Wife*, where her expertise in sentence structure and story development elevated the narrative, helping it achieve the honor of becoming an Amazon bestseller. Cheers, Laura! Let's make it two-for-two.

THANK YOU
AND A SMALL FAVOR

Before you go, may I ask a small favor? If you enjoyed *Unbreakable*, would you take just a minute to leave a short review on Amazon?

For independent authors like me, reviews make all the difference. They help other readers discover the book, and your honest feedback keeps stories like this alive and reaching new hearts.

It doesn't need to be long—just a sentence or two sharing your thoughts is more than enough. Your voice matters, and I would be deeply grateful for your support.

Thank you for reading, and for being part of this journey.

About the Author

EDMUND KRUSZYNSKI, also known as Ed, was born in Cleveland, Ohio, to second-generation Polish immigrants. He is the Amazon bestselling author of *The Medic's Wife* and *Unbreakable*. His work blends historical accuracy with gripping, human-centered storytelling—bringing forgotten lives and real events to vivid life. With praise from institutions like the Holocaust & Humanity Center, Kruszynski's books are trusted by readers who crave authentic, immersive historical fiction that makes them feel—and remember.

You can check out Ed's other book, *The Medic's Wife*, by visiting his author website at www.edmundkruszynski.com

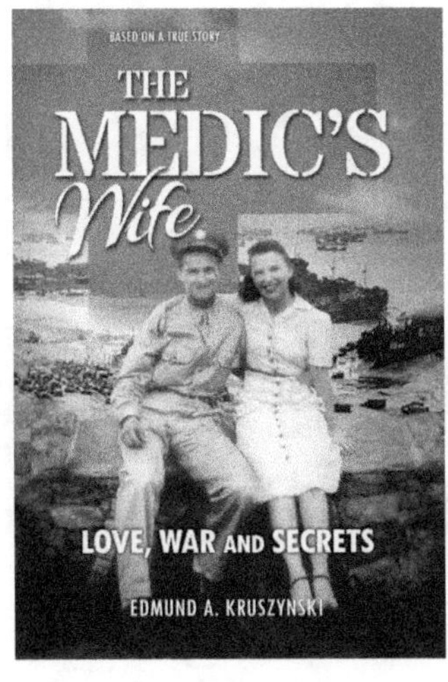

How far would you go to protect the one you love?

1944. Amid the chaos of WWII Staff Sergeant **Edmund "Ed" Kruszynski** runs toward danger while others run from it. As a young combat medic, he saves lives on the blood-soaked beaches of Normandy, through the frozen forests of the Ardennes, and deep inside **Nazi Germany**. Each day, he patches the wounded, buries the fallen, and prays his luck will hold. Then he enters **Buchenwald,** and the world goes silent. Amid the horror, Ed discovers a fragile light in the darkness—**a connection so unexpected it will change him forever.**

When the war ends, Ed returns home draped in medals but haunted by ghosts no one else can see. **Mary,** the woman who waited for him, fights a different kind of battle—against the silence between them, against the secrets he carries, and against a war that refuses to stay buried.

Their love once survived a world at war.
Now it must survive the aftermath.

The Medic's Wife reminds us that some wars never truly end—and that love may be the most heroic act of all.

Scan the QR code below to snag a copy of—*The Medic's Wife!*

www.ingramcontent.com/pod-product-compliance
Lightning Source LLC
Chambersburg PA
CBHW071156100726
47908CB00002B/403